MYTHS AND MANUSCRIPTS

PANDORA PIERCE

MYTHS AND MANUSCRIPTS

Cover Design: The Book Brander Boutique

Interior Illustrations: Della Claire

Formatting: Sara Vertuan of Stardust Book Services

Book Coach: Cathy Yardley

Book Coach: Rachel May of Golden May Editing

Developmental Editor: HEA Author Services

Line Editor: Empowered Writing

First Edition: October 2025

ISBN: 9781960239082 (paperback)

ISBN: 9781960239143 (ebook)

Published by Pandora Pierce LLC

www.pandorapierce.com

Table of Contents

Chapter 1
Willow

The soothing sound of Gran's mortar and pestle filled our apothecary shop as I hung another fresh bundle of herbs from the ceiling to dry. Our garden was growing great this year thanks to the help of a mossmew family that had nested outside. The little cat-like creatures had mossy fur that absorbed water, keeping the air around them humid and the perfect temperature for plants.

One such feline was currently slinking through the shelves, chasing a beam of sunlight between the glass storage jars. I moved the jars aside, cupping the tiny mossmew in my hands.

"This isn't the best place to play." Her moss was so fluffy that my fingers easily got lost in it when she nuzzled against my hand. I placed the delicate creature inside a potted lavender plant, smiling as she nestled between the stems. "Thank you for helping our plants thrive."

I moved away from the plant just in time to see Gran bending her wrists back and forth like they were sore. I glanced away so she didn't accuse me of spying on her, but listened carefully when she started grinding herbs again. The once steady rhythm of her mortar and pestle had begun to falter as the ache of her many years of being an apothecary weighed on her. If she wasn't careful, she'd overwork herself just like Grandpa had. Aging wasn't easy, but stubbornly working long hours certainly didn't help.

Every time I suggested she take a break, she'd work twice as hard just to prove how fine she was. It had only gotten worse after Grandpa passed away a few years ago. This shop was their dream and being here reminded her of him. I didn't have the heart to tell her to give that up while she was still grieving, but she really should think about retiring.

I'd never seen somebody fall apart like she had after losing the love of her life. It terrified me. Love might be a wonderful thing, but I never wanted to feel the kind of heartbreak Gran did. I took a deep breath, inhaling the earthy scent of our shop. That smell had calmed me ever since I'd moved in with Gran after my parents passed away, helping her and Grandpa gather plants and mix medicines before I even knew how to write. Now it was my time to step up, to show Gran how capable I really was so she could rest after so many years of hard work.

"I can feel you staring." Gran glanced over at me accusingly as she poured the ground herbs onto a set of brass scales. "What's on your mind? And don't you dare mention my age again."

I winced. "Sorry, just daydreaming, that's all."

"Daydreaming, huh?" Her eyes softened. "Thinking about the book again?"

That damned book. I used to brainstorm stories with Grandpa all the time, but I'd never actually written any of them down. Not until the Tales and Tomes Festival last month. Gran had insisted I try it, to honor Grandpa's memory and all that, but it hadn't ended well.

I pulled a well-worn note from my pocket, staring at the story gods' words once again: *the story speaks, but the heart is silent.*

How ridiculous. I'd been so excited when that note had appeared on the surface of the book well, but the gods were practically mocking me. I'd put my heart *and* soul into that book and they had the gall to tell me that the heart was silent? They could have just said they hated my book. I would have gotten over it. The only reason I even wrote the book was to make Gran happy.

"Come sit down and have some tea." Gran motioned at the chair across from her. "If you're still that worried about the note, maybe you should write another book for next year's festival. See what the story gods say then."

"No, that was just a one-time thing." I stuffed the paper back into my pocket. "We've got a lot of inventory to do still, so I should—"

"Sit down." She nudged my chair out as she added leaves to the teapot. "Whenever I decide to retire, and I'm not saying that's anytime soon, the shop is yours. You don't need to prove anything by working yourself to the bone." She stared at me so intensely that I sank onto the chair like she wanted. "Honestly, I'm still not convinced it's what will even make you happy. Just because it was my dream doesn't mean it has to be yours."

"But it *is* my dream. I love tending to our gardens, crafting medicines that can heal people in need, checking in with our repeat customers, all of it. This shop is my home and it's my dream just as much as yours."

I knew every nook and cranny of this place, from the gnarled and pockmarked wood of the worktable to the smooth wood of the stools that every member of my family had sat on. My grandparents had opened this shop before my parents were even born and they were supposed to take over before their accident. Now it was up to me.

"You don't need to worry about me." I reached for the teapot to pour us both a drink as the sweet and nutty scent of rooibos tea swept over us.

This kind of tea was often used to brighten somebody's mood, a fact that was not lost on me at all. I smiled against my teacup as the steam curled around my face. Helping people was the part of the job I enjoyed the most, and Gran was an expert at it. It was like she knew what was wrong with somebody before they even told her. Many believed she had magical powers at this point. I'd spread a few of those rumors myself in my younger years, but that didn't mean she was *always* right.

Because right now she was acting like I was just here to fulfill some duty to my family, not because I actually wanted to be here. I loved this shop and all the memories it held. It kept me connected to what little family I had, and I refused to give that up for anything.

"Okay." Gran sighed dramatically. "But I'm here if you ever want to talk about your writing. You and your grandpa always came up with such wonderful stories."

He's the one who'd gotten me into reading, gifting me books like they were golden treasures. Then Gran would bring me up the mountain with her to gather herbs and I'd sometimes wander off to the Misty Mountain Library to read for a bit. Books had been a huge part of my life for as long as I could remember, but that didn't mean I had to be the one writing them.

Writing a book was like sharing your biggest dream with a stranger and hoping they didn't crush it. There was no control or defense. You just had to accept whatever people thought, even if their thoughts were like a dagger to the heart.

"Maybe if you let me read it..." Gran's offer faded when she caught my expression. "Fine, I don't need to read it, but one day I truly hope you feel confident enough to share your joy with others."

"Thank you, Gran." I gripped her callused hands tight. "You're the only reason I even tried in the first place. You've always got my back, so I'll let you read it. One day. Maybe when you retire."

She barked a laugh as she poured herself more tea. We both knew that book was locked up in my dresser never to be seen again after the Tales and Tomes fiasco. Another opinion might not be terrible though. Maybe the gods had meant something else and their note was supposed to be helpful? That was probably wishful thinking.

The bell above our front door chimed as a customer walked in. I motioned for Gran to stay where she was and got up to greet them.

"Welcome to Bloom and Bramble Apothecary, how may I–" my voice caught in my throat when I saw the telltale black horns and shadows curling around the man. What was the

Demon Lord doing here?? I cleared my throat, trying not to stare. "How may I help you?"

"Nyssa forced me to run errands. A demon lord running errands." He scoffed, pushing a bag of books at me. "Guess she's really growing into that head librarian role, but here, these are yours. You put them on hold last week but never came to pick them up. It was uncharacteristic of you, so everyone was worried."

"That's so sweet you were worried about me." I looked through the books while his intense gaze swept over me. "And thanks for bringing these."

"I never said *I* was worried," the demon lord grumbled, but he moved closer instead of leaving now that his errand was complete. "So you're an apothecary?"

His voice sounded more curious than usual, so I motioned for him to come inside. I honestly didn't know very much about him beyond that he was the tall, dark, mysterious kind of guy, but he had come all the way out here just to drop off these books. The least I could do was show him around.

"This is my Gran's shop." I nodded at her as she picked up her mortar and pestle again. "Her name's Mable and my Grandpa always said she was the most beautiful flower." I leaned closer to whisper. "He also said she was a bit prickly, so she's actually the bloom and the bramble in our shop's name."

The Demon Lord gave me a small smile as he browsed our wares in silence. It wasn't an awkward silence though, more like he was so focused that talking would have interrupted him. His long dark hair brushed against the jars as he leaned closer, carefully examining each one.

He picked up a healing tonic, his slender fingers far more delicate than I'd expected, and held it up to the light. The green hue shimmered across his strong jawline, illuminating a genuine curiosity in his eyes that drew me in. He was entirely focused, as if the rest of the shop had faded away and that bottle the most precious thing in the world to him.

What would it feel like to have that intense gaze of his focused on me?

Heat crept up the back of my neck so I whipped around to help Gran before he caught me staring. I clearly read too much dark romance if I was getting flustered over the leader of a demonic army.

"Who's your friend?" Gran whispered. "He's very handsome."

"Did you miss the demon horns?" I asked with a laugh. I knew she'd been having problems reading the tiny ledgers lately, but there was no way she missed those. "He's one of the story spirits from the library. He's the Demon Lord from the book series *I Just Wanted a Peaceful Life, but Now I Have to Stop the Demon Lord and His Entire Army!*"

Gran's eyebrows shot up. "A story spirit in our shop? I didn't think they left the mountain."

That was a good point. What had Nyssa been thinking sending him into town on his own? Sure, the town had changed their tune about the library, but the Demon Lord was still the scariest of them all. At least, to most people he was.

The barest hint of a smile touched his lips as he noticed the mossmew curled up in the lavender. He pet the tiny cat-like creature so quickly I would have missed it if I hadn't been watching.

Did the Demon Lord... actually like cute animals? The way he acted at the library made me think they were all a bother to him, but maybe that was an act. Like the big grumpy type of character with the heart of a cinnamon roll?

No, that was what Gran would say was my imagination running away with me again. He was the villain of his story, not some romance hero about to woo anyone who crossed his path. Not that I'd want that anyway, not even if that little smile of his gave me butterflies.

"So he's not your friend now," Gran said slowly, "but you'd like him to be?"

I laughed, pouring the ground herbs into a pouch. "No, nothing like that. He just dropped some books off for me."

"Riiight." She got to her feet, wandering over to the Demon Lord before I could stop her. She was still pretty spry when she wanted to be. "Hello, can I help you with anything?"

The Demon Lord bowed his head. "No, wise one. I was just browsing."

I would have been annoyed if he'd used his usual sass on my Gran, but him being polite was kind of shocking. I didn't know he had it in him. Maybe there was more to him, a quiet puzzle to solve if I had the time.

"You seem at home here, dear." Gran patted his hand. "Feel free to stay as long as you like."

"Gran!" I hissed, clamping my lips closed when the Demon Lord glanced at me. "I mean, yes, stay as long as you like."

That little smile tugged at his lips again, but this time, his eyes were on me. I rubbed my palms against my pants, suddenly feeling warmer than usual. Maybe too many mossmews had come inside, filling the air with their humidity.

"I think I will stay a while, thank you. It reminds me of...." His brow furrowed and he turned away, studying what we had on the shelves instead of finishing his thought. "The library is too noisy lately. It's refreshing to be somewhere quiet."

Gran gave me a look that said get over there and talk to him. I sighed, doing what she wanted just to stop the conversation I knew would come if I didn't. She always wished I'd find a nice man to share my life with like her and Grandpa, but she didn't realize how risky that was.

I couldn't even handle sharing my book with anyone, let alone my heart. One harsh note from the story gods and I was like a wounded animal in need of a life-saving tonic. The pain just wouldn't go away. The thought of going through that again, but multiplied by however much I cared about another human being, was unimaginable.

There was no way I wanted to let myself care for somebody, not for real anyway. Gran was the only person I needed in my life.

I still knew how to be pleasant to customers though, so I smiled at the Demon Lord and picked up my inventory logs to keep my hands busy. "So the library's doing well then? That's great."

He scowled. "It's terrible. The place is crawling with humans all wanting to talk to me."

"Yeah, that sounds absolutely terrible." I gave him a wry grin. "So you have fans, what's wrong with that? You're from an extremely popular book series. I'm just sad that we'll never get to know how it ends."

The author of his story had passed away after writing seven amazing book and leaving the final one unfinished.

"Not you too." His scowl deepened as his shadows snapped in the air. "I don't know how it ends any more than you do so everyone needs to stop asking."

His voice was almost a shout by the end, and he looked ferocious with those shadows whipping around him, his eyes set in a glare.

"Are you really that mad about having fans?" I snapped, gripping my inventory book tight. "Having people actually enjoy your story is a great thing. Some of us will never get that chance."

His glare softened, but he didn't respond, and the silence stretched between us. It was thick and awkward this time too.

"Sorry, I didn't mean to yell at you." I opened a container to count how many elderberries we had. "My book just didn't get the praise I was hoping for, that's all."

"That's unfortunate." He watched closely as I counted our stock of herbs, writing them down for a bit before opening the next jar himself. He started counting the ginger roots, moving them around in the jar. "Three."

I raised an eyebrow. Was he helping me do inventory?

We continued on like that for a few hours, spending the afternoon inventorying the entire shop in amiable silence, which seemed to be the thing he craved most right now. As the sun set, he turned to leave with just a nod and a bow to my Gran.

"See you again soon?" I hated how hopeful that question sounded. "I mean, if you need another escape from the library that is. We can always find work for you here."

He smiled a real smile for the first time. "I might take you up on that. Farewell."

Then he walked out the door, bell chiming as he vanished in the shadows.

"Well, follow him, quick," Gran urged, nudging me towards the door. "Seize the moment! He's not used to this world, so you should walk him to the mountain at least."

I shook my head, laughing. "He's a Demon Lord, Gran. He doesn't need me to walk him home."

"Doesn't need it, no, but maybe he wants it."

I rolled my eyes, forcing myself to move deeper into the shop before my feet betrayed me and ran outside to see if she was right. He'd probably be offended by the idea of me walking him home anyway.

My place was here. At the shop. With Gran.

That was the only thing I could focus on right now. The faster I learned everything I needed to know, the sooner she could retire and rest up. I wanted her to enjoy life after all these years working, not work herself sick.

I was an apothecary and that was all I needed to be happy.

Chapter 2
Demon Lord

The quietest place in the library was on the second floor, in the corner of the old research wing that hadn't been restocked yet. Warm light shone through the multi-paneled windows, each pane of glass tinted slightly different for a beautiful array of golden light. It was a remnant from before the wild magic storm had changed this library and it was my favorite place to hide away from the world.

Nobody came up here, so it was just me and blissful silence.

Or at least, that used to be true, but on top of the stack of epic fantasies Lisa had found for me was a handwritten novel titled *Love in the Shadows: a fanfiction* with a note scribbled across the front.

You're my favorite character! I hope you love my story.

I sank onto a chair, tossing the cursed story back on the table. The fans were getting out of control. It would be so much easier to chase them off the mountain and be done with it, but the new rules forbade me from scaring people. What a joke. I was the Demon Lord; scaring people was what I should be doing.

Instead, I hid myself away upstairs reading books all day. Thankfully Lisa took her role as a librarian seriously even though she was a story spirit like me, so she always managed to find stories worthy of my time.

Each one was full of love and heartache, joy and sorrow, good and evil. Reading let me feel what those characters felt in a way that I never could with my own story since my book series wasn't about me. I was just a footnote in the hero's claim to fame, the big villain he'd eventually defeat to save the world. He'd been fighting against my demonic forces for seven books while I conquered territory after territory, building an army.

He was humanity's golden hero ready to save the world from my evil plans.

Too bad I didn't know what those plans were yet. The author hadn't written me on the page, and he'd passed away before finishing the last book, so my side of things were a little fuzzy. All I knew was that I had to beat that hero into the dirt. I picked up another epic fantasy and dove in, hoping to find inspiration for my villain quest. The endings were always so impressive, but the bad guys never seemed to win. I should ask Lisa if there were any stories told from the villain's point of view next.

As I was reading, a tiny purple dragon landed on my horns, flapping his wings to keep his balance. They'd been doing that a lot lately, landing on every available body part like I was some kind of flying lizard perch.

"How many times do I have to tell you not to do that?" I swatted the dragon away and he tumbled through the air. "I don't want your company."

The dragon roared at me, but it came out more adorable than he'd probably intended due to his size. The glare on his face was clear though: he was not happy with me.

"Oh fine, come burn something for me." I snatched up the fanfiction, holding it out to him like a treat. "Just don't sit on my horns. Give me that much dignity at least."

He swooped down, flaming the papers quickly so I never had to see that abomination again. Writing fanfiction about me might have been okay before I stepped out of my book, but I was a real person now and that was just weird. Even weirder to give it to me like some kind of love letter. I was a Demon Lord, not somebody's crush. Villains never got their happily ever after anyway, it always doom and gloom for us. Flames danced across the pages, devouring any chance of me reading that story.

Burning love letters was exactly something a villain would do, so at least I was getting one thing right today. I dropped the last bits on a plate so I didn't burn my fingers and leaned back in my chair with a grin. The dragon took that as an opening and settled on my lap, snuggling closer as I groaned. It was better than sitting on my horns at least, so I let him be and went back to reading, absently stroking his scales.

My gaze kept drifting to the ashes of that fanfiction though. What if that was the author's only copy? My stomach clenched. No way would they have given me the original. It had to be a duplicate...

Well, there was no saving it now either way, so I'd just have to embrace it as an evil deed marked off my list for today.

It would be extra evil if it was the original, so I should feel good about that. Too bad my stomach didn't agree. Thankfully squeals of joy from downstairs distracted me, drawing me over to the second-floor railing against my better judgement.

A group of patrons filled the lobby, talking excitedly with Lisa and Nyssa. I squinted, recognizing a few of them as my so-called fans. They hounded me, day after day, asking questions and wanting to know more about my books. They somehow expected *me* to know how it should end just because I was a character from the series, but I only knew as much as the author had written, just like everyone else.

"Demon Lord," Lisa shouted up at me, "they've got good news to share with you. Come down here."

The urge to pretend like I hadn't heard her was strong, but she'd probably march up here and drag me down if I didn't answer. I'd rather the fans didn't realize this was my secret hiding spot either, so I walked downstairs filled with trepidation.

"What's going on?" I asked gruffly, trying to keep my interest low.

One of the fans had a flyer gripped in her hands so tight it was crinkling.

"Um, there's a contest, for your um, your book series." She handed me the crumpled piece of paper, blushing. "Sorry."

I shrugged. "It will read just as well, crinkled or not."

Lisa smirked behind her teacup as the girl beamed at me. Oh no, had I somehow just made her even more interested? I never knew what would set these fans off in shrieks of joy or anguish, so I shut my mouth and read the flyer. Humans were far too much work.

A publishing company was announcing a contest to write the last book in my series. The author's family would choose the winner, so everyone would finally know how it ended. I swallowed hard, trying to process what that meant.

Somebody, a total stranger, was going to be deciding my fate, telling me who I should be and why. Not my author, just some random fan. A chill sank into my bones. What would happen to me once the last book was written? Would I change based on how they portrayed me? I couldn't risk that. There had to be a way to stop this.

"They're going to finish your story." Lisa gripped my arm encouragingly, smiling like this was something amazing. "You'll finally get to know more about yourself."

The fans started chattering, filling my head with nonsense about all the ways the books could end. Everyone obviously wanted this, but the idea of the contest settled into my stomach like lead.

Didn't they realize that having an ending might be even worse than never knowing? What if the author they chose never gave me a good reason for all my villainous acts or made me lose the final battle in a pathetic way? They might make me trip over a rock and accidentally fall off a cliff like in the last story I read. I deserved a better ending than that.

Panic raced through me as people crowded in so close I could barely breathe. I needed to get out of here, away from all of this.

"How do you think the hero will win?" the fan from earlier asked. "I mean, the good guys always win right?"

My chest tightened. Every book I'd read had ended like that. There were so many ways for the heroes to slay the villains, so many ways for them to crush us under their boots. That was not how my story was supposed to end. It couldn't be. I was the Demon Lord who'd been whispered about for seven books! My end should be mind-blowing and memorable, not a joke or an easy fight.

"If you really think the hero can defeat me, then what are you even doing here?" My hands shook as my shadows plunged the room into darkness, snapping and coiling until they snuffed out every light. "I'm the Demon Lord for a reason. There's no way a puny hero can defeat me so easily. I'll snuff out the sun if I have to and drag every human into a world of everlasting shadows if he even dares to lay a hand on me."

There. That should intimidate them, right?

"He did it!" A woman squealed. "The Demon Lord cast his shadow magic on us just like that general did in book 3!"

Screams of delight crashed over me as the entire library filled with excitement. I cringed. My shadows used to make people flee in terror, screaming down the mountain as they ran for safety. But now they just made the fans *love* me.

I was a terrible villain.

My shadows dissipated in an instant as my fans' happiness doused every bit of rage I'd managed to muster up. They snapped a few pictures, standing next to me and hanging off my side like I was some kind of display piece. This was not what my author had had in mind when he was planning my big ending. I was sure of that.

Lisa's shoulders shook with silent laughter as a grin spread across her face. "And that's the kind of darkness you'll see in the final book everyone. I wish you all the best entering the contest!"

"Gee, thanks for your help." I rolled my eyes, jerking away from the newest fan who was clutching at me. "As if I need a group of amateurs writing my book."

"Oh, he's just kidding, you know how he gets." Lisa waved the rest of the fans away with a smile before focusing her attention on me. "What were you thinking? You're lucky they enjoyed that."

"I'm the bad guy, what do you expect? I know the library needs patrons, but these fans are getting too forward. I can't deal with them every day, not when a contest means there's going to be even more of them prying into my life."

She sighed. "I know this has been an adjustment, but we'll make it work somehow."

The library used to be a quiet, wonderful place, until the Tales and Tomes Festival. It had been such a success that our home was now filled to the brim with people wanting to talk to us, poking and prodding as if we were a carnival act just because we were characters from their favorite books come to life.

I rubbed my hand over my face, leaning against a book-shelf. "I just...miss when there was nobody here but us. Is that so wrong?"

"No, but scaring patrons is," she said softly. "I thought we moved past that. Let me talk to Nyssa and see what we can come up with. You shouldn't have to feel this uncomfortable. I really thought you'd be happy..."

She glanced away, busying herself with reorganizing books on a shelf. She'd been the one finding me all the fantasy books I'd been reading, helping me see what kind of stories were out there. She wanted me to figure out my story just as much as I did. She'd understand if I told her my fears about being a joke of a Demon Lord, but somehow, I just couldn't bring myself to do it. Saying it out loud would make it real and ruin all my hard work trying to be evil.

I took a deep breath. "I *am* happy. Thanks for letting me know about the contest."

"You're welcome." She frowned at me like she could sense I wasn't telling the truth. "Look, if you're that worried about it, you should just find your own writer and work with them on the story."

I blinked at her, frozen in place. What an absurd idea. "You want me to find my own writer?"

"Of course, take your story into your own hands. Make it what you want it to be. You deserve whatever kind of ending you see fit, and you've got the rare opportunity to make it happen." She smiled, hugging a book tight to her chest. "We're characters from stories, but that doesn't mean we have to be governed by those stories. You can be whoever you want to be."

That didn't feel right. Characters were written by somebody else. I couldn't just go rogue and become something my author hadn't intended. We might have stepped out of our books, but we were still part of them.

Finding my own writer wasn't a bad idea though. Somebody who would do my story justice while staying true to the original author's plans. I wanted to go out with such a bang that everyone would remember it. I wanted an epic ending, one full of meaning and emotion that explained why I did all the things they claimed.

I wanted a real story. And maybe, just maybe, I'd even get a name.

It felt a little crazy, but a tiny spark of hope flickered in my chest. This contest might be exactly what I needed after all.

Chapter 3
Willow

The mountain air was crisp, verging on chilly, now that I'd taken a break from herb-gathering. I leaned back against a large tree, staring at the blank pages of my journal. Why had I even brought it with me? I was done with my book, so I didn't need a journal on hand to jot down any bursts of inspiration. Not that they'd helped anyway. My book was obviously terrible. I shoved the journal back in my bag, glaring at the manuscript I'd hidden in there too. I'd put so much work into that story, but the gods had rejected it almost immediately.

I ran my fingers over the faded and well-worn piece of paper they'd sent me, staring at the words written on it.

The story speaks, but the heart is silent.

If that was my reward for all the time I spent writing, for all the nights I lost sleep just to get a few hundred more words in, then it definitely wasn't worth it. There was no way I'd put all that effort into a book again, not after that reaction. I assumed they'd love my book just as much as I did and I hated this gross feeling in my stomach now, like I'd failed something important.

This was exactly why I never should have tried in the first place. Getting attached to something only ever led to pain. Which was why the main character in my book succeeded *without* falling in love. The opportunity was there when her greatest enemy turned into an ally, and they even had sparks and good chemistry, but she chose her duty as a Queen. She saved her kingdom from a long war and named a new ruler, ending the story as a powerful woman who didn't need anyone else.

It was dark and a little tragic, but full of emotion. That apparently wasn't enough for the story gods though.

"What will it take to get this book out of my head?" I muttered, staring at the bright blue sky. "I just need to get over it and move on."

"Hard to do when you keep talking to yourself about it," a familiar voice said.

I jumped to my feet, dropping my bag as I whipped around to see the Demon Lord of all people. He waltzed up to my tree as if he owned the mountain, dark shadows contrasting with the bright noon sun. I'd never seen him outside in the middle of the day like this, not to mention all the dragons flying around him like he was some kind of shepherd and they were his flock.

"Are you stalking me?" My heartbeat pounded in my ears. "First my apothecary shop and now here?"

"If I was stalking you, you'd never even see me. I can literally blend in with the shadows and you're the most un-observant human I've ever met. You didn't even hear me coming up the path."

"I was distracted." I let out a breath as I gathered everything that had fallen out of my bag. Pencils, pens, journal, all sorts of stuff that an apothecary didn't need. "So what *are* you doing here then?"

"Preventing a rampage." He frowned at the dragons. "These lizards are chaos incarnate."

One of those chaotic dragons chose that moment to land on the Demon Lord's horns like an adorable purple sidekick. The Demon Lord swatted at him, snarling obscenities, which only made the whole thing more ridiculous. I snorted, turning it into a cough when he glared at me.

"What? It was cute," I said, not even bothering to apologize. "You should thank the dragon for making you look good."

Not that he had any trouble doing that on his own, but he was kind of fun to tease.

He grinned. "If you think they're so cute, then you should love that one stealing your stuff."

I glanced behind me just in time to see a sapphire dragon flying off with the note the story gods had left me.

"Hey! Give that back!" I tried to snatch the note away, but the dragon darted out of reach every time I got close, like we were playing a game. If I wasn't careful, he'd burn the note to a crisp. I took a deep breath and looked at the Demon Lord. "Mind helping me out?"

His smile turned devious. "Maybe. If you say please."

It was like he was daring me to say it, to fall on my knees and beg for his help. I'd have refused immediately, but the way his dark eyes roved over me had my throat in a vice grip. Did he realize how attractive that look was?

Probably. But there was no way I actually *liked* him. This was just a game and two could play at that.

"Oh dark and terrifying Demon Lord, please save my notes from these dragons before all is lost."

He stared at me for a while before shaking his head. "You really aren't afraid of me, are you?"

"Only in your dreams. Now can you help me or not?" I nodded at the dragon chewing on my note.

Shadows swirled around him, reaching out to the dragon in question. The dragon tilted his head, dropping the note in favor of chasing the shadows instead. More dragons joined in, zooming around the Demon Lord as his shadows zipped around the clearing. They'd obviously played this game before and loved it. Even the Demon Lord had a little smile on his face as he watched them.

When he caught me looking, his brow furrowed. "What's so important about a scrap of paper anyway?"

I caught the note as it fluttered through the air, stuffing it safely in the pocket of my work overalls.

"Nothing." I snatched up an empty basket I'd brought with me. "I'm going to go pick herbs. Thanks for your help."

He nodded, following me as I moved to a patch of knee-high feverfern that was a beautiful silvery-green right now. When steeped in tea or ground up into a tonic, the fern boosted a person's immune system and helped lower fevers. It was the most potent at the end of autumn, so we always tried to have a large stock gathered in preparation for winter.

My back twitched as the Demon Lord continued to study me, ever watchful and intense. After a few minutes, he knelt beside me and started picking the ferns too. I sighed, letting my shoulders relax. Of course he'd just been watching how to properly deal with the ferns.

I had to get my thoughts under control if we were going to keep running into each other like this.

"It didn't seem like nothing," he said softly, adding the plants to my basket with care. "The paper, I mean."

He really wasn't going to let that go, huh? I focused on digging up the delicate roots without damaging them, before answering. "It was the reply from the story gods at the festival."

"And?"

I yanked a root a little too hard, snapping it in half. "And it's none of your business, that's what."

He added herbs to the basket as if nothing happened. My guilt said it all though. He was only trying to help, and I'd snapped at him like a jerk. He was even keeping the dragons occupied while we worked so they didn't nip at the plants or knock over my basket.

I dug another plant up carefully. "Sorry. The story gods just didn't like my book, that's all. They said it had no heart, but it's fine. I never wanted to be a writer anyway."

Silence stretched between us as we continued filling the basket, but I could feel his gaze on me like an itch I couldn't scratch. He obviously had something to say but was keeping quiet for some reason. Once we'd dug up half the patch of feverfern, I brushed off my hands and turned to him.

"Just say it."

He carefully rearranged the ferns and their roots to fit as many as possible in the basket. "I was just wondering if the story gods were really that harsh or if maybe you took it wrong? Nyssa said they provide guidance to writers, not crush their spirits."

"My spirits are not crushed." I scoffed. "And there was really no other way to take it. My book sucks. End of story."

"I somehow doubt that. What did your Gran say about it?"

I scuffed my boot in the dirt, avoiding his gaze. "Well, she hasn't read it yet."

"Okay, what about your friends?"

I bit my lip, refusing to admit I didn't have any of those. Acquaintances sure, but nobody close enough that I'd let them read my book.

The Demon Lord reached out, lifting my chin so I had no choice but to look him in the eyes. "You didn't let a single soul read your story before deciding it was terrible, did you?"

"No, that's what the story gods were for." I jerked out of his grip, heat burning my cheeks. "What's it matter to you anyway? You're supposed to be evil incarnate, but it sounds like you're trying to encourage me."

"So what if I am?" He crossed his arms, staring at me. "I think you're just afraid to let anyone read it."

I tried to laugh it off, but it sounded hollow even to me. I winced. "You don't get it. If Gran read it, she'd feel obligated to tell me it was amazing. She's sweet like that and my stories remind her of Grandpa, so there's no way she'd tell me it was bad. And the same thing would happen with friends too. If they said something nice, I'd probably think they were sugar-coating it to spare my feelings."

Or maybe I was just too afraid of what their response would be. A harsh answer from the story gods was one thing, but from Gran? I wasn't sure I could deal with that. Not that it mattered. I was an apothecary. I knelt in the dirt again, digging up each plant with the care they deserved. This was where I felt most at home, with my hands in the dirt and the smell of fresh herbs in the air.

The Demon Lord leaned down next to me, his voice soft. "I'm not your friend or your family. Let me read it."

I froze, fingers entrenched in the dirt. He wanted to... read my book? That was ridiculous, why would he care about my story?

Except somebody who didn't care about me or my story might actually be the perfect person to read it. He was right: he wasn't my friend *or* my family. He barely knew me, so he shouldn't feel bad giving me his honest thoughts. It would be nice to be able to talk to somebody about it and see where I might need to edit. Not that I was planning on wasting any more time on that story, but it was good to have options.

I wiped my hands on my overalls, getting them as clean as possible before opening my bag. I'd brought my manuscript with me in case Gran's curiosity got the better of her and she tried to read it while I was away, which was silly, so maybe I just hadn't felt comfortable leaving it behind after so many days of having it in my bag.

"Here." I held the pages out to him with trepidation. "It's the only copy I have, so be careful."

His shadows curled around it as if they were extra hands, pulling it to him. He didn't even look at it before tucking it away and adding the last of the herbs to the basket.

"Really? That's it?" I asked.

"Well, I can't say anything until I read it." Exasperation filled his voice. "Unless you expect me to do that now with you watching me."

"Uh, yeah, I pretty much do."

He stared at me, as if trying to figure out if I was serious or not. Honestly, I wasn't sure either, but the moment I'd handed my story over to him it was like my entire body had filled with anxiety. I wanted to know what he thought as soon as possible, but I was also afraid of knowing it.

What a pickle I'd gotten myself into.

"On second thought, I don't need you to read it. It's fine." I held my hand out for the book, but he took a step back instead. "What are you doing? Give it back."

A faint smile tugged at his lips. "Not until I read it. You can't tempt me with a good story and then take it away."

He was insufferable. I should get out of here before I did anything embarrassing like sit him down and force him to read. "Fine. Just let me know what you think and don't let anyone else read it."

He handed me the basket of herbs, leaning close enough for his long hair to brush against me. "I swear, I'm the only one who will touch it."

My breath caught in my chest. He was even more handsome up close with those long lashes and gorgeous purple eyes. Like amethysts sparkling in the sunlight. My pulse pounded in my ears as I grabbed the basket from him, careful not to accidentally brush against his hands. That was the last thing I needed. Words escaped me, so I just nodded and fled down the mountain.

This was going to be a long few days waiting for him to read my book. I'd have to stay busy with work and hope Gran didn't tease me too much for giving him my story when I'd refused to let anyone else read it.

No, she was definitely going to tease me about that. Ugh. He better read like the wind.

Chapter 4
Demon Lord

I stepped out of the pages of my book carefully, hoping nobody would be waiting to ambush me when I returned to the Misty Mountain Library. The pages glowed with a bright golden light whenever we came or went, drawing far too much attention for my liking.

We'd had so many patrons visiting since the festival, which was great for Misty, but tiresome for me. Now that I had to dodge fans as a daily occurrence, my home no longer felt like my home, and I wasn't sure what to do about it.

The bond between the library and me warmed as it checked in. It never spoke in words, but I could feel what it meant all the same. It was worried.

"Don't waste your time on me." I tucked my book away in its hiding spot behind an old shelf. "I'm fine, honestly, it's just different now."

A book rose in the air, flying over to me and landing in my outstretched hands. It was Willow's manuscript. I walked to the edge of the upper floor, gazing at the book tree over the railing.

"What am I supposed to do with this?" I held the pages Willow had worked so hard on tight. "It's not like she really needs me to finish reading it today or anything."

The library sent a jolt of magic at me that felt like an eye-roll. I sighed, unable to hide anything from Misty.

I'd spent every moment since I got back from meeting with Willow reading and was already three-fourths of the way done. I assumed it would be awful like she said, so I was going to be the bad guy and tell her that, but it was surprisingly good. The worldbuilding was intricate, putting me right in the story along with her characters, and the plot was excellent. There wasn't a single reason I could think of to have the little dragons burn *this* story.

Well, maybe one thing. Her characters obviously had feelings for each other, but they just flirted and never did anything about it. I kept thinking that would change, but I was nearing the end, and still nothing. It was pretty frustrating actually. The characters just didn't feel realistic, like they had a lot of self-discovery left to do.

Huh, maybe that's what the story gods had meant about it not having heart. I'd have to read the note to be sure, but that would mean it was supposed to be constructive instead of harsh, so it made sense.

If Willow spent the time editing this with more emotion, it would be an amazing story. Maybe I should ask her to enter the contest for the last book in my series too. My story didn't have any romance in it, and besides that aspect, she was a really talented writer. If I had to trust somebody to finish my story, she felt like a good choice.

The library tugged on our bond again, pulling my attention to a vibrant red-haired woman walking inside. Willow stopped to chat with Nyssa, her eyes bright as they roamed the library, looking for something.

Or someone.

No, that was ridiculous. It had only been a day, there was no way she'd expect me to be done already.

Even so, I walked down the stairs to the main floor and sat at a table close enough to overhear them. I flipped to the last page I'd read in Willow's book. The Queen was describing her big plan to defeat the enemy, and I couldn't wait to see how it all played out. If it was an easy victory, I'd be pretty disappointed, but I had a feeling the bad guy would have a big dramatic ending like he deserved.

Nyssa's voice carried over as she pointed at a pile of logbooks. "Here's our donations list. If you could sort through all the new books we've gotten and write down who donated what, that would be great. Then you can add tags to the books as well."

"Sure, no problem." Willow nodded, but her gaze kept drifting over to me as if she could feel me staring.

I buried myself in her book. What was she doing here? It sounded like she was volunteering, but she'd never done that before. So maybe waiting to hear what I thought of her book was driving her so crazy that she couldn't stay away...

That idea filled me with an odd sense of pleasure. Everyone was always bothering me about my own story, but having her seek my opinion on something that had nothing to do with the insufferable hero of my book was refreshing.

I read another chapter as she gathered up all the books that had been donated to the library over the past week, laying them out on a table suspiciously close to me. I could feel her attention on me more than once, watching me read the story she cared so much about.

"What are you grinning about?" she finally asked me.

"Shhh, I'm reading." I forced a serious look on my face and focused on the book.

I hadn't even realized I *was* grinning, but she smiled that overly happy smile of hers and hauled even more books over. The clanking of metal drew my attention to the floor where dozens of tiny knights rushed to Willow's side. I ignored them as best I could and kept reading.

Their commander bowed low. "Lady Willow, welcome back to the Misty Mountain Library. May we be of any assistance?"

Willow smiled. "Sure, I could use some help writing names on these tags and putting them in their books."

They chatted a bit more as she lifted each knight onto the table, handing them pens and labels as she organized the books into what I assumed were stacks based on who donated them. Other libraries had sent some over, but the bulk of the donations had come from the townsfolk, offering up whatever books they had lying around as an apology for abandoning Misty after the wild magic storm.

I'd have refused them outright if it was me, but the library had literally glowed with happiness when they stopped by with their wagon full of books. It reminded me of the first time Nyssa had shown up. Eager and determined, just like the whole town seemed to be now.

I flipped to the next chapter, getting closer and closer to the end of Willow's book. Now that she was standing right in front of me, I wanted to finish reading as soon as possible so we could talk about it. Except, every time her gaze wandered over to me, I felt myself re-reading the same paragraph over and over, as if the words weren't sinking in. I'd never been so unfocused in my life.

"So, how's it going?" She peered over my shoulder at the book. "Ohhh, that's a good chapter! You're close to the end now." The warmth of her body seeped into my back and her hair tickled my cheek as she leaned closer, pointing at something on the page. "That was my favorite part."

The excitement in her voice made my heart flutter in a way I'd never felt before. I was so distracted by her closeness that I didn't catch what part she pointed at. I was the Demon Lord, a villain so terrifying that it took seven books to build up to meeting me. I was not the type of man who got flustered over a cute girl.

I cleared my throat. "You know, I'm never going to finish reading if you keep hovering. The knights look like they could use your help too."

One of them was trying to lift a heavy book, but his tiny arms were shaking, and I had a feeling it was about to squash him. Willow gasped, racing over to catch the heavy tome just in time. The knight sank to the table in relief as Willow comforted him. The knights might be meddlesome, but they were a good distraction when you needed one. Now I had to get back to reading.

Willow was counting on me for my opinion, and I would not let her down. Nobody else had read this. Just me and the story gods.

She needed *my* help.

I dove back in, reading chapter after chapter as the story reached its climax. The Queen overthrew her enemies in a resounding victory but decided that it was time to end her reign and let somebody else take over. Instead of heading off into the sunset with the guy she obviously loved, she gave him her crown. She apparently trusted him with her kingdom, but not with her heart. They could have easily ruled together, and it would have been a beautiful ending, but instead she just left to start her life over in solitude after the long hard-fought war.

The End.

Finishing a good book was usually so satisfying, but with hers I felt cheated out of something that could have been great. Willow had written those characters so that I *knew* they loved each other, but then she completely ignored the whole concept. She was probably going for a strong female character who didn't need a man, but the way she wrote it felt like the Queen *wanted* the guy even if she didn't technically need him. Women could be strong and still be in relationships. Nyssa did it every day, and I'd read about so many other strong female characters too.

How could Willow be such a good writer, but miss such an important element? No wonder the story gods thought it had no heart. Willow didn't let her characters admit any of their true feelings.

She must have seen me set the book down, because she dropped the three-headed dog's ball and was heading my way with an eager look on her face that I really didn't want to crush. She was the first person who was excited to hear my thoughts on something that didn't relate to my book. She didn't want hints about how the hero would win or how I would die. She just wanted to know what I thought about *her* book.

And that was a wonderful feeling.

Before she made it over to me, a group of young teenage boys approached my table.

"These books are amazing," one of them said, beaming as he held up the first book in my series. "Are you really the Demon Lord?"

Children were the few fans I didn't mind talking to because I didn't have to answer any annoying questions. I just had to be scary and amuse them.

"Yes, I am the Demon Lord." I stretched my shadows out, swirling them around the children as I bared my teeth. "So watch out."

Their eyes widened as I formed my hands into claws, rawring just enough to make them laugh. Then I let my shadows do the rest, putting on a little play with dancing demons and cute animals all hopping around. That would entertain them for hours.

"Rawr?" Willow asked, her voice filled with mirth. "That's adorable."

"I think you mean terrifying."

My face burned as I focused on the kids to avoid any more of her teasing. Of course she'd been standing close enough to hear that.

After a while, she nudged the manuscript I'd left on the table. "So....what did you think?"

"Honestly?" I paused, intensely aware of how much I could hurt her with a wrong word or blunt comment. "I could use some time to put my thoughts together. And I'd like to read that note, if you still have it."

She glanced away from me, pulling a very worn and tattered piece of paper out of her pocket. It was a bit singed, with tiny teeth marks at the top from the dragons yesterday. I took it carefully, not wanting to put a single extra wrinkle in it.

The story speaks, but the heart is silent.

That was a little different than saying the book had no heart, but I understood what it meant entirely. Willow had shied away from her characters' feelings instead of letting them shine. Emotions were what let a reader connect to a story, but she'd left a lot of them out. All the aspects of the war and losing their kingdom felt emotionally charged, but anything more personal like falling in love fell flat. That should be an easy fix for a good writer like her though, so maybe if I explained it well enough, she'd see what the story gods meant.

And then be ready to write my final book next.

"The suspense is killing me." Willow let out a breath, exasperation clear on her face. "Why don't we get a drink while you mull this over."

I nodded and handed the note back to her. Willow deserved the truth, but in a way that didn't hurt her feelings so much that she'd want to stop writing entirely. I wasn't really good at being delicate or comforting, but I had to try with her. She was too good of a writer to let slip through my fingers. Especially since she didn't treat me like the others. She'd never demanded answers about my books, fawned over me, or run away in terror. She treated me like any other person and that was something I'd never experienced before.

But I found myself craving more of it. More of her view of me.

I bet my ending would be more than satisfying if she was the one who wrote it. Now I just had to convince her of that.

Open
ho
(ma
and t

CHAPTER 5
WILLOW

I'd brought the Demon Lord to Mochi's Snack Shack while he gathered his thoughts, but the longer we sat here, the more my mind raced. He was the very first person to read my book and he was like an emotionless stone! I had no idea what he was thinking. Did he hate it? Did he love it?

Nothing. He just kept flipping through my manuscript and casually scribbling notes on another piece of paper like this whole experience wasn't stressing me out. I wished I'd never given him my story in the first place. Then I'd be at the apothecary shop all nice and cozy mixing herbs. Instead I was here, trying not to grind my teeth too hard.

Mochi slid a third mug of hot cocoa across the counter to me. I caught it and took a long drink, downing the warm cocoa like it was nectar from the gods. It warmed me up and gave me a nice sugar rush as I licked whipped cream off my lip. Mochi had even added marshmallows to this one, upping the sugar content with each mug he'd given me.

"One more please, Mochi." I took a deep breath to calm my nerves. I wished the Demon Lord would just say something. Anything. "With cookies too maybe?"

A soft furry paw patted my arm as if the red panda was consoling me. His fluffy tail swayed behind him as he chirped something incomprehensible.

The Demon Lord smirked. "He's cutting you off."

"What?" I glanced at all the empty mugs next to me. Maybe I had had a bit too much. "But it's just cocoa! It's not like I'm drinking dragon's breath ale or something."

Plus, it was the only thing distracting me from the Demon Lord's very slow notetaking. I just wanted to know what he thought already. Was that really so hard? I sighed, lying my head on the wooden counter as I traced a tiny scorch mark the dragons must have left behind. It was sweet how they had all worked together making this for Mochi.

The red panda tilted his head at me, his ears twitching as one more mug of cocoa appeared in his paws. This one had whipped cream, marshmallows, chocolate shavings, and mini cookies in it too.

"Thank the gods," I murmured, then winced. "I mean, thank the pandas!"

Mochi's chatter almost sounded like a laugh as he pawed my hand one more time. I scratched behind his ears, my fingers getting lost in the soft fur of his coat. He was one of my favorite story spirits, so adorable and always watching out for everyone. I just wished I could understand him like the other story spirits could.

He leaned into my hand, eyes closed in bliss. If a good scratch was all he wanted in return for the many, many cocoas and good company, I'd gladly oblige.

Mochi chirped and moved away as he busied himself with setting up food for the lunch rush later.

"Okay, I can't take this anymore. Give it to me straight." I sat up, steeling myself for the Demon Lord's response. "You hated it, right? That's why you're taking so long to answer?"

He paused, actually paused, and the whole world felt like it was crashing down on my shoulders. My pulse raced as I rubbed my sweaty palms on my pants. Maybe drinking that much hot cocoa wasn't the best idea. I was burning up here.

"I liked it," he finally admitted. "It's got a lot of potential."

Potential? Having potential was what people said about houses that were falling apart but could be nice if you put years worth of work into them.

I downed more cocoa. "So you didn't love it, huh?"

"What, no, I said I liked it." He frowned at me. "You've got a bit of, well, you're covered in whipped cream."

My face warmed as I wiped the cream off my lip, waiting for him to say more.

"You've got a unique voice." He glanced at his notes, but my mind was already racing.

Unique voice usually meant it was super weird and not something a person would enjoy reading. The book was about a Queen giving up her right to the throne once she accomplished all her goals. She also proved she didn't need love to get anything done, which admittedly wasn't the expected route to take.

Maybe that had been a terrible idea and the story really didn't have a chance. I should just forget about it and move on. Grandpa would be proud that I'd given writing a try finally and that was all that mattered...right? Gran would have to be okay with that.

The Demon Lord sighed. "Why does it seem like everything I say is sending you into a depressed cocoa binge? You wanted the truth, but you're barely listening."

"Sorry...go on."

"Since you seem to want the bad news first, here it is: your characters are hard to identify with." He paused, as if waiting for me to freak out again, before continuing. "The plot is really good and I love the worldbuilding, but it's missing the raw emotions. The story has such big highs and lows with a tragic ending for the romance, but their feelings barely scratched the surface. With a plot like that, I should have been emotionally destroyed by the end and cursing your name, but I kind of just set the book down and was done. Personally, I think it would satisfy a lot more readers if you let them get together in the end. It felt...abrupt when the Queen left."

Was romance really all that mattered to people? Sure, it was the bestselling genre out there, but there had to be a place for realistic endings too. Sometimes people just didn't work together and that was fine. I'd had plenty of old boyfriends call me cold and distant, but we still managed to be friendly when we saw each other. That's just how life went sometimes.

I guess I could have made it clearer that my characters were ending as friends. Maybe that would help...

"Wait." I threw an arm out toward him. "Do you actually read romance novels?"

He shrugged, taking a small sip of the cocoa Mochi had given him a half hour ago. "A few. There was only so much to do in an empty library for months."

The image of him reading fluffy romances hidden away in his corner of the library made me laugh. It felt good to laugh and forget about my own book for a moment.

"So what kind do you like?" I leaned forward on my elbows. "Sweet romances with lots of fluff or dark romances where the villain gets the girl?"

His eyes widened. "There are romances about villains?"

"So, so many," I said with a grin. "Actually, you're kind of like some of them. A shadow daddy in the flesh."

He choked on his cocoa, sputtering. "What in the nine realms is a shadow daddy?"

I scooted closer, as if I was telling him some big secret. "Well, it's basically a guy who's dark and mysterious. And he has control over shadows, of course." I nodded at the shadows suddenly flitting around him. "Usually, he's morally gray or a straight up villain with *touch her and you die* vibes that are extremely sexy."

A tiny blush swept across his face. "And you think *I'm* one of these...shadow daddies?"

I couldn't help but laugh at the awkward way he said it, like the words were something completely ridiculous.

"Definitely, you're the biggest shadow daddy I've ever met."

He drank his cocoa slowly, avoiding eye contact until, eventually, he mumbled, "thank you."

My stomach fluttered. That sincerity of his always caught me off guard.

"Anytime." I downed the rest of my cocoa in one big gulp. "Now, back to my book. Thanks for reading it, but I think I've got the picture."

"I don't think you understand anything. I liked your story. Truly."

I reached for my book, but his shadows curled around it possessively. I crossed my arms over my chest and glared at him. "You were supposed to be honest, remember? The whole you're not my friend or my family thing?"

"You really haven't been listening, have you?" He picked up my book, holding it like it was something precious. "I said I *like* your book. It needs some work, sure, but the bones are good. You just need to stop holding back and let your emotions flow."

I blinked at him, staring at his ashen gray skin and dark purple eyes. He was from a book, so he should know what made a story good. I'd let him read it for a reason, so if I was just going to ignore everything he said, what was the point?

"So you... you actually liked it?" I whispered. "You're not just saying that to make me feel better?"

He raised an eyebrow, giving me his trusty are-you-an-idiot look. "I said I liked it. Honestly, I liked it so much I was going to ask you to write the last book in my series too, but if this is how you respond to compliments maybe I shouldn't."

"Wait, what?" I clenched my empty cocoa mug tight. "Do you realize how famous your series is? Everyone's been waiting for that final book for years. There's no way a no-name like me could do it justice."

"There's a contest going on right now and anyone can join." He gave me a blank stare. "Even no-names like you."

"That's not really the issue here. People not liking my book is one thing, since I'm the only one who really cares about that, but messing up your series? Oh boy would that suck. Thousands, no, hundreds of thousands of fans would be knocking down my door ready to tell me what a bad job I did."

And the pain of that massive failure would eat me alive. It had already hurt so much hearing that the story gods didn't like my book, so I couldn't imagine hearing that from thousands of people at once. Even if they said it in a polite way, it would still hurt like daggers in my chest. Why would I risk that? I bit my lip as the Demon Lord patiently waited for me to calm down. He was the one I'd really hurt if I messed up that final book, and I especially didn't want to disappoint him.

"I'd probably just mess it up." I glanced away from the surprisingly kind gaze of his. "I'm too new to this writing thing, and you said it yourself: my book lacks emotion. So what if I ruined your ending?"

He sighed. "I'm worried that's what everyone else is going to do. All anyone's talked about is the big battle between me and the hero. They just assume I'm going to get killed off so the golden boy can be victorious, but nobody seems to care about me or my side of the story."

Sadness tinged his words, real enough that I caught myself looking at him again. Worry lines creased his forehead and his lips were tight. Now that I'd met him, and gotten to know him a bit, that kind of ending didn't feel right for his story.

"So you want the hero to lose?" I asked.

"No, it's his book, so the hero has to win, but I don't want to be just a stepping stone to his victory. I want to be a mountain standing in his way." He glanced up at me. "That kind of ending is something only a writer with a unique voice like you could pull off."

Suddenly, the word unique sounded like high praise instead of the insult I thought it was earlier. He'd put a lot of thought into this and was trusting me to give him the kind of ending he deserved, instead of just letting the hero defeat him in the classic good vs evil showdown.

But was I good enough to do that? What if I let him down?

"I don't think–"

"You're too afraid to write my last book, aren't you?" His shoulders slumped. "Fine. I'll find somebody else." The Demon Lord stood up and started walking away with the saddest look on his face, making me feel like I'd failed him before I even tried. I said I was never going to write another book again though. I couldn't go back on that just because a handsome guy was giving me puppy dog eyes, right? I wasn't a real writer. I was an apothecary.

I took a deep breath and forced a smile. "Finding another writer sounds like a good idea. I can help you look for somebody if you want."

"Really?" He frowned at me, confusion clear in his eyes. "I thought it would be a great opportunity for you. If you're worried about your skills, don't. I promise, you're talented. I wouldn't have asked you to write my story if I didn't believe that. The world deserves to read your books, and my series can help you with that." He moved closer, putting his hands on the snack shack on either side of me. "If you're worried about the emotional parts, I can help you with those. I want to feel something real. Something my story never let me feel before. We can make this book amazing. Together."

The familiar scent of old parchment and something smokey, almost like vanilla, enveloped me as he stood there, staring into my eyes. His confident gaze soothed my panic. He not only liked my story, but he wanted me to write his too. That was baffling, but it also felt kind of nice. If the Demon Lord believed I could do this, then maybe I should have a little confidence in myself too.

It was only one book. How hard could it be to write?

Memories of the Tales and Tomes Festival invaded my mind. I couldn't just forget all the long nights, early mornings, and exhausted editing sessions where words barely even felt real anymore. Writing that last book had been the hardest thing I'd ever done, and the gods just laughed it off. My chest ached, remembering the despair I'd felt reading that note in front of all those people at the festival.

"I just can't do it." I shook my head, pushing past him as I got off my stool. "I don't want to feel like that ever again. I'm an apothecary, not a writer. Find somebody else."

Tears burned my eyes, and I couldn't bring myself to look at him. Not when that kindness of his had almost swayed me into doing something I'd regret. This was for the best. I didn't need to write some book to feel fulfilled. I was already happy as an apothecary.

I wiped the tears from my cheeks as I slowly left the library, each step feeling worse and worse. If this was really the right decision, then why did it feel so awful?

CHAPTER 6
WILLOW

The long trudge back into town gave me plenty of time to think about what the Demon Lord had said. Some writers were naturals, and their stories were the ones who touched people's hearts, sticking with them for years to come. Other writers had good ideas but weren't as skilled at bringing them to life. I was apparently in that second category, which was fine. I'd given writing a try, and now I knew it wasn't for me. I'd made the right decision, even if the Demon Lord wasn't happy about it.

I pulled open the door to our shop, inhaling the calming scents of honey and ginger. Gran must have been cooking a new batch of cough syrup. This was where I wanted to be, getting lost in making medicines. I hurried inside and dropped my bag behind the counter.

"Welcome home." Gran smiled at me as she stirred a pot of honey simmering on the stove. "How'd the meeting go?"

"Fine." I headed over to the table covered in freshly harvested yarrow and twine as if she'd been in the middle of bundling them to dry. "He liked my book."

"That's great!" The corners of her eyes crinkled as her smile grew. "Now you'll let me read it too, right?"

Not a chance, but I couldn't tell her that. "Uh sure, maybe later."

The yarrow smelled sweet and earthy, grounding me in my work as I hung each new bundle from hooks on the ceiling. I used to lay on the floor as a child, gazing up at all the dried herbs like they were a mysterious upside-down garden. Grandpa had caught me doing it once and joined me, telling me wonderful stories about the tiny fairies who dried the plants out for us.

I'd spent the next few years trying to spot one until I realized he was kidding.

If only he were still here. He never wrote any of his stories down, but he loved to brainstorm and think of all the possibilities. They were my happiest memories of him, gardening or blending herbs while we talked about fantastical worlds and fictional people. Work never felt like work when he was there and coming up with stories had actually been fun. Doing it alone was completely different. Every idea was a struggle and forming them into words was even worse.

"Are you okay?" Gran asked softly, joining me at the table. "You said he liked your story, so why do you seem sad?"

"It's nothing." I hung another bundle of yarrow up, its delicate leaves soft against my skin. "Can we just focus on work for a while, please?"

She quirked an eyebrow as she leaned down to snag something out of my bag. "Nothing, huh? Then what's this crumpled up flyer all about?"

I glanced over, wincing when I saw the big illustration of the hero from the series *I Just Wanted a Peaceful Life, but Now I Have to Stop the Demon Lord and His Entire Army!* That damn demon must have snuck it in my bag on my way out. He apparently didn't take no for an answer very well.

"It doesn't mean anything, Gran." I shook my head, wishing she hadn't seen it. "I'm done writing, okay? I'm not going to enter the contest."

"But you love this series!" She rested her hand over her heart, smiling. "Do you remember when you snuck into your Grandpa's workroom and accidentally grabbed the third book instead of the first and tried to pretend like you weren't thoroughly confused? He finally gave you the first two even though you were way too young for the series, but you were hooked after that. The two of you read every book that came out, waiting in line for hours at midnight releases. I thought you were both crazy, but you were happy, and that's all that ever mattered to me."

"Of course I remember that, Gran." I just tried not to. I rubbed my eyes and focused on the work in front of me instead, bundling up the rest of the yarrow far too quickly. "Being a fan is exactly why I don't want to write the last book. Can you imagine how many people I'd disappoint if I tried?"

She frowned at the flyer, putting her glasses on to look closer. "But it says that the family of the author will be choosing the winner, not the fans. Nobody will even see your story unless they think it's good enough to win. So what's the harm in having a little fun?"

Fun was the last thing writing that book would be, but it was nice to know that the author's family would be the ones deciding. Hopefully the series would end in a way that fit the author's original vision then. Not that that was my problem. I glanced around the shop, noting all the empty jars and half-made medicines. This was our busiest time of the year preparing for winter when colds and fevers ran rampant. Writing a book just took too much time, time I didn't have right now.

I took the flyer from Gran, noting the insane deadline. "Look at that. There's no way I could write that book in a month!"

"But isn't' that how long your last one took?" Gran frowned as she took the simmering cough syrup off the fire to cool. The honeyed ginger smelled sweet and slightly spicy. "That's half the point of the Tales and Tomes Festival."

"Technically, yes, but I spent months planning for that before I actually wrote anything." I took the pot from her shaky hands, putting it safely on the table. "And you know I haven't even read the latest book yet..."

It had released the same month Grandpa passed away and I hadn't been able to bring myself to buy it. I hadn't thought about the series once since then, choosing to pack up all our books and merchandise for it rather than feel the pain of missing him every time I walked by it.

Gran didn't answer as she dipped a spoon into the cough syrup, ladling it carefully into jars. The golden syrup filled the glass, sparkling warmly in the light. Every medicine we made was like a gem, vibrant and beautiful.

"I know it's been hard," Gran whispered so softly I almost didn't hear her, "but you can't just stop living, Willow. It's not healthy to shut yourself off from the world like this." The bell above the door chimed, saving me from responding as Gran pinned me with a stern look. "This isn't over, so don't even think about going anywhere."

"Fine, fine." I held my hands up in surrender. "I'll just wait here and keep bottling cough syrup."

Gran turned to greet two of our regular customers. "Welcome, Professor Ashford and Professor Min. It's good to see you. Thanks again for helping us with those mossmews."

They smiled back at her, the three of them chatting for a bit to catch up. Gran had a personal touch with all our customers like that, which was why I preferred to stay in the back. I was perfectly polite to everyone, but I had no interest in crossing that business casual line like Gran did. They weren't part of our family no matter how many times she said they were. They were just our customers.

Professor Ashford *had* been nice enough to help us with the mossmews who moved into our garden a few weeks ago though. He was the leading expert on caring for magical creatures, but somehow, he always managed to injure himself when he was around them. One time he'd come in with burns from a fire spirit living in his fireplace, another time he'd been limping from falling off an over-excitable pegasus. I looked him over, trying to guess what was wrong this time. The dark circles under his eyes, extra pale skin, and the way his wife was fretting over him more than usual made me think sleep deprivation again, but we'd given him more sleeping drafts the last time he was here.

Gran smiled warmly at them. "Hmmm, it looks like you both could use a nap. Are your sleeping drafts not working anymore?"

"No, well, yes?" Professor Ashford winced, glancing between me and Gran. "One of the slimes I'm caring for might have drank some of them."

Professor Min scoffed. "Some of them? Try all of them. The man didn't get a single potion for himself, and he kept waking me up with all his tossing and turning." Her eyes softened as she looped her arm through his. "You know I don't sleep well unless you do too."

The way he smiled at her made me smile too. They always seemed so happy together. People like them were willing to risk the pain of heartache to be happy. I admired that. I couldn't do it myself, but I could respect those who tried.

Professor Ashford smiled sheepishly at Gran. "I'm sorry I wasted your tonics. The slime just loves the valerian root inside of them and proceeded to sleep all cozy by the fire. It was adorable, so I couldn't be that upset at him."

I raised an eyebrow. "And what about you? How have *you* been sleeping then?"

"I'm fine, Min's just a worrier." He rubbed the back of his head, smiling bashfully as he handed us the usual payment for his order.

He always seemed to care more about the health of the creatures he was caring for than himself and those dark circles proved it. He'd probably stayed up late watching the slimes instead of even trying to rest. I sighed, adding as many sleeping drafts as we had to a box along with some valerian root as a treat for the slime. Maybe he'd let the professor have his sleeping draft if he had his own snack too.

Gran crossed her arms, staring him down. "I expect you to take one of these every night. Lock the box to keep the slimes out if you must, but you need your rest. If you don't sleep, you'll start hallucinating. Or worse."

"Or worse?" His eyes widened. "Okay. I'll be more careful."

I pressed my lips together to keep my laughter to myself. Gran was so tough sometimes, resorting to scare tactics on difficult customers. The professor needed a bit of that, otherwise he'd keep putting his beloved animals before himself. He had to realize that the only way to care for others was to take care of yourself first, right?

"Try some chamomile tea during the day too." I added a few bags to his order. "It's on the house."

"Oh, I can't accept that."

"It's for helping us with the mossmews then." I motioned at the tiny cat-like creatures slinking over to them like they had catnip in their pockets. "Just let us know if the tea helps or not."

Professor Min leaned closer to Gran with a smile. "You've raised a good one there, haven't you? You should both come over for dinner sometime."

I gave Gran a look that clearly said no way, but she just smiled and accepted the invite. Great. So much for professional distance. At least I'd get to see all the cool magical creatures though.

Professor Ashford smiled and held his hand out to a mossmew who was weaving figure 8's around his legs. The mossmew purred softly, leaning into his hand like they were old friends. We couldn't have made such a good home for them without him giving us tips on how to keep them comfortable and what to feed them.

"They're really thriving here, aren't they?" He glanced at the back door. "Mind if I take a peek at your garden? See how the rest of them are doing?"

Gran shoved the box of medication in his arms. "Another time. Right now, you need to go home and sleep."

"But I've got class—"

"Not today, you don't." Min nudged him towards the exit. "I'll handle everything. You just need to sleep."

He leaned over and kissed her on the temple. "I honestly don't know what I'd do without you. Thank you."

They really did seem great together. Too bad they were leaving. Gran would probably want to continue our earlier conversation. The cough syrup needed to be dated and labeled though, so I bent my head down and pretended like I was really, *really* focused on that task.

Gran clicked her tongue against her teeth. "That's not going to distract me, you know. Are you really done writing? For good or just for now?"

"For good. I gave it a try, but it just wasn't fun. I know you want me to love it because of Grandpa, but, well, he's not here anymore." I swallowed hard, my hands shaking just enough to mess up the tiny labels on the jars. "I can let it go if I want to."

My shoulders tightened and I hated how final that sounded. Like I was giving up. But that's what people did all the time. They tried a hobby and stopped if they didn't like it, right? This wasn't some big, horrible thing. When I glanced up at Gran, she had such a sad look on her face though. Like she was losing Grandpa all over again.

"I'm sorry," I whispered. "I just can't go through that again."

Gran pulled me into a hug, patting my back softly. "Oh honey, you don't have to if you don't want to. I won't be disappointed, but I'm worried that *you* will be. You don't seem to remember how much you loved writing that book." She pulled back, her eyes softening as she smiled at me. "Sure, some days were hard and you seemed downright miserable, but when the words came out just right, your eyes would light up and you'd be so excited."

"Really? I don't remember that happening very often..."

She gave me a wry grin. "Well of course not. The tough times always seem to overwhelm a person's joy, but that doesn't mean it wasn't there. Or that you can't be happy writing again. The way you talked about your story is the happiest I've ever seen you. It always was. That's why I keep bringing up times with your Grandpa, not because I want you to feel guilty, but because I don't want you to forget about the things you love deep down. Writing is hard, I understand that, but if it's something that makes you feel fulfilled, then you shouldn't give it up so easily."

My chest ached the more she talked, like her words were digging into my very soul. Words were powerful like that, which was one of the reasons I really did enjoy writing. Maybe she was right and I had more fun than I was remembering. Parts of the process felt downright magical as I went from initial idea to something people could hold in their hands and read. The Demon Lord said it lacked some depth, but that didn't mean I couldn't grow and get better next time.

But did I want there to be a next time? And was the Demon Lord's book really the one I should be working on if I did?

"I don't know, Gran." I gathered the jars of cough syrup in my arms, carrying them over to the proper shelf. When I went back from another handful, she was still watching me with those sad eyes. "I'll think about it, okay?"

She nodded, gathering up a few jars of her own to shelve. "Okay, just like I'm thinking about retiring someday."

"No, that's totally different. You're just being stubborn."

"And you're being what? Honest with yourself?" Gran snorted. "I know you use our shop as an excuse not to do things sometimes. That was fine when it was getting you through all the pain of losing your parents and then your Grandpa, but you can't hide away here forever."

She said it so matter-of-factly that I couldn't help but stare at her. "Really? This has nothing to do with my parents."

They'd passed away when I was young, which was why I'd started living here in the first place. Being together helped us all heal, but it also gave me a way to stay connected to my parents. This shop was like part of our family with all of us working here at one point or another. I bet Gran would have retired already if mom was running the place instead of me...

Gran leaned over to pat my hand. "They've got everything to do with this. So please, just give writing another chance. If not for yourself, then for me."

Gran never asked for anything, not even when we were so busy we almost couldn't finish the orders. And the way she was looking at me right now made me feel so...unsettled. Like she was truly worried about me. I hated seeing that expression on her face more than anything else.

"Fine, but if I hate it, then I'm really done for good." I crossed my arms, giving her my best serious face. "No more talking about my dreams or making me feel bad for giving up on writing. Deal?"

"Deal." Gran nodded. "But if you enjoy it, then I get to actually read the book this time."

"Fine. You can read it when you retire."

We both laughed and I went back to shelving the cough syrup while Gran started grinding herbs for our next project. It was so easy to fall into a comfortable work pattern with her as the calming scent of our shop washed over me. I loved working here, but maybe she was right, and maybe I loved writing too. There was only one way to find out.

I groaned, hanging my head in my hands. "I've gotta go talk to the Demon Lord again, don't I?"

"How terrible," Gran said with a wicked grin. "Try not to have too much fun working side by side with him all day."

"Gran!"

"What?" She shrugged innocently. "He's going to be your best source of information for writing that book. It's probably every writer's dream to talk to one of their characters in person like that. Take full advantage of the opportunity."

She had a good point, and the Demon Lord had seemed eager for his last book to get written. But could I really do the series justice? I guess it wouldn't hurt to try. Like Gran said, only the family of the author would be reading it. So if it was terrible, nobody had to know.

Except me, of course.

If that was the price of finally putting this writing nonsense to bed, then I'd do it. I'd write one more book, and if I failed again, then I'd know I'd given it my all.

Chapter 7
Demon Lord

Since Willow had refused to write the last book in my series, I was forced to come up with a new plan yesterday. She wasn't the only good writer out there, she wasn't even the most qualified one, so all I had to do was host interviews and see who else was worthy of writing my ending. Which was how I'd gotten stuck for hours talking to super fans and a few authors who'd never even read the books.

It was exhausting. I slumped back in my chair as yet another author strolled into the library's conference room, bright-eyed and full of far too much excitement.

"It's so nice to meet you!" The woman rushed over, shaking my hand with enough vigor to pull me right out of my chair. "When I heard you wanted to work with an author for the contest, I hopped on the first sky ship! Ten hours later and here I am, full of ideas and ready to write!"

"Okay, let's cut to the chase then." I extracted my hand from hers. "How do you see this ending?"

"Well, first you're going to hire me, then we're going to make some magic happen, and we'll probably fall in love too." She hugged a copy of the first book to her chest, smiling brightly. "With you on my team, there's no way we won't win this competition."

"I meant how do you see the book ending?" I sighed, rubbing my temples. If I tried to scare her away, she'd only get more excited. I'd learned that lesson the hard way with a woman who thought the hero and I were secretly soulmates and should end up as a couple. The more I argued, the more convinced she was. "Nevermind. You can just go."

"But I didn't even tell you my name yet. It's Sage and I've got a wonderful ending planned for your book, I promise." She rushed to pull a bunch of papers out of her bag, dropping more than a few in her haste. "Sorry, just let me find my notes."

"Fine, but if you choose to stay, you'll only get one chance." I stepped closer, looming over her as my shadows swirled through the air. "If you disappoint me, I'll send you to a shadow realm and I swear you will not enjoy it."

More papers fell from her hands, fluttering to the floor as she took a step back. "Seriously? But that's a fictional place..."

"And I'm a fictional character. Try me. I dare you."

Sage gulped, pushing her glasses higher up her nose. "Wait, you have to say that, don't you? Playing the part of an evil villain and all that."

Now that hit a little too close to home. Her laughter set my teeth on edge as she bent to pick up her notes scattered across the floor. Didn't anyone believe that I was actually an evil demon lord who was destined to destroy the hero and take over the world? Or was I honestly just a joke to all of them?

If only Willow hadn't said no. She was one of the few people I'd met since coming out of my book that seemed to take me seriously. Or at least, didn't try to make me into some overly dramatic caricature of myself. Without her, I was probably doomed to lose to the hero in some horrific way.

"Mr. Demon Lord?" Sage stood up, papers in hand. "I think that once the hero kills you, your dark power should flow to another, creating a new Demon Lord with your will and rage fueling them to get revenge in a new series."

That would work, but forcing my will onto someone else when I barely even knew what I wanted myself felt wrong. It was the most reasonable ending presented so far though, so I should probably take her up on it...

"Fine, let's–" A pop of red hair drew my attention to the doorway where Willow stood smiling at me. Wait, had she changed her mind about writing my book? Excitement surged through me, but I clamped down on it as her eyes drifted to the writer next to me. No, she was probably here to meet and greet with all the authors I'd gathered, that's all. I crossed my arms, trying not to let my disappointment show. "I knew you'd come crawling back eventually, but as you can see, I'm already interviewing other writers. You had your chance, and you lost it."

She rolled her eyes. "Hello to you too. Excuse me for thinking the offer might still be good barely a day later."

"Does that mean you changed your mind?" I felt myself moving closer to her against my will, hope blazing in my chest.

She was the one I'd wanted all along, not some super fan trying to show off. "I might be willing to reconsider. If you ask nicely."

"Excuse me." Sage pushed between us, nudging Willow out of the way. "This is *my* interview. You'll need to wait your turn just like everyone else."

"Oh, sorry." Willow winced and started walking away, but there was no way I'd let that happen again. Not after this exhausting day of interviews had proven just how perfect she was for my book. I flooded the far side of the room with shadows, casting her exit in pitch black darkness. She turned back with a grin. "You want me to stay that badly, huh? But I thought I was supposed to beg for the job."

That's what I probably should do, but the fear of losing her was far too strong. I didn't have the time or patience to continue these interviews, especially when the author I wanted was standing right in front of me.

And a lord should get what they wanted, right?

"You *will* write my final book," I commanded her. "I let you leave once, but you're stuck with me now until you finish it and it better be outstanding."

"Seriously?" Sage huffed, clutching her papers tight. "I can't believe I flew all the way here for this. It's your loss, I promise you that."

Willow raised her eyebrows as Sage stormed through my shadows, exiting the room with flair. A minute later and I'd have been working with her instead of Willow. Thank the gods for good timing.

"So where do we start?" Willow asked. "We could go through the series as a whole, jump right to the end, or focus on plot holes maybe?" She glanced up at me with an eager expression that was so different from the anguish on her face yesterday. She'd looked like she was holding back tears then, but now she was completely fine. If she could flip her emotions that easily, what was stopping her from changing her mind again and dropping the project after a few days?

"First, tell me what changed your mind." I pinned her with my most imposing stare. "You were so dead set against writing this book yesterday. I don't buy that you had a change of heart."

"Caught me." She picked up a book, flipping through the pages without really looking at them. "My Gran heard about the competition and thought it would be a great opportunity for me, so yeah, I'm doing it to make her happy. I promise I'll give it my all, but..." Her fingers brushed tentatively over the cover of the most recent book in my series before pulling away from it. "I'll admit that I haven't read the newest book yet."

"Wait, you haven't even read all the books??" I shoved the book in question at her. "Here. Read it as fast as you can."

She glanced from me to the thick book. "Right now? With you staring at me?"

"Oh how the tables have turned." I grimaced, knowing exactly how strange it was to read with somebody watching you. "Okay, maybe you can save that for later. You're familiar with the other books, right?"

"The early ones yes, I've reread them multiple times." She tilted her head, staring at the rest of the books on the table. "The later ones I'm a little fuzzier on." I must have been letting my frustration show because she raised her hands defensively. "What? You're the one who asked me to write this, remember?"

Oh, I remembered. It sounded like a perfect idea at that time, but I just assumed she knew the series like the back of her hand. Everyone else seemed to and wouldn't shut up about it. No wonder she hadn't bombarded me with questions like everyone else: she wasn't a super fan.

Any other day that would be refreshing, but right now it felt like a bucket of cold water. If we were going to pull off this ending, I *needed* a super fan.

I sighed. "This would be so much easier if you could step inside my book like I can. Then you'd be surrounded by the story, living it."

And probably running in terror because of the war that was about to happen between the demons and the hero. Maybe it was a good thing she couldn't come inside my book. It was no place for somebody as warm and kind as her.

"Too bad jumping into books isn't a thing," she said with a laugh. "I'm sorry, just give me a day or two. I'll refresh myself on everything and catch up on the last book. Then we can start planning."

"Fine, go read, but don't forget a single detail."

"Yes, My Lord!" She saluted me with mock seriousness before turning to leave. "I'm going to need a cozier chair though."

Before she made it two steps away, the book in her arms started glowing with a warm golden light. She stopped, turning back to look at me as if I'd know what was going on. Then all of the other books in my series started glowing too until the table was bathed in sunlight.

"What in the nine realms," she muttered, walking back to the table. "What's happening?"

Warmth spread through my connection to the library, like it was telling me it would all be okay. Which only made this whole situation stranger. That light looked like the light that appeared when we were going in or out of our books. Why would that be happening now?

The last book's cover flipped open. I had a really bad feeling about this.

"Hold on–"

The light engulfed me before I could finish. I blinked, waiting for it to dim. The stone walls surrounding me were instantly recognizable: we were inside my castle. But this wasn't like every other time I'd gone into my book, because this time, I wasn't alone.

Willow was right beside me, inside my book! Her red hair was the brightest color in the drab room and her green eyes were full of confusion.

No, no, no. This was not happening. Had the library heard me joking about her stepping inside my book? I hadn't been serious! It was too dangerous, too unpredictable.

I clenched my hands. "We need to leave. Now."

"No way." She shook her head as her gaze swept across the barren room. "Not until you tell me what just happened. We were in the library and then poof, we're...where are we exactly?"

If I told her, she'd probably get excited and refuse to leave, but this magic was a big unknown. Had a human ever gone inside a book before? How would it affect her?

"This isn't part of the library." Willow ran her fingers over the cold stone slab against the far side of the room, frowning. "Is this...a bed? Who would sleep on something so uncomfortable?"

"Me." I sighed. There was no way she'd let this go without an explanation. "We're in my room. In my castle."

Her eyes widened. "Wait, we're inside your book? I didn't know you could do that! Why didn't you say something?"

"I *can't* do that." And even if I could, I wouldn't have. "It's got to be the library trying out new magic. Misty's the one who brought us out of our books, so it makes sense that it would be involved with you coming inside."

"That is so cool." Her excitement faded a bit as she studied the rest of the sparse gray room. "But is this really where you live? It feels so harsh and uncomfortable. The books always had such vivid descriptions, but this just..."

Her voice trailed off like she didn't want to insult me.

"Looks like the author didn't give a damn," I finished for her. "The castle might be detailed on the outside, but the inside is pretty bleak."

That felt like a metaphor for my entire life. The outside looked good, but the inside was a blank canvas.

Willow crossed her arms, staring intensely at the bed. "That just isn't right. Not even a Demon Lord should live like this, so it's a good thing I'm here." She grinned, her eyes lighting up. "Ohhh, we should get some really cozy blankets, maybe a few pillows, really make this place comfortable."

"It's fine, let's just get out of here."

"Really? You don't want even one pillow?" She sank onto the hard excuse for a bed. "I don't think you know what you're missing. This is not what a bed should feel like. It should be so comfortable that you can barely force yourself out of it in the morning."

Something about her being on my bed, stone slab that it was, felt strange. She didn't belong here.

"If I agree to get a blanket, will you leave?" I asked. "For your safety."

"You think I'm not safe here? I'm in the Demon Lord's castle, literally in your bed." The corners of her lips quirked up. "Who in this entire book would dare harm me here?"

She dropped her bag at the edge of the bed and then leaned back on her hands to watch me. Seeing her belongings in my room felt like she was claiming it, making herself at home in my world. And I couldn't decide if I should throw the bag out the window or stand in front of it so she'd stay a little longer...

I swallowed hard. This was not how the story went, and it wouldn't help us finish the book at all.

"We're leaving." I grabbed her arm, ignoring her laughing protests as I willed us out of my book.

The golden light came back, reaching down for me like it always did, transporting me out of my book and back into the safety of the Misty Mountain Library. I let out a breath, happy to have that whole mess behind us.

Except, where my hand used to be gripping her arm, I just felt empty air.

Willow wasn't there.

My stomach dropped as the glowing light around my book dimmed without releasing her. Was she stuck inside the book?

"Misty!" I shouted, marching toward the book tree as shadows snapped and whirled around me. "How could you let her inside but not let her back out?"

The branches of the tree swayed, giving me no answers at all.

"Bring her back. Now." My voice thundered in the quiet library, causing a few patrons to back away quickly. "I was just kidding about her going inside the book, you know that right?"

The tree bark groaned quietly as Misty continued to ignore me, but a trickle of pride washed through our connection. The library was pretty happy with itself, which probably meant it didn't know she was stuck. It really thought it was helping us, helping her finish my story. Which was sweet and kind, but oh so very wrong.

"Misty, Willow can't get out. You need to bring her back."

The leaves on the book tree trembled as our bond went cold in a way I'd never felt before.

"What's wrong?" I gently laid my palm against the tree's bark, but a pit was already settling in my stomach. Do you not know how to get her out?"

Our bond warmed a bit, and I could sense the rightness of that. The library had been infused with wild magic, bringing us out of our books without even truly knowing how or why at first. The wild magic had taken over and drawn on what the library wanted most, so if the same thing was happening now, it might really not know what to do.

I sucked in an unsteady breath. I couldn't be upset with the library for not knowing how its wild magic worked, but I had to fix this. It was my fault for making that offhand comment. My fault she was stuck.

"Let me talk to Nyssa." I patted the great book tree in what I hoped was a reassuring way. "We'll figure this out. Together."

That's what the overly optimistic librarian had ground into me over the past few months, that we were better together than alone. Hopefully that still held true. The tree's leaves stopped shaking and its branches seemed to perk up. It trusted Nyssa as its librarian so I'd have to trust her too. She wouldn't want news to get out that the books could suddenly lock patrons inside them after all.

Nyssa was already on her way to me by the time I started looking for her, hands on her hips and a deep frown on her face. "What did you do now? A few patrons said you were shrouding the tree in darkness or something."

"Accidentally, but there's more important things to worry about."

"Look, I know you're a Demon Lord, but you've gotta try and work on your people skills." She paused, staring at me. "Wait, what bigger things?"

"Willow is stuck inside a book."

Nyssa tilted her head and then started laughing. "Good one. What will you think of next? That people are hopping inside books like a cool vacation?"

I waited for her to stop laughing, trying to resist the urge to use my shadows to drag her over to the table of books. There was no way to prove Willow was inside. It wasn't like there would be a picture of her screaming face on the first page, hands pounding the paper.

Would there?

"Just fix it!" I snapped. "The book tree's magic is out of control again."

"Wait, you're serious? And you left her in there alone?" Nyssa gasped, shoving me toward my book. "Get back in there and take care of her, you ridiculous demon! I'll contact Oren and we'll figure something out. Check in again tomorrow if you haven't found a way out yet."

My book started glowing, as if welcoming me inside, but there was one more thing I needed to do. I grabbed a piece of paper and scribbled a note to Willow's Gran, letting her know that Willow was safe and sound but we'd be working on the book for a while.

"Give this to the apothecary for me." I forced the note into her hands. "Don't forget."

"You're nicer than you look, but hurry up." Nyssa nudged me again. "She's probably terrified."

I nodded, diving back into my book as quickly as I could. Unfortunately, Willow wasn't there either. Or at least, she wasn't where I'd left her. In her place on my bed was a note of her own that read: *Gone exploring, don't wait up.*

The paper crumbled beneath my fingers as I clenched my fists. Why hadn't she just waited for me? I was barely gone fifteen minutes!

My pulse thundered in my ears as I searched empty castle room after empty castle room. After every room had been thoroughly searched, there was only one option left.

Willow had gone outside. Even I'd never done that before...

Outside was where the story of the book took place. My character had never been part of that, I was always locked away in my castle doing evil schemey things in the background. If I tried to step outside, I'd risk not living up to people's expectations. No matter how hard I tried to be terrifying and full of darkness, I seemed to fall short at every turn. Fans swooned over me, children adored me, and dragons cuddled me. Not exactly the monster everyone thought I'd be.

But Willow needed me right now, so I'd just have to glower and push through this.

I took a deep breath and pushed the doors to my castle open for the very first time since I'd woken up in the library. I'd find Willow, drag her back, and then return her to the library where she belonged.

CHAPTER 8
WILLOW

One minute the Demon Lord was there and then the next, he was gone. The golden light just pulled him up and completely ignored me.

Now I was alone.

I tried not to worry about what that might mean, but there wasn't really anything else to occupy my mind besides the chill in the air. I shivered, rubbing my hands along my arms. The castle apparently had no heat, not even a fireplace for the supposed lord of the castle's room. If I sat here much longer my mind would race with worse and worse possibilities.

Was I stuck in here? Why and for how long?

I sank onto the Demon Lord's sorry excuse for a bed. It was cold and hard, nothing like a bed should be. Picturing him sleeping here every night, and apparently not knowing that beds could be better, made my chest hurt. Did he really think this was how things were supposed to be?

Maybe that's why he was so grumpy. I would be too if I slept on a stone slab.

There was no way he'd leave me here all by myself for too long though. So, until he came back, I might as well explore a bit. I was inside a book! I'd dreamed of going inside my favorite stories so many times, but now I was really in one. I couldn't just sit here and not even take a peek outside.

Slinging my bag over my shoulder, I wandered into the hallway. Torches lit up when I walked by them, revealing half-finished tapestries and mostly empty rooms. Some areas were just fuzzy holes in the wall, literally blank spaces, like the author had gotten bored thinking of what the rooms would be for. Which was fair since this castle was gigantic, but what stood out most were the cracks. Dozens of spider-webbed fissures breaking what should have been a strong and fortified castle.

I ran my fingers along the cracks, the walls cold and rough. With all these unfinished and broken pieces, how much of the Demon Lord's series was left unknown? If I was really going to write the final book, then I needed to see more than this castle.

I had to fill in the blanks. I needed to go outside and meet people.

Excitement rushed through me as I grasped the handles of the large entryway doors. Once I stepped outside, I'd be talking to other characters from a story, just like the Demon Lord. Would they know they were inside a book like he did? Or would they think their world was the real world?

Depending on how much I could explore, maybe I could find all the answers I needed to write an ending the fans would appreciate.

I flung the doors open, gazing out at a sky covered in a dense miasma cloud that turned the sunlight a surprisingly beautiful shade of purple. A forest of stark white trees surrounded the castle, fencing a sprawling village in on all sides. A shout drew my attention to the right as I hid behind the doors, half expecting the village to be full of monsters.

But what I saw instead took my breath away.

People of all shapes and sizes, some with horns and others with fluffy ears and tails, were putting pies on their windowsills to cool and playing with children. Stalls lined the main road like a marketplace full of everything from bakers to tailors, all with the same ashen skin as the Demon Lord.

This was a demon town!

I stepped forward, my curiosity bubbling up inside of me like the book well itself. I had to see this. I had to know what the town was like because I couldn't remember it being mentioned in the books.

Voices hushed as the demons turned to stare at me one by one.

"Hello." I smiled at them warmly. "My name's Willow."

A short demon with a plump loaf of bread in his paws gulped, his tail twitching. "Hu-hu-human!"

He dropped the bread and fled, hiding behind one of the buildings.

"Wait, no." I shook my head. "I'm not here to hurt you. I came with the Demon Lord."

But instead of greeting me back, they either fled or drew weapons. Did nobody hear me? What was going on?

A group of stern-looking demons with swords marched forward, horns gleaming under the purple sky. They looked like soldiers ready to slay the evil human who'd encroached on their territory.

"Humans are not allowed here," one of the muscled demons said, gripping a spear. "You kill us on sight, but think you can just waltz into the heart of our nation? You'll pay dearly for your overconfidence."

I swallowed hard, holding my hands in the air as I slowly stepped backward. "I didn't mean to, I'm sorry. I'll just leave and you'll never have to see me again..."

The tip of his spear sliced my cheek before I even noticed him moving. A small trickle of blood dripped down my face as pain pulsed through me. This was supposed to be a story, but I was bleeding for real!

I stumbled back, fleeing before things got worse. I had to get back inside the castle. Where was the Demon Lord??

Cheers rose up behind me as I ran away.

"You're safe now everyone," the demon called back to the market. "Do not fear the human; we'll take care of it!"

Seriously, were demons really that terrified of humans? They had strength and magical abilities that the humans in this book could only dream of. So why did they seem so proud of scaring off one completely non-violent woman?

Something about this town didn't feel right, but I'd be damned if I was going to continue exploring without the Demon Lord. Not that I'd admit that to him, of course.

Except, instead of going back to his castle, I'd sort of ended up in the forest. The shadows cast by the big trees seemed to move on their own, taunting me, leading me deeper inside. The trees were white, like ghosts in the night, and I wasn't sure where I'd entered. I turned around, searching for the castle, but all I saw were trees. Trees with demonic red eyes in their branches.

My pulse pounded in my ears. I'd barely taken two steps into the forest, so how could I be lost already? I stared at the stark white trees as memories tugged at my mind.

Grandpa had always skipped over the scary parts about this story when I was young, but there had definitely been a white forest. One that the hero was never supposed to enter for fear of getting lost inside for eternity.

My eyes widened. This had to be the Wandering Woods!

It was supposedly the Demon Lord's best defense against intruders, and I'd walked right into it. Sure, I'd wanted first-hand knowledge of the book, but why oh why did I have to get caught in that grumpy demon's trap while doing it?

Dead leaves covered the ground, crunching with each step I took. I swore I saw movement too, like little creatures dashing through the leaves, leaping from tree to tree, laughing at me.

I clutched my bag, wishing I had magical defense potions in here instead of books, snacks, and healing herbs.

"Calm down," I muttered to myself, "just calm down. Everything's going to be okay. The Demon Lord will return, and he'll get me out of here."

A soft keening sound pushed through my growing terror. It sounded like something was in pain.

I searched for the noise, spotting a small bunny-like creature beside a tree holding its paw strangely. The bunny had gorgeous long black fur and big floppy ears with horns curling back over its head. Its bright red eyes landed on me as black and red flames sprouted in the air around it in a defensive circle.

"Don't be scared," I said, kneeling slowly. "Are you hurt?"

The demon bunny grew bigger, as if trying to intimidate me into walking away, but there was no chance I'd leave an injured animal. Not even a demonic one in a storybook. I reached into my bag, pulling out a container of dried fruit and some herbs I'd seen wild bunnies eating on the mountain before.

"Here, have some."

The bunny's black nose twitched. It hopped closer, flames inching toward me as it cautiously nibbled some of the herbs. Heat licked my fingertips, but I didn't move. The bunny lunged forward to gobble them up, chubby cheeks bouncing as it chewed. My fears faded as the demon bunny happily ate the dried fruit too.

I exhaled in relief, finally regaining some control over my senses. Just because it was part demon didn't mean it wasn't adorable.

"Okay, let's get that paw of yours fixed next." I pulled out a bandage and healing salve that I was supposed to drop off for a client on my way back from the library, and reached for the bunny. It leapt back, snarling like no bunny ever should. "Okay, okay, no need to flame me. Why don't I try it on myself first?"

My cheek was throbbing at this point, so it would be good to clean it up anyway. I spread some of the bright green salve onto my face and secured a bandage over it.

"See?" I leaned down, letting the bunny examine it. "It's just a healing salve. It'll help your paw."

The bunny hopped one step toward me, then another, before it held out its paw, head turned away like it couldn't be bothered with this nonsense.

"Well aren't you the proud little thing," I said with a laugh as I spread the salve over the cut on its leg and wrapped it up. "There, you're all set! You should stay close so I can remove that bandage later and reapply the salve."

Its deep red eyes blinked up at me. Could demon bunnies understand humans?

We stared at each other for a bit, question unanswered, before the bunny scurried into my bag, nibbling on all the other treats I had in there.

"Hey, those are mine too!" I laughed, daring to pet the adorable demon. It purred, settling into my bag like it was its new home.

I let out a breath. That had gone much better than I thought it would. If I could get on the good side of this demon bunny, then maybe I could show the townsfolk that they didn't need to kill me on sight. I could at least stay safe until the Demon Lord returned and got me out of this book

I carefully stood up, trying not to jostle the bunny, but noticed the dead leaves had blown away revealing a path. I frowned, hoping this wasn't some trick that would lead me deeper inside forest.

"What do you think Bun, should I follow it?" I opened the flap on my bag so the bunny's head and big floppy ears could poke out over the edge. It chittered at me, nibbling some herbs and motioning its head the other way. "You want me to go that way?"

When the bunny's head bobbed in what I took as a nod, I turned around. "Okay, let's hope this is the way out."

After what felt like hours, I stumbled out of the forest and back onto fresh grass. I grinned, taking a deep breath of the magic-infused air. I could see the castle! And the town! And the demons...

The demon with the spear whirled on me, like he'd been waiting here the whole time.

"It'll be okay, little bunny." I clutched my bag tight in case we had to run.

"How did you get out?" he demanded. "Did you kidnap a demon bunny?"

"I don't think so? It just hopped in my bag all on its own." The townsfolk stared in disbelief as I reached down to scratch behind the bunny's ears. "I promise I didn't come here to hurt you all. I'm here to help. I think."

Whispers surrounded me as the baker demon slowly approached. "You said you came here with the Demon Lord, right?"

"Yes, but he had to run an errand," I lied, "he'll be back soon."

The bunny hummed and chittered, making a bunch of bunny talking noises that reminded me of when Mochi spoke and I couldn't understand him. The rest of the demons nodded.

"Cinder, the bunny, says you healed her?" When I nodded, the spear wielder continued. "Can you heal others too?"

"Of course!" I frowned, scrounging through my bag. "Well, I don't have many supplies with me, so I'd need to gather a few things. I'm not even sure what this world has actually. I'm an apothecary where I'm from."

I was babbling, but they were all staring at me, making me nervous. The bunny hopped out of my bag, as if my rummaging around had disturbed her peace. She sat between my feet, staring right back at all the demons. My little bunny defender.

"Your name's Cinder, huh?" I bent down to pet her. "It's nice to meet you. My name's Willow."

Cinder's nose twitched as I handed the bunny a few more herbs. She stuffed them in her mouth, chubby cheeks chewing fast. The demons around me relaxed, smiling at the bunny.

The baker from earlier stepped forward. "Do you really know the Demon Lord? Like you've talked to him in person?"

"Well, yeah?" I frowned, glancing at their curious faces. "Haven't you?"

The soldier crossed his arms, muscles bulging. "Of course not. Our lord is far too busy to be talking to random demons like us. I bet you've never even met him. You're just trying to infiltrate our town. You and your bunny are not welcome here."

Interesting. How had nobody talked to him before? His generals had to get orders somehow, otherwise they'd never have been sent out on all those missions in the previous books. Unless the Demon Lord *only* talked to his generals and deemed everyone else unworthy of conversation. That felt right for the character I'd read about, but odd for the person I'd been getting to know. Like there was a disconnect between what I'd read and what I'd seen in person.

The delicious scent of spiced meat wafted through the air, making my stomach rumble. I'd intended to stop by Mochi for a snack before all this happened, but I'd just have to find something in the castle while I waited for the Demon Lord. Would eating storybook food still be filling?

"I'll just leave you all be then," I said as I backed away toward the castle. "I'll wait inside for him to come back."

"Inside?" The baker gasped. "She's been inside the castle! We can't turn her away. What if she truly is the Demon Lord's...?"

"Friend," I finished for him. "We're friends."

Or at least, I thought we were. It sounded better than acquaintances writing a book together.

The baker raised his eyebrows. "Come along, little human. Let me get you a plate of food and you can tell me all about this *friendship* you have with our lord."

Before I knew it, I'd been pulled into their circle, surrounded by tasty food and laughter. It was like a switch had flipped and their curiosity about the Demon Lord had taken over. I gladly sampled every food they gave me, marveling at how real it tasted. This world didn't feel like a story at all. It was all so homey and warm, I never would have guessed we were in the infamous demon village.

That disconnect I'd felt earlier was growing. Something about this village just didn't seem right. Demons were supposed to be evil incarnate, so why were they feeding me pastries and chatting about their day? Whatever the reason, it seemed like writing this final book just got a whole lot more difficult.

CHAPTER 9
DEMON LORD

The sky was full of the purple miasma I'd only ever seen from my castle windows. Breathing it in felt strange, like power coiled in the air waiting to strike. If I stepped outside, stepped into this book's world, I'd finally become part of it and people would see who I really was. A demon trying to act like a lord. I could probably fool normal people by just walking around with a glower on my face, but if I ran into any of my generals, they'd realize I wasn't who I was supposed to be.

They were strong and terrifying, just like I aimed to be myself, and I was purposefully avoiding them until I achieved the villainy they'd expect. I was their leader, and I refused to let them down.

Honestly, it might be better to stay inside and leave Willow to fend for herself. Sure, I was partially responsible for her being here, but she was the one who'd run off on her own. So why was I the one walking outside as if my feet had a will of their own? Each step felt heavier and heavier and my back tensed up like people were watching me.

I inhaled the magically charged air, staring at the village ahead of me with its crooked rooftops, glowing lanterns, and bustling market full of demons. If something happened to Willow, I'd never hear the end of it. Nyssa and Roan would be furious, probably banning me from the library and interacting with patrons. Actually, that part didn't sound half bad.

Maybe I should just return to the castle after all. Either Willow would find her way back or I'd finally get out of talking to people. It seemed like win-win.

But before I could retreat, the sound of Willow's voice drifted over. She was laughing with one of the demons in town, smiling like she'd known them all her life. I couldn't believe I'd been worried about her. I shook my head as she laughed again, brushing a strand of hair behind her ear.

A bandage covered her cheek.

Shadows twisted against my skin as something even darker surged in my chest. That bandage hadn't been there before. I stormed into town, each step fueling my anger as I searched for other injuries. Her pale skin was unblemished besides the bandage, but that didn't mean she was fine. She was literally surrounded. By demons.

My long strides ate up the distance between us as my shadows swallowed everything in my path. Somebody had touched her. Hurt her. And they were going to pay.

"Hey, look who's finally back." Willow's grin faltered when her gaze fell on my shadows. "I know I probably should have waited for you, but I was just too curious. And it's totally fine. Turns out these demons are really nice."

The demons in question froze in terror as I marched up to her. Her cheek was swollen and there was a tiny smear of blood on her skin. I reached out my hand, hovering just over the bandage. "Who did this to you?"

"What?" Her eyes widened. "Oh, that? It's nothing. Just a misunderstanding."

"It's not nothing." My voice was low, full of barely contained rage. I'd only left her for fifteen minutes. How had she gotten injured in such a short time? "Who hurt you?"

A hulking demon with a spear fell to his knees. "I'm sorry, My Lord. If I'd known she was *your* woman, I'd never have touched her."

My shadows coiled around him like a boa constrictor before my mind caught up to what he'd called her. Willow was definitely not my woman.

"Well aren't you two just full of spit and vinegar." Willow crossed her arms, glaring up at me. "If we're going to put labels on me, I'd prefer consort."

"Consort?" My shadows sputtered as my face warmed. "I think I'd remember if we'd....if we'd..."

"If we'd what?" Willow asked. "Got married?"

Being a demon's consort went far beyond marriage. It was a sacred bond that formed when two souls and bodies melded into one so profoundly that their magic intertwined. Whispers about my consort made my face burn even hotter. I disappeared into the shadows between two houses so none of them saw, especially Willow. She had no idea what she'd just implied.

I would never have a consort. Not now. Not ever. I was the villain of this story.

Willow stepped into the space between the houses, turning this way and that as if looking for me. "Uh, did you run away or something? I thought it was a good plot twist. You know, a reason for me to be in your castle."

My shadows licked her skin, testing her, as if the very mention of a consort had them curious. I clamped down on them hard. "This isn't a game. You can't just joke about being my consort."

"Sorry, I was only trying to help." Her eyes widened when I pulled out of the shadows just enough for her to know I was there. "Is being your consort really that terrible?"

I rubbed a hand over my face, laughing despite myself. "You know nothing about demons."

"So teach me. If I'm going to write your story, then I need to know everything."

I peered at her over my fingers. Her bright green eyes met mine, full of curiosity as she lightly touched my arm in reassurance. That simple touch lit a fire in me, sending my shadows spiraling around us both. She had no idea what this conversation was doing to me. Once she understood, she'd never call herself that again and this would be over.

"Being a demon's consort isn't like a human marriage." I wrapped my arm around her, pulling her against my chest. "It's a bond so deep that you can feel the other even when they're not there." I traced the curve of her cheek, carefully avoiding the bandage. "When one is hurt, the other feels it. Like a tether you'll never escape. You'd be bound to me, body and soul."

That had to be enough to scare her away, but instead of laughing it off, she moved closer, leaning into my touch and making my skin tingle.

All thought of explaining the bond disappeared as she bit her lip, staring at me with something that looked like longing in her beautiful green eyes. My breath caught in my chest, and even though I knew better, I didn't pull away. I'd been trying to shock her into taking back her joke, but instead I'd gotten swept up in her charms.

"Mating bond," I blurted out.

She blinked, thankfully pulling away like I'd hoped. "What?"

"Uh, sorry, it's a romance novel thing." I scratched the base of my horns and stepped back so I wouldn't get caught up in the moment again. "Calling yourself my consort is like saying we're fated mates."

Her mouth dropped open. "Demons have fated mates? And I just told the whole town that I was yours??"

"Basically, yes."

There, that's the reaction I was hoping for. Her skin was as red as her hair as she stumbled back. My shadows reached for her as the pleasure of hearing her call herself mine, even in jest, pulsed through me. I should be happy she understood enough to never use that phrase again, but something about her reaction irritated me too. Being my mate wasn't that awful of an idea, was it?

No. Thinking like that was dangerous. If I got my hopes up for any kind of partner, let alone a true mate, the end of my story with the hero would be the least painful part of this adventure.

I was the villain, and villains never got a happy ending.

"You need to tell everyone the truth," I said. "Before this gets out of hand."

She shook her head. "No way. The demons already don't trust me, so if I go out there and tell them I was just kidding, they'll write me off entirely. I'll never get any answers out of them then."

"And who's fault is that?" I asked with a groan. "They'll think I'm weak if I take a human as my consort. So just tell them it was a cultural misunderstanding or something."

"That's a terrible idea." She glared at me, eyes bright with defiance. "If you want me to write your book quickly, then I need to be in a position of power here. Being your consort gives me that. It also explains why I'll be in your castle when nobody else has ever been there."

I opened my mouth to shoot back a witty retort, but nothing came. Her logic was sound. The deadline for the competition was looming and she needed to be as immersed in my story as possible. Even if it meant pretending to be my *consort*.

"Fine, what else do you need?" I took a deep breath, ready to do whatever it took to help her on this mission.

Her eyes widened. "Well that was easier than I thought. I mainly need to talk to the hero. It's his story, so that should be our main objective."

That blasted hero again. Everything always came back around to him. I ground my teeth, dragging Willow back out by the townsfolk. My gaze landed on the soldier who'd wounded her. He was still on his knees where he belonged, awaiting punishment, which suited me perfectly.

"You there, stand up," I commanded him. "You dared to point a weapon at my consort. You even drew blood. That cannot be easily forgiven."

He gulped. "Yes, sir. I understand."

"What are you doing," Willow whispered, leaning close so nobody would overhear. "I said I need the hero, not some macho show of force."

I ignored her, focusing on the soldier in front of me. "You have one chance of redeeming yourself. Kidnap the hero and bring him to me. Alive."

The soldier slammed his fist against his chest, bowing low in fealty. "I will not fail you again."

"Wait a minute, that's not what I meant at all." Willow shook her head, reaching for the soldier's arm. "I'm sure you have a family and friends who will worry about you if you do that. You'd be going on a suicide mission."

"I'm stronger than you think." The demon raised his head and met my gaze straight on. "And I'm honored to be trusted with this mission."

Willow sighed deeply before glaring at me. "Do something about this. You can't just let him die over a silly scratch that'll heal in a few days."

My chest tightened. Willow might not really be my consort, but the world was about to believe she was. I couldn't let anyone think hurting her was a way they could get to me. It was my fault she was stuck in here and I'd be damned if I let her get hurt again because of it. If I couldn't get her out right away, then I had to protect her. Maybe the soldier could come in handy another way...

"Fine, if my consort wants you to live, then you'll live for her. From now on, you'll be her bodyguard. Your life will protect hers. Don't let anyone harm her again."

"As you command." The soldier bowed so low his forehead slammed against the ground before finally standing up.

"Looks like I have a new job! The protector of the Demon Lord's Consort!"

A few demons dared to walk up to him, patting him on the back and congratulating him like he'd won some big prize. Willow even joined in, chatting with them as comfortably as when I first saw her outside. It was like she had an innate ability to put people at ease and talk like they were old friends. They even started handing her gifts like bread, jam, and vegetables. They all seemed thrilled to meet my consort. It was such a joke, but seeing them welcome her like that warmed my heart a little.

This wasn't what I'd expected when I walked outside, but she was safe, and the town had seen my leadership in person. That had to be good enough for now.

As I turned to leave, a small demon with antlers bowed to me. "Thank you for saving me, My Lord."

"I don't remember doing anything of the kind." I frowned as a few more villagers bowed, saying the same thing. Apparently they thought I'd saved most of the town, rescuing them from humans, but that had to be wrong. I was the villain, not a savior. Plus, I never even left my castle.

Willow moved beside the demon child, wiping smudges of ash off his cheeks. "I'm glad you're safe. Who brought you here?"

The boy's eyes lit up. "The Demon Lord sent his most trusted generals to rescue me after I got snatched up by humans!"

"His generals, huh?" Willow frowned, moving closer to me to whisper. "Do you think those are the big fights in the previous books? Could the generals be rescuing captured demons to grow this village of yours?"

"Of course not," I scoffed. "They're pillaging towns and destroying armies. They're not saving children." Except, there did seem to be a lot of demons here all thanking me for saving their lives. "No, if that was true, it would be in the previous books, right? They couldn't skew it so far as to make saving children seem like an evil deed, right?"

Willow shrugged. "Maybe they're doing both. Pillaging and saving? There's always two sides to a story, after all. I need to see both sides if I'm going to write the ending." She glanced back at me, her eyes softening. "Don't you want to know too?"

More than I thought I would. Before, all I'd wanted was to live up to the author's expectation of me. To be the villain I was always meant to be. But if there was something missing, I had to know what it was. Maybe it would finally explain why I was so disconnected from my role. If it helped make the ending memorable, I'd do whatever it took. Even meet the hero if Willow required it.

CHAPTER 10
WILLOW

The villagers had given us so many gifts from fresh vegetables still covered in dirt to giant pieces of unidentifiable meat, all bundled up in my arms as we walked back inside the castle. Most of the food looked pretty normal: carrots, potatoes, and things like that. I'd expected demon veggies to be a bit more...peculiar. Honestly, I'd expected the entire village to be stranger. Everyone seemed so normal, besides the horns and animalistic features of course.

From what I remembered of the book series, *I Just Wanted a Peaceful Life, but Now I Have to Stop the Demon Lord and His Entire Army!* was all about a hero saving humanity from an evil demon overlord trying to take over the world. It was a classic plot, but done really well, full of heart with a fun writing style. But what I'd read didn't match with what I'd just seen. The demons seemed kind so far, nothing like the aggressive and violent beasts they'd been in the books.

Well, one of them had attacked me on sight, but it was only a scratch. If this really was the world of those books, his spear should have ended me, but this scratch was no worse than I'd gotten in the past while picking herbs on the mountain. Plus, the healing salve had already stopped the throbbing, numbing the pain enough that it was barely noticeable.

"I really need to read the last book in your series because I'm obviously missing something big here." I glanced at the Demon Lord. "Let's head back to the library and scour the whole series for details. Something just isn't adding up and I need to know why. Was there foreshadowing for this kind of village? Or is it a product of us being here and there's no deeper meaning to the story?"

"About that..." He stopped abruptly, falling behind me a few steps. "You know I intended to take us both out of the book earlier, right?"

"Well yeah, but it didn't work for some reason." I turned around, pinning him with a stare. "Wait, why didn't it work?"

His purple eyes darkened as he looked away from me, cast in the shadows of the sconces. "I don't know."

"You don't know?" I clutched the food to my chest, accidentally smushing the bread a little. "But the library knows, right? I'm assuming that's how I got in here to begin with at least."

"Yeah." His shoulders rose as he took a deep breath before finally meeting my gaze. "But the library doesn't always know how its magic works now that wild magic is mixed in. You're not a character from a story, you're a person, and I don't think the library knows how that works yet." He stepped closer, putting a hand on my shoulder. "I promise we'll get you out of here. Nyssa's already working on it, and I'll do everything I can to assist. You will not be stuck here for long."

I swallowed hard. The intensity of his words washed over me, but his reassurance wasn't quite enough to stop my growing concern. Gran needed me at the apothecary shop. I couldn't just waste my time here while Misty figured out its magic. I needed to go home!

"Look, I've already been here for so long. Can't you just try and leave with me again? Maybe we need to be holding hands or something. The connection could help?"

He frowned. "What do you mean you've been here for so long? It's probably only been a half hour."

"Half an hour?" I tilted my head. "No, it feels more like half a day. I mean, I explored the castle, got attacked by that soldier, got lost in the Wandering Woods—"

"You went into the Wandering Woods?" His grip on my shoulder tightened. "Are you okay?"

"Cinder made sure I got out safely."

The little bunny poked her nose out of my bag, reaching up like she wanted to nibble on some of the food the villagers had given us. If more time really was passing here than outside, then maybe it was okay to wait a little bit. Nyssa was very good at her job, so there was no way she'd leave me stuck inside a book for too long.

Even so, I was supposed to be helping Gran prepare for winter, gathering what herbs we could and making fresh batches of cold and fever medicines. Sure, I'd agreed to work on this book, but I hadn't intended to abandon her entirely like this. Not during our busiest season of the year.

"Did Nyssa seem confident about getting me out of here?" I asked softly.

"Yes." The word escaped his lips like a promise, a vow that I wouldn't get trapped here forever. "You're safe for now. And maybe we can use this time difference to our benefit. If we have more time, we can plan the last book even better." He winced, pulling away. "If you still want to write it, I mean. I know I'm the one who did this to you. I never meant to put you in danger like this. I just..."

As his voice trailed off, it felt like the temperature in the castle dropped a few degrees. I shivered, hating that this fun adventure suddenly felt more like a nightmare. If I really was stuck here, then I shouldn't spend my time moping. Gran wouldn't want that. She'd want me to use this opportunity to write the best story I could.

"Let's make something for dinner and figure out a plan." I shoved the food I was carrying into his arms, holding Cinder closer for warmth. "And maybe find a fireplace? What's with this cold air all of the sudden?"

"The castle's always been drafty." He started walking again, leading me to what I hoped was a kitchen with a big blazing fireplace. "So you're really okay with this? You're not upset with me?"

I shook my head. "What's to be upset about? It's not like you or the library did this on purpose. Plus, what other author can say they got to literally go inside their favorite book for ideas? I feel lucky, not angry." Lucky. I had to believe that. This was a great opportunity for me. I blinked back what felt like tears and scratched behind Cinder's ears. The bunny cooed, leaning into my hand. "Nobody's at fault here. I just wish I'd been able to let Gran know. Maybe you can hop out of the book and tell her?"

"I actually did that already." He stopped to open a door that led into what looked like a kitchen. "Well, I wrote her a note and had Nyssa deliver it."

"Really?" My chest warmed. He really was a lot nicer than the books portrayed him. "What did you say?"

"That we were working hard on the book and you'd be back in a few days. Not to worry."

I laughed. "Oh man, she already thinks you're a shadow daddy, now she's going to think you've seduced me too."

Which he definitely hadn't, but he was sure getting close. Sending a message to Gran so she didn't worry was beyond sweet, but falling in love only opened yourself up to loss and I'd had enough of that already. There was no way I'd fall head over heels for him, no matter how charming his whole grumpy demon thing was.

He was about to set the food on the counter but pulled out a towel and set everything on that instead. "It's a bit dusty in here. Let me clean up."

I nodded and carefully placed my bag on the floor so Cinder could hop out. Her little nose twitched as she explored the kitchen, hopping from corner to corner. The Demon Lord moved quickly as he cleaned, shadows whipping all over, removing every speck of dust with the intensity of a general off to war. Soon the kitchen was shining.

Man, I could get used to that, if only he wasn't staring at Cinder like she was vermin he wanted to toss out with the trash.

"Do you not like bunnies?" I asked while I washed the vegetables in the sink. "I've seen you with the dragons in the library and you adore them. So what's with the look?"

He froze, a faint blush sweeping his ashen cheeks. "I do not adore those flying lizards. They use my horns as a perch. What's to like about that?"

"Oh, nothing." I grinned, watching Cinder hop right onto his shoe. "But I think that bunny might like you."

"Animals always seem to. It's a demon thing. At least this one led you out of the Wandering Woods, so I guess it can stay here." He bent down to pat Cinder on the head stiffly, as if he wasn't used to showing such affection. "As long as it behaves."

Cinder bowed her head low, then hopped off his shoe and went back to my bag as if she was looking for snacks. Food sounded good, even after trying so many different things in the village. A hot meal and good company could shoo away any chill, sending the nightmare vibe away for good. The tension in the Demon Lord's shoulders made me think he could use that even more than me.

"So what kind of dinner are you thinking? I could probably make soup with this, or maybe you'd prefer grilled meat?" I frowned. "Actually, I don't know that much about you. What foods do you like?"

"I'm...not sure." That pause told me everything as he fumbled trying to peel a carrot with a dagger more suited to throwing than peeling vegetables. "Maybe sweets? Mochi always has good food."

"Sweets, huh?" That's the one thing the villagers hadn't given me anything for, of course. "Well, I'll see what we can do tomorrow. Maybe we can try lots of food and see what you think of it. Gotta learn more about you somehow."

A small smile tugged at his lips. "That sounds nice."

It did sound nice. We could explore the village more, try out some tasty food, and get ideas for his story. It honestly almost sounded like a–no. I was not going on a date with the Demon Lord! This was work. Just gathering information for my book, that's all.

I busied myself with putting a pot of water on the stove and dicing up the vegetables. Little bits of skin still remained on all of them, like he'd never peeled vegetables before. Not that he'd admit that, of course. It felt like everything was a new experience for him and I was determined to make them good ones. Everyone deserved happy memories to drown out the inevitable bad ones. Even a Demon Lord.

If only I had some chicken stock or bouillon. Something to really make this soup pop, because right now, it tasted more like hot vegetable water.

I rummaged through the cabinets, searching for spices or salt or anything that could liven the dish up, but found nothing. Besides a few pots and utensils, the room was empty.

"What do you usually cook with?" I frowned at yet another empty cabinet. "There's nothing here. How do you eat?"

"When I go into the library? It's not really a big deal. I don't need much."

"Don't need much?" I sighed. "You really don't take care of yourself well, you know that? Honestly, what have you been doing this whole time?"

He turned his back, searching for something in the cabinets. Since they were empty, it felt more like he was avoiding the question. Maybe I shouldn't have pried, but how did he think this was okay? He slept on a stone slab and now he didn't even seem to eat? That wasn't how anyone should be living, especially not somebody like him. He might seem grumpy, but I could see the kindness in him too. He'd asked me to be his writer because he believed in me. He believed that I could write him a better ending than anyone else.

Maybe part of that was getting him to believe in himself too. Believe that he deserved a good life. Why else was he doing all this? He'd said something about wanting an ending worthy of a Demon Lord, but that couldn't be the whole story, right? He had to want more than an impressive ending; he probably wanted a good ending too. A happy one.

Or maybe that's what *I* wanted for him...

I stirred the hot vegetable water. There had to be something I could do for him. Something like....

"Hey, Demon Lord?" I waited for him to turn towards me. "Is there something else I can call you? Demon Lord feels so official and I think we've gotten close enough to drop the formalities. I mean, we are about to eat dinner together and I did follow you into a book of all things."

"Demon Lord is fine," he said gruffly. "It's the only name I've got."

"That can't be right." I paused, thinking back on the previous books. The Demon Lord really had only ever been called just that, like a dramatic name to frighten children. "Huh, okay, so maybe we start there. Let's give you a name!" I glanced down at Cinder, getting an idea so silly I couldn't help but grin. "What about Lord Shadowbuns?"

He rolled his eyes, sinking onto one of the stools by a small wooden table in the corner.

"Okay, so not that name," I said, chuckling. "Maybe Sir Broodsalot then."

As I bounced various names off him, each sillier than the last to lighten the mood, I poured two bowls of soup and took a carrot over to the table for Cinder too. The demon bunny's red eyes lit up as she took it in her furry little paws to nibble on. The Demon Lord eyed the soup like he wasn't sure if it would be edible, but dug in anyway, barely even giving it time to cool. I picked up a spoon and blew on it, sipping on the kind of watery, but not half bad concoction.

The soup was warm, at least, and comforting. It reminded me of Gran. What would she do in this situation?

Pry into his personal life, probably, in a loving way of course.

"If you don't use the kitchen much," I said, swirling the soup in my bowl, "and you don't care about a good night's rest, what *do* you do for fun around here?"

He blinked. "For fun?"

"Yeah, you know, the thing that makes life worth living?" I frowned as he averted his eyes, suddenly very interested in Cinder, even going so far as to feed her a chunk of carrot from his soup. "You do have fun sometimes, don't you? Like hang out with friends or read a good book?"

"Of course I do," he snapped. "I've read almost every book in the library."

I nodded, eating my soup slowly. I knew for a fact that the story spirits weren't at the library all the time. Each of them spent at least a portion of their day inside their books, to sleep and recover, but also to let the library rest and give others a chance to come out. Plus, the villagers had been shocked to see him, which meant he probably didn't go outside much...

So, what did he do all day?

He lifted his bowl of soup, drinking the last of the watery broth. If I didn't ask him soon, this little cozy dinner of ours would be over and I might lose my nerve.

"Could we, maybe, visit the village tomorrow?"

He pinned me with a death stare.

I froze with my spoon halfway to my lips, my mouth suddenly so dry I had to get a glass of water. "I mean, the villagers seemed pretty excited to see you, and I could really use some supplies. Like paper and a pen. You know, to write your book?"

He didn't answer, so I peeked over my shoulder at him. His eyebrows were pinched together as he studied his empty bowl, running his fingers along the edge in circles. He usually said whatever thought popped into his mind, so why was he so quiet now?

"What's wrong?" I rejoined him at the table. "You don't have to come, if you don't want. I can explore on my own."

"No, that's not it. I just don't really go outside." His voice was soft as he sank lower in his chair, dissolving into his shadows. "Today was the first time."

"Wait, what?" I almost dropped my glass in shock. "So you just stay inside this castle? All alone?"

Between the shadows swirling around him and the bad lighting, I could barely make him out anymore, but it seemed like he nodded. Really? He had *never* stepped outside his castle? That was basically the first thing I did once I realized the castle had nothing interesting in it. It was cold, dark, and lonely. Not a place for anyone to hole up in for months or years.

"But why?" I felt myself reaching for his hand, hovering next to the shadows. "Weren't you lonely?"

"Not really, and if I ever was, I'd just look out the windows at all the townsfolk. I'd make up stories about their lives and it was oddly comforting."

His shadows flickered, betraying his light-hearted tone. There was no way watching everyone live their lives while he was locked up in here alone had been comforting. It had probably made him even lonelier. So why had he done it?

"I used to make up stories with my Grandpa all the time too." A familiar twinge went through my chest, like an old ache that came and went with the rain, as I traced the rings in the wooden table. "It hasn't felt the same since he passed away. Now it's just me and my thoughts and it's not nearly as much fun. I'm guessing it's the same for you." My gaze darted up, like I was hoping to see some kind of connection in his eyes, but he was too lost in shadow for me to see. "Why didn't you ever talk to the townsfolk?"

"I'm the villain of the story, Willow." His shadows snapped around us both now, pulling me into the darkness with him. His face was contorted with such pain that I did take his hand this time. It was cold against mine. His eyes widened at the touch, but he still wouldn't meet my eyes. "I'm supposed to be terrifying and monstrous. The only one strong enough to unite the demon generals and rule this land." His throat bobbed as his hand tightened around mine. "Do I seem terrifying to you?"

"No, of course not." The instant the words left my lips, I knew they were wrong. His face fell and he started tugging away from me, but I laced my fingers through his. "I mean, you don't seem terrifying because you've never tried to scare me. You've been a good friend, actually, so if you want to be terrifying, I'll help you. I'm your writer, so I can make you whatever you want to be."

"That's true, you're the one in control here. That's why I wanted it to be you. You never make light of me, and you take your stories seriously. Well, I seriously need to live up to what my author wanted me to be, but I just don't feel it. I'm always worried the fans will think I'm a joke when they meet me in person. Will you help me?"

His shadows drifted over my skin, velvety soft and more comforting than I'd expected. They curled around our interlaced fingers far too intimately for my taste. Warmth spread through my stomach, and I jerked my hand back with an awkward laugh.

"Of course I'll help you, but is being terrifying really all there is to being a villain?" My skin was still tingling from his shadows as I clenched my hands in my lap. "Like, why are you the villain? What drives you?"

His mouth opened like he was going to answer, but he snapped it closed as a deep frown marred his forehead. "Honestly, I have no idea. The books never said. I really am useless."

"No, you're not." I crossed my arms as another chill swept through the air. "Let's make finding out your villain origin story our mission tomorrow then. While we're out gathering supplies, we'll gather information too. I'm sure once you know why you're the bad guy, you'll feel connected to the role. Based on what I saw, I'd guess it has something to do with the villagers. They were all thanking you for protecting them and stuff."

"You think I'm evil so I can protect them?" He leaned forward, resting his elbows on the table. "That's an interesting idea and it would give me something to fight the hero over..."

"Yeah, great, now what's with the heat in this castle?" I stood up, holding my hands over the stove that only had a little warmth remaining. "Isn't there a single room that's warm?"

He chuckled and his shadows dissipated like they were never there. "Come, let's find you a blanket."

"Do you actually have one of those?" I picked up Cinder along with my bag. "Feels a bit too cozy for a big bad Demon Lord, don't you think?"

A small smile tugged at his lips. "Even big bad Demon Lords need to warm up sometimes."

"Careful, you're starting to sound like me." I laughed, following him into the hallway. "I should probably find somewhere to sleep too since I'm going to be here for a while."

"You can use my room. It's the best in the castle."

"Your room, huh?" I looped my arm through his, leaning into him a bit. "Well my, my. I didn't think we'd be moving *that* quickly."

"I will sleep elsewhere, of course." He tried to glare at me, but the little half smile ruined the vibe. "Just take the room or sleep outside."

"The grass outside might be softer." I gave him a sideways glance and laughed. "I'm kidding. I'll be fine anywhere as long as you've got blankets. Thank you."

He stopped so fast I bumped into him. Cinder whimpered, sticking her head out of my bag with a glare.

"Sorry." I pet the bunny until her gaze softened. Then I walked around to look at the Demon Lord. "What's up with the sudden freezing? You could warn me, you know."

His gaze was locked on a soft golden glow coming out of one of the rooms. I'd searched the castle top to bottom before I went outside and there hadn't been a room with lights on before.

"Is somebody else here?" I whispered.

He put his finger to his lips, moving slowly towards the room. The light brightened as the crackle of a fire filled the air, which was deliciously warm and inviting. It felt almost magical, like something was giving me exactly what I wanted. The Demon Lord held his arm in front of me before I walked inside. The room was full of floor to ceiling shelves heaped with books. Hundreds of them, just waiting to be read. There were thick tomes, what looked like journals, and even some old leatherbound rarities.

It reminded me of Misty.

"Since when does your castle have a library?" I asked.

"Since never," he growled, storming into the room. "This isn't possible. I've been in every single room, and all of them were cold and empty. If this was here, I'd have known it."

"But it is here."

I walked inside, taking the large room in from the warm fireplace to the cozy-looking couch positioned between two massive bookshelves. A table sat in the middle of the room, covered in books as if somebody had been reading here just a moment ago. The Demon Lord searched every nook and cranny, but there was nobody else here. Eventually, he just stared into the fire like he was lost in thought. I sank onto the plush couch, relaxing into the cushions with a sigh of contentment.

"Now this is a couch I could fall asleep on." I snuggled deeper, easing into the comfort of the warm fire and the cozy cushions. "Maybe I'll just–"

"Nope, not a chance." The Demon Lord yanked me up so fast I thought my arm might fall off. "There's no way I'd let you fall asleep here. What if it's a trap?"

I raised an eyebrow. "And what kind of trap would it be?"

"You could get stuck here and never leave. I mean, you kind of already are, but that's not my point."

"At least I'd be in a warm room with enough books to keep me occupied for years." I walked back into the hallway, hopping over the threshold back and forth a few times. "See? No trap."

He crossed his arms, glowering at the books. "Then what is it?"

"A gift." I trailed my fingers along their spines, reading each title as I went by, but none of them sounded familiar. "Maybe it's Misty's magic?"

"If Misty was going to change something, it probably would be to add a library." He browsed through a few of the books, flipping their pages open. "But these all seem to be empty."

I snagged a few books off the shelf, opening them for myself. He was right. Every book had a pretty cover, but the pages inside were as blank as newly purchased paper. It felt just like the castle: pretty on the outside, and empty on the inside. I sighed, setting the books back on their shelf. What was the point of a book you couldn't read? I covered up a yawn, feeling the excitement of the day taking its toll on me.

"Well, whatever it is, I'm grateful." I sprawled out on the couch, closing my eyes before the Demon Lord could haul me out of here with more warnings of danger. "Goodnight, Lord Shadowbuns."

He snorted. "Goodnight, Willow. I'll be right over here if you need me."

He sank onto the floor, lying with his back to me so he could watch the doorway. I couldn't imagine the floor was any more comfortable than that stone bed of his.

"We could share the couch, if you wanted," I said softly. "All jokes aside. You deserve a good night's rest."

"I'm perfectly fine here." His long black hair trailed over his shoulders as he settled in. "Sleep well. I will guard you while you dream."

He would guard me while I dream? My stomach fluttered as I laid back on the couch again, all thoughts of sleep forgotten. How could I when that adorable demon was just a few feet away?

Chapter 11
Willow

I'd managed to get a very good night's rest in the comfort of the castle's library, lulled to sleep by the crackling fireplace and the deep, even breathing of the Demon Lord. A few quiet movements, like the sound of pages flipping softly, made me think he was awake now though. I opened my eyes, peeking over at him as he browsed a stack of books.

"Find anything useful?" I asked, but he just shook his head. "Well, if I'm going to write, I need a pen, lots of paper, and you need answers." I forced myself to sit up, rubbing sleep out of my eyes. "There's only one place we're going to find all of that. In town."

"If we must." He ran a hand through his silky black hair, brushing it over his shoulders in one smooth movement that made me wonder what kind of rat's nest mine looked like. "Let's get going then."

I patted my hair, finding more than a few frizzy tangles. Great. Just great. "Let me freshen up quick first. Give me like ten minutes."

He nodded, absently paging through another book. Thankfully, this library had an attached bathroom with all the necessary amenities. I'd need to find an extra set of clothes so I could wash mine soon though. I added new clothes to my mental list of things to look for in town as I hurried to get ready before heading to the entrance hall.

The big double doors that led outside had to be tall enough for giants to walk through, but I knew they weren't as heavy as they looked. The Demon Lord grasped the handles tight, but didn't pull the doors open. Or push. He just stood there, flexing his hands. He sighed, dropping them back to his side. Then he grabbed the handles again, looking more determined than last time.

But after a few more attempts, he still hadn't opened the doors. It would have been funny if we hadn't had that conversation last night, but now his words echoed in my mind. He'd only left his castle once and that was probably just because I'd gone out on my own and he was worried. Picturing him staring out over the town from those big windows made my chest ache.

He deserved to step outside every day. To experience what this life of his really was.

"If you're not going to open that door, then I am." I pushed off the wall. "It's time to put yourself out there. Nobody will think you're a joke."

He stared at me for a moment and I didn't have the heart to actually open the door if he didn't want me to. Wanting to stay inside was a vibe and taking that away from him by force didn't feel like the right move here. He had to want to leave, not be forced to. After a few more moments, he sighed, pulling the door open on his own.

"Let's go," he grumbled. "You need paper, right?"

"Oh, so this is all for me, huh?" I grinned, resisting the urge to pat him on the head and call him a good boy as a joke. "Maybe we should get something nice for you too while we're out. Maybe a new bed?"

"Why would I need a new bed?"

I rolled my eyes at him. "Because yours is literally a stone slab. Every side of it is the wrong side to wake up on. Believe me, your life will completely change after sleeping in a cozy bed for the first time."

The purple in his eyes shimmered. "How so?"

My grin widened, but before I could respond, I noticed a burly soldier with a familiar-looking spear slumped against the wall of the castle. His frumpled uniform made me think he'd been here all night, waiting for us. I touched the scrape on my cheek, which was healing slowly and still throbbed a bit. If he was trying to make up for that, I respected it, but he didn't need to. Sleeping outside against a cold castle wall was just as bad as a stone slab.

"Don't any of you demons know how to get a good night's sleep around here?" I nudged my supposed bodyguard awake. "Good morning. Have you been here all night?"

He rubbed his eyes, mumbling something about being the Demon Lord's right hand, then jerked awake. His eyes widened as he took us in, leaping to his feet.

"I'm so sorry, My Lord!" He brushed off his clothes, trying to tug the wrinkles out before bowing deeply. "I'm at your command. What would you like me to do today?" The Demon Lord glanced back at me as if I should know, but the soldier seemed to take that as his cue. "Guard your consort. Of course!"

I snorted, trying to cover my laughter with a cough. Shadows swirled around the Demon Lord as he took off towards the village in silence. Grumpy, grumpy. It had to be the bed.

"So, what's your name, soldier?" I glanced back to where he'd taken guard a few steps behind us. "If you're going to be following me around, I'd like to at least know that much."

"Dain, my lady."

His eyes roved the surroundings, as if waiting for an enemy to jump out at us. It reminded me of the Demon Lord yesterday. Was this land really so rough? The villagers had been nothing but kind yesterday, minus the incident with Dain of course. But everywhere I looked, there was such beauty and wonder that I couldn't imagine it being dangerous here.

Purple veins of light glowed from the stone pathways, as if the earth itself was steeped in magic, and lanterns were strung between the buildings. They shone softly in the morning light, but I bet they looked beautiful at night.

Demons were bustling around, opening their shops and bowing to the Demon Lord. The shock on every face was understandable. He really did make for an imposing figure, with his long black hair, perfect horns, and shadows curling around him like a cloak.

Unfortunately, he was walking pretty fast, and I kept missing all the good-looking places to visit. The scent of roasted nuts filled the air, and my stomach rumbled, wishing we'd grabbed breakfast. I didn't have any coins that worked in this realm, so I'd need to rely on the Demon Lord for now. But those nuts smelled so good that I felt myself wandering over anyway.

"Here, try some," a kind woman said, scooping nuts into a bag. "They're on me."

"Oh no, I couldn't do that." I shook my head, but my hands had a mind of their own and were already reaching out. The woman laughed and handed me the bag. They tasted like pecans, rich and buttery from some kind of coating they were roasted in. I closed my eyes, savoring the flavor. "These are amazing."

"I'm glad you think so." She smiled, leaning in closer to whisper. "Take a few more, as thanks for bringing our Lord outside."

I smiled and took the nuts gratefully before hurrying to catch up to the Demon Lord. "You should walk slower and talk to people. You're supposed to be getting to know why you're a villain, remember?"

"Oh, right." He slowed enough for me to shove a bag of the nuts into his hands. He frowned at them suspiciously but tried one, and then proceeded to devour the entire bag as we walked.

I ate mine slower, enjoying not only the flavor, but what they represented. These people loved the Demon Lord. They respected him and wanted to help him however they could. They were kind and so different from what I'd imagined when reading the series.

How could the books have gotten these people so wrong? It had to be intentional, like how history was only told by the victors. Had the author planned some big plot twist where the demons weren't the bad guys? If so, what would that even look like and how was I going to write it?

"We're here." The Demon Lord paused outside of a shop with a quill and parchment on the sign. "We can get supplies and information all in the same place."

"I don't think being efficient is the way to go here, but I never say no to a stationery shop."

He smirked and held the door open for me. Parchment flew through the air, dipping and spinning like some kind of dance, while shelves of beautiful ink beckoned me in like jewels. There were rows and rows of paper in varying colors and styles, along with notebooks and binding equipment. Then there were the pens. They were scribbling on notepads without anyone touching them!

"What are those?" I gasped, rushing over to the aisle of moving pens. "How do they work?"

But the Demon Lord just shrugged, awkwardly looking around the warm shop like he was completely at a loss. Maybe it was the first time he'd seen floating pens too. Thankfully an elderly racoon demon joined us, adjusting his round glasses carefully.

"Welcome to The Quillery. What can I help you with today?" His voice was soft and calming as he smiled at me. "Oh, I see the pens have caught your eye. They're our specialty. They not only take notes on their own, but they're the best brainstorming partners. Ask them a question and they'll offer opinions." He scowled at one of the pens scribbling something about the harsh realities of life. "Some opinions you might like better than others. Choose your pen wisely."

"Do they have different personalities?" I asked, leaning down to study all the pens.

Some were shiny black while others were made of warm wood or bright colors. They were all fountain pens, which I preferred myself. The brightly colored ones seemed to be the most hyper, dashing across the pages as fast as possible with excited comments about how weird I looked. Hmmm... that felt a bit rude, but it seemed like they hadn't seen a human before, so I let it go. I moved on to the sleek black pens which wrote at a languid pace, their writing formal and a bit too high-brow for me.

The wooden pens seemed pretty chill, writing notes when they felt like it, dozing off when they didn't. It didn't seem like they'd even noticed me yet as they laid against the paper, rolling around once in a while. Maybe they weren't my kind of pen either, not when I was on a tight deadline at least.

"Hmmm...I'm looking for a pen that will notice things I don't," I said. "Maybe one who has a sense of humor and can write casually. The kind of pen who finds this world fascinating and wants to explore it more. I'd really love the brainstorming help."

The racoon demon stroked the fur on his chin. "Maybe you'd prefer the crystal pens. They're a bit sarcastic sometimes, but they're also the best brainstormers. They bring a sense of magic and whimsy to the process."

He led me further down the aisle past a group of quills with brilliant feathers to a section of pens with crystals on the top, shimmering like gems. Most of them were pretty fancy, but one in the back drew my eye. It had a charcoal base with swirls of silver running through it and a beautiful deep purple feather on top. I glanced sideways at the Demon Lord. That feather was the color of his eyes...

The scritch scratch of a pen scribbling on paper pulled my attention back to the pen. It had written something on the paper, but before I could read it, the proprietor shook his head.

"Oh, this one must have been shelved wrong." He picked the pen up, holding it in a way that I couldn't see the paper. "It's meant to be with the other feathered pens."

I raised an eyebrow. "Did it write something bad?"

"No, not exactly…" He glanced between me and the Demon Lord. "I just don't think our Lord would want a pen like this commenting on his life, that's all."

Okay, well now I was beyond curious what it had written down.

"You'd be fine with whatever pen I choose, right?" I asked, nudging the Demon Lord. "No matter what it says about you?"

He sighed. "Just show her the pen. There's no way she's letting this go until she sees its personality now."

"You know me so well." I grinned, holding my hand out for the pen and notepad. "Now, let's see what you had to say that got you snatched away so fast."

That guy behind you is sexy as hell. You should get on that. Or under that. Whatever your preference is.

I dropped the notepad, but it floated in the air next to me, its words staring me right in the face. The pen thought the Demon Lord was sexy?? A laugh bubbled up in my chest and soon I was cackling in the stationery store as the Demon Lord leaned over to read it too. His shadows snapped around him, engulfing the pen and its paper.

"What kind of store are you running?" he asked the racoon demon. "Is that normal?"

The demon wrung his hands. "Well, it was used by a romance writer for many years before it was returned to us, and it picked up a few...interesting habits."

More scratching followed that, and I reached into the shadows to rescue the little pen.

You know I'm right, so what's the problem here?

"Well, I'm not really writing a romance," I said. "It's actually more like an epic fantasy. The last book in a big series about the hero fighting off the demons."

Oh, so you're one of those humans. As if the demons would lose to any pompous heroes.

The purple feather stood tall, as if proclaiming its allegiance with the demons. Interesting. Maybe it already knew more about the world than I did. That could be really useful, but maybe I should pick a pen who didn't have such strong opinions about heroes. It was his book after all.

I glanced at the other pens who were eagerly scribbling, obviously trying to get my attention too. I started moving toward them, but the charcoal feather pen swooped in front of me, angling its notebook so I could easily read it.

Fine, fine. If heroes are your thing, I'll help you write the best hero ever. Manly and full of...what are heroes full of? Justice? Ego? What are we going for here?

"Honestly, he's kind of the clueless type." I smiled, remembering all the fond memories I had of reading the books with Grandpa. "He's kind and eager to help, but doesn't always go about it the right way. He sometimes takes things at face value and is a bit naive, but he's got such heart. Loveable and honorable to a fault."

Oh, so he's a himbo. Got it. I can help with that.

"A himbo??" I burst out laughing again. "Okay, maybe he is a bit, but he's really sweet."

Sweet only gets you so far. Somebody's probably going to take advantage of that some day. Maybe lead him down a bad path in the name of justice.

I froze, staring at the pen's words. What if that was actually the plot twist? That the hero fully believed he was doing the right thing, when in reality, it was completely wrong? Oh, that gave me so many other ideas and I had to write them down.

"Okay Penny, now we're getting somewhere." I frowned. "Inky? Penpen? Scribbles?"

The name's Inkheart.

"Inkheart, hello!" I turned to the shopkeeper. "We'll take this pen, please."

He readjusted his glasses, looking pointedly at the Demon Lord before nodding. "Okay, I think you've chosen a fine pen. Let's pick out a flying book worthy of following you around all day."

The pen was already standing tall on a floating notepad, but maybe those were just for show. The idea of a flying notebook and pen that could take its own notes trailing behind me at all times was enough to make anyone smile. This world was the absolute coolest. As we browsed through leatherbound books, wood-covered books, and every other kind of journal I could ever imagine, I paused.

"How is it that this village has so many cool things?" I asked the Demon Lord softly so the shopkeep wouldn't overhear us. "I mean, the human villages had magical devices too, but nothing on this scale. They didn't have personalities, not like this. They were more like tools than true magic. So what's with this place?"

"Demons have innate magic," he responded, leaning in closer. "And that purple glow outside feels like it's connected too."

The shopkeep rubbed his hands together. "Exactly! Us demons are wonderful craftsmen, unlike those thieves you call humans."

"Thieves, huh?" The Demon Lord loomed behind me, his shadows curling around us like a dark cloak. "Do you think we've done enough to stop them or are they getting too close again?"

The raccoon demon froze, his timid eyes flicking to me. "Please forgive me. You are wonderful." He wrung his hands, his fur puffed out awkwardly as he lifted his gaze to the Demon Lord. "You saved us when you created the Wandering Woods. I know you're doing everything you can to protect us. I didn't mean to imply anything else."

I elbowed the Demon Lord. "You're scaring him, knock it off." Once his shadows shrank a bit, I smiled at the shopkeep. "Sorry about him, he doesn't know when to turn off the dark lord vibes. I'll admit I'm still learning about this village. What are the humans stealing?"

He frowned. "Well, our magic of course. We have so much that the very land around us is gifted with it, imbuing the minerals in the ground with magic even lowly humans can use. That's why they keep attacking us. For our resources."

I gripped the notebook I was holding so tight my knuckles whitened. "That can't be right. I've never heard anything like that before."

"Well, humans are awful." The Demon Lord shrugged. "It doesn't really surprise me that they'd bend the truth."

I rolled my eyes. "As a human, I resent that."

"You're...okay so far." His words might have sounded harsh, but his lips were tugged up in a little half smile that made my stomach flutter. "If you stick around, maybe my opinion of humans will change."

"Guess I'll have to stick around to save the human race's reputation then, huh?" I grinned, leaning my shoulder into him to add to the teasing. "Keep bringing me to awesome places like this and I might just be tempted to."

His deep purple eyes met mine, holding my gaze. "I'd come here every day if you wished it."

I swallowed hard. I'd been teasing him, light and joking, but suddenly this felt serious. He meant that. Not that going to a stationery shop was anything intimate, but his tone made it feel like it was. I busied myself with the notebooks again, searching through every single one on display while the Demon Lord kept his distance, his gaze following me like I was more interesting than every pen and notebook here. It made my hands kind of clammy, if I was honest. It had to be nerves from a powerful man like him studying me so intently.

Eventually, I settled on a black and silver book that felt more like a witch's grimoire than anything else, but it suited the pen the best.

"What do you think?" I moved Inkheart from the temporary notepad to the beautiful new notebook. "Keep looking? Or do you like this one?"

Its feather swayed as the pen danced across the pages, swirling and dipping hypnotically.

This is perfect.

Excellent, now I just had to grab some ink and we'd be out of here. Which was good because it felt like the heat was turned up way too high in this store. I stepped up to the register, feeling intensely awkward as I realized none of my human money worked here. The poor shopkeeper just wrung his hands, apologizing over and over for no currency exchanges.

"It's fine. I can purchase anything you need," the Demon Lord said. "It'll be payment for writing my book."

The shopkeeper's eyes widened. "She's writing a book about you, My Lord? Oh, then she can have this all on the house." He leaned closer, whispering behind his hand. "Just let me be the first to read it, okay?"

"No, I can't possibly take this all for free." I shook my head, pleading silently with the Demon Lord. "I'd prefer the payment for writing your book deal, if you would."

"Of course." His shadows curled around me for a moment, reaching out for something I wasn't sure of, before he paid the shopkeep for me. "Please deliver more ink and paper to the castle in a few days. We'll probably need it."

A warm fuzzy feeling swept over me as he predicted exactly what I'd need and moved to handle it before I even asked. "How are you so good at taking care of other people, but so terrible at taking care of yourself?"

He shrugged. "I get by just fine on my own. Stop worrying and focus on the book."

"I'd worry less if we went and looked for that bed we talked about."

A sigh that felt like it was being pulled from the depths of his soul escaped his lips. "Okay. If improving my sleeping arrangements would make you feel better, then let's go look for a new mattress."

I grinned, linking my arm through his as he picked up my bags from the shop. Inkheart flew through the air behind us as the raccoon demon waved goodbye. This had been such an interesting store and I couldn't wait to see what else this demon village had in store for us.

The demons were apparently more like magical artisans than beasts spawned by dark magic like the books had led me to believe. There was so much to learn and so little time to figure it all out. Getting stuck in this book might be the best thing that could have happened if I really did want to finish this series. There was no way I'd find all these secrets out otherwise.

As we strolled through the town, hope washed over me. Maybe I could actually pull this off.

Chapter 12
Willow

Turns out mattresses were a big thing in the land of demons, so big that they had multiple stores dedicated to them. Ironic considering the stone slab the Demon Lord had been sleeping on all this time. Why would the author flesh out this village before the castle? It just didn't make any sense, unless they were the type of author who got really distracted by random details and forget about the important things.

Ha. Who would do that?

I leaned back in a chair in the shop's lobby, watching as the Demon Lord glowered at the rows of mattresses without trying any of them. I'd convinced him that this was a necessary step in figuring out who he was, but really, I'd wanted to give him the opportunity to talk to people on his own. If he really was a villain, we needed to know why, and the best way to do that was to see how people interacted with him.

Unfortunately, the intense gloom emanating off him in waves was too thick to penetrate. A few customers had gotten close, but they'd changed direction when his shadows had darkened the area. The woman behind the counter also seemed interested, but she was more focused on keeping the little girl peeking out from behind the back curtain from running out to greet him.

"Leave him be, Rosie," she whispered. "He's a customer right now and you know the rule about customers."

The little girl sighed. "Don't bother them unless they need help." She peeked at the Demon Lord again, exasperation clear on her face. "But mom, look at him! If anyone needs help, it's him."

I laughed softly, but the girl's mom must have heard me. She bowed her head and shooed the little girl back behind the curtains like they were never there. Those were the kind of people he should be talking to, but instead, he was just standing there like a statue! The girl was right about one thing: he needed help.

I meandered over by him, glaring at the mattresses like he was. "You know, you could try sitting on one to see if you like it."

"Sitting on one?" His eyebrows shot up. "Why don't you just pick one? This was your idea after all."

Well, he had me there. I flopped onto the closest mattress, sinking into its pillowy surface so far that it was cradling my entire body. That was weird, and yet, it was kind of comforting. Like one of those weighted blankets. Except, I'd sank in so far that I couldn't see the Demon Lord anymore. Or get back out.

I struggled against the coziness to no avail. "Uhhh, any help would be appreciated."

He snorted. "You're the one who hopped on a magical mattress without checking its properties first."

Magical mattresses? Sure, there was a lot of magic in this village, but even the mattresses were full of it? I gazed up at the ceiling, watching as big needles and thread flew overhead, zipping back and forth between seamstresses. Okay, maybe I should have guessed that.

From now on, I'd assume everything in this village had some kind of magic. Even those toasted nuts I'd sampled earlier. My stomach growled, remembering their buttery flavor. We'd need to stop for lunch soon if this mattress shopping took as long as the stationery shop did.

Suddenly, a strong hand grasped mine, yanking me out of the bed hard enough to send me flying through the air. I stumbled against the Demon Lord's chest, his arm resting against my waist to steady me. His eyes were full of laughter and my face burned.

"Fine, show me what bed you think we should try next then." I forced myself to step out of his warm and safe grip, moving to read the sign on a nearby mattress. "This one supposedly makes you feel like you're sleeping on a cloud. That sounds nice, right?"

He leaned over my shoulder to read the tag. "It also literally floats. Can you imagine being half asleep and forgetting you were in the air? That bed sounds like a health hazard."

"I'd totally do that," I said with a laugh. "Okay, moving on then. What about this one? It plays soft music for you until you fall asleep."

He pinned me with an icy stare. "Demon Lords do not need lullabies."

"Oh forgive me, your Demon-nes, I forgot you were too good for silly things like music." I dragged him through the aisles, checking out what other mattresses he might like. "Honestly, the magic isn't the most important part. First, we should find out what kind of firmness you like. Do you like hard beds or soft ones? Maybe you're in the middle?"

"I'm not sure..."

His voice was soft, changing his entire vibe from grumpy demon to lost puppy. I kept forgetting that he was a character from a book, so he'd probably never actually slept in a comfortable bed before. Well, there was only one way to fix that. He'd have to lay down on every single mattress until he found one he loved.

I straightened my shoulders. "If you want a good night's sleep, there's only one thing you can do: sit on that mattress. Sit on every mattress. Lay down and roll around on them. Figure out what you like and what you don't like. Your coziness demands it!"

"You want me to lay down?" His eyebrows pinched together. "Maybe you should just do that part for me. It wouldn't look good for a Demon Lord to be rolling around like a dog."

I pressed my lips together, picturing him flicking his ears and pawing at the sheets. Ohhh the silly things I could write. Speaking of writing, I could hear the furious scribbling of Inkheart behind me. I glanced over at the book.

You might as well pick a mattress for him. That way you'll enjoy it when you inevitably end up using it.

"Inkheart!"

The pen wasn't even trying to tame the quirks it had picked up from its former owner. I was in no way about to share a bed with the Demon Lord. Not a chance. Things would get all sorts of messy if that happened.

You know you want to. So go, try some beds with him, have some fun. He obviously needs help in that department.

That was true. The Demon Lord really didn't seem to know how to have fun on his own yet. And how could he if he had no idea what he enjoyed doing? I took a deep breath, then flopped onto the next mattress. This one said it magically controlled the temperature, but I wasn't sure how.

"Aren't you going to join me?" I stared up at the Demon Lord until he relented. I grinned as he sat on the very edge of the bed, barely even touching its surface. "There you go. How's it feel?"

"Fine." He grunted, but I could see him scoot backwards just a tiny bit. "Are they always this soft?"

"No, they can be firmer too." I sat up, moving on to the next bed. "This one might be more your style."

This time he sat on it without me asking him to, even leaning his hands back like he was ready to relax. I smiled, happy to see him finally letting loose just a bit. Maybe if we kept this vibe going, he'd be willing to actually talk to people too. So we kept trying beds, ranging from so soft we both got lost in them to so hard they almost felt like that stone slab, but he seemed to prefer the ones in the middle. Which actually did suit me pretty well, but I wasn't about to admit that to the chatty pen full of sassy commentary. Its feather tilted to the side, as if it knew what I was thinking.

"Okay, now what kind of magic do you want?" I asked. "Honestly, I'd lean towards sleep magic to make sure you feel well-rested in the morning."

He laid back on one of the beds, his long black hair sprawled across the mattress, seemingly deep in thought. I'd never seen him let his guard down like that before. He really was trying to find something he liked, which felt like such a win for today.

Not to mention how good he looks doing it, right?

For once, I couldn't even chastise the pen. He did look good on that bed. My heartbeat quickened and I wiped my hands on my pants, forcing myself to look away. This was for research, not pleasure. Getting distracted by those long lashes of his wasn't going to do me any good. I'd gone down that road with other men before and it always ended the same: they left.

After it had happened four times in a row, I realized there were better things to spend my time on than men who were so flighty they couldn't stick around for more than a few months. This Demon Lord would do the same thing. He was literally a character in a book, and depending on how his last book went, we had no idea what would happen to him. Getting attached to him was a terrible idea.

But, seeing him smile and take care of himself did feel good. Even if we weren't together, making his life a little better felt like it was worth doing. For the story, of course.

My stomach grumbled again, apparently so loud that the Demon Lord sat up. He got off the bed, tugging his clothes straighter. "I think we're done here. Let's get something to eat."

And just like that, all my hard work was ruined.

"Oh no, you've got to order the mattress first." I nudged him towards the shopkeep I'd seen earlier with beautiful rose-gold horns. "We'd like to buy a mattress, please."

"Of course." She smiled wide as she rang up the order, her gaze never leaving the Demon Lord for long. "I was hoping to thank you in person one day. For saving my Rosie a few years back." The little girl ran out from the back room, clinging to her mother's side with far more shyness than I'd expected. "Rosie, this is the man who united our people and created the barrier between our land and the humans. The Wandering Woods protects us so that you never have to worry about getting taken again."

Rosie looked up at him from her position behind her mother. "It's nice to meet you, My Lord."

He nodded curtly, shoulders as stiff as the bed he'd been sleeping on. I shook my head and stepped closer to the girl. "Hello, Rosie. My name's Willow and this big grump is just a little shy. We're happy you're safe."

"Really?" The little girl's mouth dropped open. "Mom, he's shy just like me!"

I laughed and patted her on the head, my fingers brushing over her cracked and ashen horns that looked nothing like her mother's vibrant ones. The shopkeep jerked her daughter away from me, shooing her into the back room again. Her eyes looked haunted, pinched with worry for her child. I dropped my hand to my side and took a few steps back.

"Sorry." I bit my lip, not sure what else to say. Something was wrong with the girl, but it didn't feel like my place to ask since I was one of the humans her mom obviously feared. "I'll just wait outside if you want."

"You're not leaving." The Demon Lord put his hand on my shoulder, grasping it tight enough that I couldn't move even if I wanted to. His shadows enveloped me with all the warmth his tone lacked as he leaned closer to whisper in my ear. "We're on a mission, remember? Ask her about the child."

He really had a problem reading the room sometimes. I took a deep breath and turned my attention back to the mother who was looking like she was the one who wanted to flee.

"I'm sorry," I repeated, bowing my head like I'd seen her do earlier. "I shouldn't have spoken so casually to your daughter, but I promise I meant no harm. When I came to this village, I had no idea what to expect, but after spending the day talking to people, I can tell I'm missing something. Why did the humans take your daughter?"

Her fingers dug into her arm, pressing in so deep they left white marks in her skin. "You don't know? They drain our magic to fuel their tools. Most of us can withstand it and regain our magic eventually, but the young are still developing. If their horns crumble, that's it. Their magic is gone for good. That's what your kind are doing to us every day."

The Demon Lord sucked in a breath, but thankfully didn't react otherwise. If that's what was really going on during all those fight scenes in the books, then he was justifiably evil. Who drove him to be that way though? There had to be something bigger going on, a plot that I hadn't wrapped my mind around yet. It just didn't make sense with what I'd read in the previous books.

"I didn't know." I shook my head, moving until my back was up against the Demon Lord's firm chest. He hadn't budged or cried out in anger. He was still as stone, like always. "But why would they do that? Humans might not have innate magic, but they can mine magical ore that powers everything they'd need." Magical ore a lot like all those purple stones I'd been seeing around town. I gasped, spinning back to the Demon Lord. "You said demons are innately magical, right? So if that seeps into the earth and humans mine it, then all the magic humans use here is really from the demons, right?"

His gaze hardened as he spotted the little girl peeking out from the curtains again. "And since humans are the greediest of all the species, they wouldn't be satisfied with just our leftovers like that. No. They'd want our magic straight from the source."

That changed everything. He wasn't just waging a war to take over the world, he was waging a war to stop his people from being used like living spellstones that were drained and recharged over and over again until they broke. I suddenly felt the need to sit down as the series I'd loved so much shattered around me.

The hero was meant to stand for justice and all things good in the world, but if he was secretly working to steal everyone's magic then I couldn't ever read those books again. I couldn't write an ending like that, not a chance. It was too horrific.

My stomach grumbled again, but I clenched my arms around my abdomen and tried to hide it. Going out to eat seemed so callous now, like I was on a fun date while they were fighting for their lives. What was the author thinking adding in a plot twist like that? Now I just wanted to end it all with the Demon Lord winning and throw the whole series on its head.

Who cared if fans hated it? After seeing that little girl, it felt like the right thing to do.

After a few minutes, the shopkeep walked over to me and handed me a bottle of water. "I'm sorry, I shouldn't have dumped that all on you like it was your fault. If our lord sees something in you enough to make you his consort, then I know you're not like them. I know you've got a good heart just from how you reacted to my story."

I took a few gulps of water to steady my nerves. "Thank you. I really had no idea that was happening, and I bet most humans don't either. We'll figure out what's really going on and put a stop to it."

"Of course we will." The Demon Lord's hands clenched into fists, his knuckles white as he stared at the child behind the curtain. It was like he was burning the image of her into his memory so he'd never forget what he was fighting for. "I'll do anything to protect our people."

Chills raced down my spine. *There* was the villain I'd expected based on the books. He was like a morally gray avenger, waiting to wipe out the enemy by any means necessary. I smiled just a bit. At least he'd finally gotten in touch with his inner bad guy.

Knowing why he was the bad guy was a huge step forward. Now I could work on planning the rest of the book. I finished up the water and handed the empty bottle back to the shopkeep with a smile. "Thank you."

She nodded and handed the Demon Lord a slip of paper. "We'll have your mattress ready for you in a few days. Stop by again if you ever need a magical seamstress."

He nodded and waited for me to join him by the door. "Let's get you some food."

I almost said no but Dain was still standing guard outside like he'd been doing all day. He'd slept outside the castle last night too and refused the nuts I'd tried giving him, so he must be hungry by now. We needed to stop for food so he could finally take a break. Then we could plan our next steps.

Chapter 13
Willow

The weight of everything we'd just learned was so heavy that the Demon Lord had walked by three restaurants without even looking at them. I didn't know how to lighten the mood or if I should even try, so I just ignored my rumbling stomach and kept walking beside him.

Until one rumble was so loud that the Demon Lord stopped to stare at me. "We never got any food, did we?"

"No, but I'm fine." I rested my hand on his arm and his gaze softened. "Do you want to keep exploring or call it a day?"

"I want to make sure you're well fed." He turned to talk to Dain. "Where's a good place to eat? Somewhere quiet so Willow can write, if she wants to."

"Oh, I definitely want to. Right, Inkheart?" I laughed as the pen practically danced on its notebook. "Thanks for thinking of that."

"Okay then." Dain's face scrunched up. "Maybe Bunny Brews? Since you like bunnies, there are loads of them there."

"Wait, it's a bunny cafe?" I grabbed the Demon Lord's arm. "We have to go there!"

"Okay? I don't really get it, but whatever makes you happy."

Inkheart fluttered across the page, flying closer to me so I could take a look.

Gotta love a man who spoils his Queen.

"What?" I nudged the pen away, laughing awkwardly. "It's not like that at all."

He'd just bought me a magical pen, all the paper I could ever want, and sworn to protect his people no matter what. It reminded me of why I'd had a crush on the hero when I was a kid. There was just something about a guy willing to do anything to save the people he cared about. Not that the hero and him were anything alike, of course, or that I was crushing on the Demon Lord now too.

The back of my neck warmed as I walked beside the Demon Lord. "That was nice, you know. How you reassured that woman."

He made a noncommittal noise and kept walking, but something was different than before. He was easier to keep up with now and he glanced at the shops and the people around him like they were important. Nobody had to stumble out of his way this time either. That encounter seemed to have opened his eyes a bit, and I couldn't help but be grateful for it.

"It's nice that you have a purpose now," I said, keeping pace with him easily. "Plus, we know why you're such a big grump now. Your people trust you to keep them safe and that's an important role. You can't be bothered with silly things like humans and soft beds, right?"

His steps faltered. "You really think they trust me?"

Dain and I shared a confused look. "Well, yeah?"

The Demon Lord scratched the base of his horns, a slight red tint staining his cheeks. "I need to run some errands on my own, okay?" He shoved a pouch that clinked like it was full of coins into my hands before turning to Dain. "Make sure nobody touches her while I'm gone."

Dain saluted him, standing so tall and proud that you'd think he was just given a mission to save the world even though the Demon Lord was already fleeing at top speed. Inkheart scribbled, flying in front of me.

Did you hear that? He doesn't want anyone to touch you. He wants to be the only demon doing that!

I rolled my eyes at the pen. "I don't think *he* wants to touch me either. Otherwise there wouldn't be half a street between us already." I cupped my hand to my mouth to call out. "Don't take too long! I'll miss you!"

He spun around, mouth dropped open like I'd said something scandalous. I grinned as his shadows rose up, hiding his awkwardness behind a mask of darkness. He was kind of adorable for a Demon Lord.

"My lady?" Dain prompted, holding the door to the cafe open. "Are you still going inside?"

"Oh, right, yes."

I moved through the doorway and into the warm, cozy cafe. The gentle buzz of people chatting softly mingled with the scent of coffee and sweets in the air. There was a gate around the entrance to ensure the little demon bunnies didn't escape when the door was open and they were lined up inside of it, noses pushing through the mesh. The bunnies ranged from black like Cinder to golden or stark white. Their flames were different colors too, lighting up the room like holiday lanterns.

"Welcome to Bunny Brews," a young demon with a menu in her hands said. Her long bunny ears stood tall, twitching as she eyed me up. "Are you a human?"

An older woman swatted her with a towel. "Coco, you can't just ask somebody if they're a human like that. Try to have better manners." She smiled warmly at me. "Excuse my daughter, she's never seen a human before. Why don't I show you to our best seat in the house?"

"No problem at all."

We followed her through a few rows of mismatched wooden tables, all a bit worn down as if people had spent years using them. Tables like these, covered in dents and grooves, had untold histories that Grandpa and I used to love making up stories about.

We'd explain small indentations away by saying that students must have spent hours studying there, absentmindedly dragging their pens against the wood. For extra smooth spots in the middle of a table, we'd craft a beautiful story about two lovers who couldn't help but hold hands all day. Everything was a story when we were together, but now that he was gone, I felt a bit silly bringing it up to anyone else.

I missed the days of getting lost in dreams like that.

"Here we are," the woman said, motioning to a large table by the window with a plush chair. "I hope it's to your liking."

"It'll be great, thank you." I sank into the comfortable chair, already feeling like this might be my new spot as a few bunnies wound around my feet. "Do you mind if I write while I'm here?"

"No, not as long as you order a drink and some food if you're peckish." Her smile was warm and bright as she leaned closer. "You're the Demon Lord's consort, right?"

"Yup, that's me." I grinned, picturing how much he'd hate being reminded of that little ruse. "I've never been to a demon run cafe before. What kind of drinks do you have?"

She passed me a menu. "We've got everything from black coffee to flavored, iced coffee, and even some teas if you're looking for something different."

"I'll have a caramel mocha and a hazelnut croissant, please." I glanced over at the soldier who was positioned against the wall five feet away. "Dain? What will you have?"

He stood up straighter. "Nothing for me. I'm on duty."

"We're in a cafe. A bunny cafe!" I rolled my eyes. "I think I'm perfectly safe for a while."

The woman cocked her hip out, staring him down. "If you want to stay, you've gotta order something." She turned to wink at me, whispering. "That works every time on the strong stoic types."

My shoulders shook with silent laughter. This woman sure knew what she was doing, understanding the situation in mere moments. She probably saw all types of people working here.

"You better listen to her," I said with as much authority as I could. "Otherwise the Demon Lord might be disappointed."

Dain practically leapt forward. "I'll take a double shot of espresso, please."

The owner and I shared a secret smile before Inkheart scribbled its own order.

I'd love some tasty ink if you've got any. Something dark and spicy?

"Hmmm...I doubt they'll have any of that." I rummaged through my bag for the half-empty bottle of ink I had. "And the Demon Lord has the new ink we bought at the stationery store too. I'm sorry."

"Oh, it's no problem." The woman smiled, writing Inkheart's order down too. "We serve all sorts here, even magical pens."

The pen leapt into the air, swirling its feathers in excitement as a few bunnies hopped, following the pen back and forth. It was all so magical and kind of ridiculous, which made it even better. Warmth radiated from every aspect of the cafe, breathing new life into my concept of a demon village once again.

"I might love this place already." I picked up a demon bunny, petting it on my lap. I should have brought Cinder, but the bunny had been nowhere to be found when I woke up. "I'll have to stop by again with my own demon bunny."

"You are always welcome, my dear. Now get to writing." The woman made a shooing motion. "I'll bring your orders out soon."

Her kind encouragement really set the right tone, making me pull out my new paper and lay it on the table proudly. I glanced at the pen flying through the air, wondering how I was supposed to actually write with it. Maybe I should have bought a normal pen as well? While I debated it, Inkheart scribbled a note to me.

Finally ready to put me to use? Just say the word!

"How does that work? Do you write for me?"

I'd never do that. The words are up to you, so use me like any other pen when you're writing. But feel free to put me back on my notepad if you want to chat or need any encouragement.

"Thank you." I swept my fingertips over Inkheart's feather like I was petting Cinder before taking the pen in my hand to write. "Guess it's time to get started. Wish me luck."

Inkheart bounced happily in my hand. I dipped the pen into the ink pot and held it inches above the clean white paper. The blank page was always the most terrifying part for me, but with Inkheart by my side, I knew we could do this.

Chapter 14
Demon Lord

I'd told Willow that I had errands to run, but really, I had just needed some time to think. She'd said that people trusted me like it was obvious, and at first I was going to say that was crazy, that people shouldn't trust a villain, but I knew she was right deep in my bones. Or maybe I just wanted her to be right.

The way everyone kept thanking me and sharing their stories like I'd been a big part of their lives felt nice. Too nice. I'd never expected something like that, but it made me understand what Willow had been talking about last night. I'd always felt like a fake because I didn't know why I was fighting the hero.

Now I did.

When I'd seen that little girl with her broken horns, something in me snapped. It had taken every ounce of self-control not to go after the hero and his cursed people right then and there. How dare they steal my peoples' magic and put that sad look in a little girl's eyes? I wanted to end them all and make them regret ever looking at magic in the first place.

People were what mattered, not what you could use them for. After reading so many books in the library, I knew that was a motivation that could drive heroes and villains alike. It had to be why the author had made me this way. He'd written me to protect the demons, no matter the cost.

For the first time, I felt like maybe I really was the right person to fight the hero. I was the Demon Lord, not just in name, but in action too. The more I got to know these people, the more I wanted to protect them and be the man they thought I was. Which meant it was time to go back and talk to Willow about all this.

The strong scent of coffee wafted out of the Bunny Brews Cafe, drawing me in with faint curiosity. Willow had suggested that the only way I could figure out who I was and what I enjoyed was to start trying everything. The mattress shopping had been quite the experience, and I was kind of excited for a softer bed. What if coffee ended up being just as pleasant? Mochi had given me many hot cocoas, but never coffee. I'd seen tired patrons downing the drink like it gave them the will to keep going.

It seemed like an interesting drink, and I wanted to try it.

Before I could open the door, a young woman with bunny ears rushed out carrying an arm full of drinks. She barreled into me with an oof, and the drinks started to tip. I grabbed the carrying case, holding on to the drinks as she stumbled, ears flopping over as she righted herself.

"Phew, that was close." She straightened her uniform and took the drinks back from me. "Thanks for the save! Tell mom to give you something on the house. She's the owner. I've gotta run."

Then she was off again, disappearing into the crowd on the street behind me as if she had no idea who she'd just run into. Walking around town like this had shown me that the demons weren't the mysterious group I'd made up stories about, but real people just working hard to live their lives to the fullest. A smile tugged at my lips as I went inside.

"Welcome to Bunny Brews, how may I help you?" An older bunny woman with the same brown coloring as the girl outside smiled at me, then tilted her head. "Wait, are you the–"

"Yes, I'm the Demon Lord." I'd let myself get lost in thought, but I did still have a role to play. I cast my smile aside and took a deep breath. "I'll have whatever you recommend. Thanks."

The woman frowned, ears twitching. "I was going to ask if you're the man Willow's been waiting for, but looks like I got my answer. Dark and grumpy. Is that how you like your coffee too?"

My eyes widened. "Dark and grumpy? Is that really how she described me?"

A quiet laugh drew me deeper into the coffee shop where Willow was sitting next to a large window. Sunlight spilled through the glass, shining warmly on her red hair. She looked so cozy, curled up in an armchair surrounded by scribbled notes, coffee, and snacks. Her coffee had so much cream and caramel on it that it looked like a snack itself. It reminded me of all the hot cocoas she'd drank at Mochi's Snack Shack.

"I think I'd like a sweet coffee like hers." I turned back to who I assumed was the owner of this cafe. "Maybe something dark as well, just to see what I like."

"Never had coffee before?" When I shook my head, the woman got an excited glint in her eye. "I'll bring you both an assortment of drinks then. The writer seems to enjoy the sweeter ones, but we've got all kinds."

I nodded my thanks as I made my way to Willow. She shuffled some papers together, stacking them so they weren't sprawled across the table. Inkheart hopped back onto its notebook with a flutter, both of them turning toward me expectantly while the bodyguard drew closer, as if he too was interested.

"So, how'd the errands go?" Willow asked sweetly. "Get anything interesting?"

The way she said that felt like a trap of some kind. I slowly pulled out a chair and sat across from her, debating my answer. I'd initially left to gather my thoughts before she could start asking questions for the book, but I actually had stopped at a few shops to make it feel like I was running errands. I was a demon of my word after all.

I reached inside the deep pockets of my outer cloak and pulled out two writing boards, sliding one across the table to her. "This is for you. It'll let us keep in touch over long distances. When you write on one, the words appear on the other."

She leaned over the table, her hair brushing against the wooden surface as she examined the device with a slight crease in her forehead. Then she picked up the attached pencil and wrote something, her green eyes filling with amusement as she smiled.

The urge to check the other writing board was too strong and I tugged it toward me.

Now I won't have to miss you so much while you're gone.

My mouth dropped open as I stumbled for words that wouldn't come. I glanced up at her to see her shoulders shaking with silent laughter. Oh, so she was teasing me then? Well, two could play at that game. I grabbed my own pencil and wrote a message just for her.

I'd stay by your side every day if that's what you require. I'll hold you close and comfort you in this terrifying demon world. You'll never want for a single thing. All you need to do is ask and it's yours.

There. She was going to be as red as a plump tomato after reading that. I felt a smug grin grace my lips as I glanced up at her, but instead of shock and embarrassment, she had an even stranger look on her face. It was almost like...she was happy? She kept staring at the words I'd written as if they were something special. Oh no, had I messed up the teasing and she thought I was serious?

"I'm sorry, I was just trying to tease you back." I awkwardly turned to the owner who was bringing over the drinks she'd promised us. What bad timing. "I didn't mean to imply anything with that."

The older bunny woman smiled as she handed us drinks that smelled like nutty chocolate and something darker. "What's he implying, dear? Anything you need help with?"

"Oh, he was just writing me a love letter." Willow took a big sip of her drink. Foam lined her upper lip, and she slowly swept her tongue across to lick it all up. My stomach fluttered and I felt unable to look away. What kind of magic was in these drinks? She leaned forward, nudging my mug towards me. "Drink up. It's delicious."

"Oh, she's a handful, huh?" The owner laughed warmly. "Go ahead and try them, Demon Lord. One is a mocha latte and the other is a plain dark roast coffee. Thought you might like to compare them to see what level of sweetness you like."

Thank the gods she'd given me an excuse not to speak because I had no words for Willow. She'd somehow taken my attempt at teasing and upped it far more than I ever could. Did she ever mean it when she flirted like that? It seemed to come so easily to her, but was there any feeling at all behind it?

Did I *want* there to be feeling behind it?

I took a cautious sip of the plain coffee. A bold almost smokey taste filled my mouth, so bitter that I felt myself making a face that wasn't exactly polite. I winced. "Sorry."

Willow burst out laughing and handed me a container of something white. "Try adding sugar, see if that helps."

The three of us proceeded to test taste different coffees with different amounts of sweetness to them, even trying different flavorings too. Eventually I settled on one I truly enjoyed: a hazelnut latte.

The owner smiled proudly. "I knew we'd find the right one for you."

Something about her was so comforting, reminding me of Willow's grandmother with her warm and soothing vibes. I relaxed into the plush chair as the coffee warmed me. I could see myself spending a lot of time in a place like this, brainstorming with Willow or chatting about anything really. As long as she was here, I felt at peace.

The coffee turned acrid in my mouth. I was supposed to be getting Willow out of the book, not enjoying my time with her. She was stuck because of me, and I should be doing everything I could to get her out, so she could return to that loving grandmother of hers and make healing potions to help her town.

I drained my mug before standing up. "I'm going back to the library to check on Nyssa's progress. She must have figured something out to get you home."

"Right now?" Willow fidgeted with the empty mug in front of her, not meeting my gaze. "I mean, sure, that makes sense. Let me know what you find out. I'll stay here and keep writing for a while."

Inkheart bobbed a nod, feathers fluttering as if to assure me it would keep Willow company. A pen wasn't enough though, not if there really was a time difference like before. A half hour outside could be hours in here. I turned to the demon who'd taken on the job of guarding her. He'd stayed outside the castle all night and remained at Willow's side here too. He might be overeager, but I had a feeling I could trust him.

"Keep her safe." I pinned him with a stare worthy of a Demon Lord, instilling every ounce of seriousness I could into it. "And give her whatever she needs while I'm away. Use my treasury if needed."

"Yes, My Lord." He bowed so low he almost tipped over. "I'll protect her with my life and make sure she wants for nothing."

"I don't need all that." Willow shook her head, waving her hands in the air. "I'm really fine here writing. Just go get the information and come back when you can."

Inkheart scribbled furiously, floating up so I could see.

I thought the whole consort thing was a ruse, but the way you look after her shows your true colors. You care for her, Demon Lord. She's safe with us.

What did a pen know? I grunted, brushing it aside. Of course I cared about her safety. It was my fault she was in this mess, so until she was safely back in her apothecary shop, all my attention would be on her. It was the least I could do. I closed my eyes, summoning the bright light that would take me back to the library.

Something tugged at my sleeve. Willow.

"Could you check on Gran too?" she asked softly. "I'm worried she's overwhelmed without me. She should probably hire some help, but there's no way she'd agree to that, so I'd feel better if you made sure she was okay."

I nodded. "Of course. I'll visit her shop myself and ensure her well-being."

Willow let out a breath and smiled. "Thank you. You can get going now."

The warm golden light started falling from the ceiling, but Willow tugged on my sleeve again.

"Sorry, but could you grab me some clothes while you're there too?" She scratched the back of her head, looking embarrassed. "And maybe some other essentials? Gran can put a bag together for you. I just have a feeling I'll be here for a while, so it would be nice to have my things."

"Anything else?" I feigned annoyance, trying to get her back for all the teasing.

Her eyes lit up. "Oh! The rest of the books in your series would be great. I left them at the library and could really use them if I'm going to make your last book amazing."

I sighed. "Am I your errand boy now? You do realize I'm the Demon Lord, right?"

"And that's why I'm sure you can handle it," she said sweetly. "My Demon Lord would never let a few errands get in the way of his mission, right?"

Her Demon Lord? A pleasant shiver raced through me. I'd never been anyone's anything before and even though I knew she was teasing, it felt really good to hear. Too good. I closed my eyes, summoning the light that would bring me back to the library again so I could run these errands and get back to working on the final book.

Chapter 15
Demon Lord

The library was just as busy as I remembered, full of patrons and overwhelmed librarians. Nyssa and her researcher friend Oren had immediately shooed me away when I asked about their progress on getting Willow out of the book, saying that it hadn't even been a day yet and even they weren't that good.

I'd wanted to protest, but there wasn't anything I could do to help them. No matter how badly I wanted to get Willow back home, I didn't know anything about library magic. They did, and pressuring them wouldn't get me anywhere. So I'd grabbed the books in my series and headed off to the next stop on my list.

The apothecary shop.

A soft bell chimed as I opened the door and stepped inside. Dried plants hung from the ceiling while living ones sat on every available shelf, throwing off a wonderfully earthy smell. Something sweet was mixed in too, like honey or fruit maybe. As I walked up to the counter, the sound of a mortar and pestle slowed.

"Welcome to Bloom and Bramble Apothecary, I'll be right with you." Willow's Grandmother's voice was soft, yet firm as she finished grinding the herbs she was working on, then slowly stood up. I could practically hear each bone creaking as she did so and rushed over to help. She waved me off. "Customers aren't supposed to come behind the counter, you know." Then she squinted at me. "Ohhh, look at those horns. My, my, looks like we've got an interesting visitor today."

She turned back as if to talk to somebody but paused. It was just her and I in the shop, nobody else. Confusion marred her features until she covered it up with a smile. My chest ached knowing how much she must miss Willow. I had to tell her what was going on, had to explain why Willow wasn't back yet.

"Elder Mable." I bowed my head to her. "Willow wanted me to check in and see how you're doing."

"If she wanted to know that, she should have come here herself." Mable tilted her head, squinting at me even harder. "Unless there's some reason my granddaughter didn't come? Is she okay?"

"Fine, perfectly fine," I rushed to say. "Just working hard on the book."

I tried not to wince as the half-truth fell from my lips. I had to tell this woman where her granddaughter was, but I didn't want her to worry too much. Maybe I'd wait until we had a plan for how to get Willow out of the book. I wasn't used to dealing with people's emotions like this. Usually,

I just said what I thought without a care, but this little old apothecary was important to Willow. The most important person in her life.

She patted my arm. "I'm glad you found a way to get her writing again. Now, sit down and help me with these hand warmers."

"What?" I glanced over at the table covered in fabric and herbs. "No, I'm just here to check on you and get some clothes for Willow."

"Youngsters these days, always in such a hurry." Mable shook her head, settling back down onto a chair. "If I stop to gather Willow's things, then these sunflowers will lose their potency, and I'll have to lay their petals outside all over again. I need to use them while they're fresh and full of the sun's warmth."

She picked up the pestle again, grinding the softly glowing sunflower petals with a clear liquid. The longer she worked, the more the liquid glowed, as if the light from the petals was being absorbed by it. I felt myself drawn to it as the sweet flowery scent filled the air.

"Grab that." She nodded at a paintbrush on the table. "And spread a thin layer of this across the fabric. Don't make it too thick or it will clump up, hear me?"

"Yes, ma'am." I sat down, grabbing the brush as if this was completely normal. The fabric was soft and so thin I could almost see through it. "Actually, I've never done this before. I don't want to mess it up."

"Messing up is part of life. You can't be worse than that so-called apprentice who stopped by earlier."

My eyebrows rose. "Oh, so you hired somebody then? Willow will be happy."

"Like I'd ever hire a good-for-nothing like that. Hmph." Her eyes narrowed, staring at me like she was debating if I was a good-for-nothing too. "Less talking, more working."

Apparently ordering demons around ran in the family. I felt myself smiling as I dipped the brush into the glowing flower mixture, spreading it as light as I could. The fabric absorbed the liquid, taking on the glow just like how the sunflower fields shined bright after asking in the sun all day. Warmth emanated off the fabric too, reminding me of the cafe with Willow. It wasn't overly warm, but just enough to stave off the chill in the air.

Once I was done, I cleaned off the brush and turned to her. "What next?"

"Cut the fabric into three-inch squares so we can make them into pouches." She handed me a pair of shears, then nudged over two jars of dark powders. "Then measure out equal parts of iron powder and charcoal with that scoop and place them in the center of each square like you're making a pastry or filled pasta. Add a heat stone to the middle and you'll be ready to wrap it up."

I'd never done any of those things, but it seemed simple enough. I set about cutting the fabric, the soft snip-snip oddly soothing. A tiny mossmew curled around my legs, meowing and rubbing up against me. I reached down to pet the mossy animal, remembering the first time I'd visited Willow. These little cat-like creatures had been playing in sunbeams, racing between all the glass jars on the shelves. Willow seemed to have a fondness for them, and I wished she was here to play with them again.

Guilt gnawed at me as I measured out the ingredients the apothecary had given me. I should really tell her where

Willow was. She could handle the truth, right? Even if we didn't have a solid plan yet, it wasn't like Willow was in danger. She just couldn't be here...

Mable slapped my hands. "I said equal amounts! Are you trying to set my shop on fire?"

I'd been so lost in my thoughts that I hadn't been paying enough attention to the hand warmers and had accidentally added triple the amount of one powder than the other. A small flame burst out right before the apothecary stamped it out with a thick pad. She picked up the last few squares I'd been working on and tossed the powders into what looked like a burn bin so the flames couldn't creep out.

"I'm sorry." I shook my head, backing away from the table of precious ingredients. "I'll pay you back for that and more. Whatever you need."

She sighed. "What I need is to get these finished by the end of the day. Why don't we take a break before we get back to it?"

"Why don't I find that apprentice you mentioned instead?"

"You're doing perfectly fine. Sit, sit!" She waved me back as she pulled a teapot over that was whistling softly. "Do you like tea? Have any preferences?"

I sank onto the chair, not sure how to answer. "Um, what's Willow's favorite? She mentioned how nice it would be if you could send some over."

"She always thinks better with a good cup of yerba mate tea. Calms her down and helps her focus." Mable smiled, grabbing a glass jar of green tea leaves, one of red, and one that was almost black. "Take all of these with you when you leave. As a thank you for helping Willow follow her dreams.

She spends so much time locked up in here, never letting herself go after what she truly wants."

"She loves being an apothecary though, doesn't she?"

Honestly, she hadn't mentioned it much since she'd gotten stuck in my book. I bet there were demon apothecaries she would like to visit. Maybe they'd even have big gardens for her to explore so she could feel like she was back home for a moment, picking herbs on the mountain like usual. Suddenly, I had the urge to go back and show her every beautiful thing the demon world had to offer. Once I found out what those things were, of course. Our trip through town had been more exploring than I'd ever done.

Mable poured me a cup of tea that smelled like grass after a long rain. "She does love being an apothecary, but I'm not sure it's what she loves most."

Steam curled around my fingers as the cup's warmth seeped into my hands. The little mossmew from earlier had somehow climbed into my lap, peeking her head above the table to sniff the tea. Then she curled up, purring as I ran my fingers through her mossy fur, waiting for the apothecary to explain what she'd meant by that.

As Mable settled back in her chair and sipped her own tea, she finally met my gaze. "Willow has experienced a lot of loss in her young life. Her parents, my wonderful daughter, passed away when she was young. And then my dear husband left us a few years back. It's made Willow afraid of getting close to anyone or really going after what she loves." She took another sip of her tea, sitting quietly for a while. "I'm afraid she's only here because of me."

The words were so quiet I almost didn't hear them. I had never experienced loss like that before, but the pain on the apothecary's face said it all. Was she really the only reason Willow was working here? That didn't feel right. The way Willow talked about her Gran was full of love and respect, not obligation and duty.

"Even if Willow is only here because of you, I don't think that's a bad thing." I sipped my tea. It was warm and tasted very earthy, verging on pungent. "Doesn't everyone want to spend more time with the ones they love?"

The apothecary barked out a laugh. "Well, when you put it like that, how can I refute it?"

We sat in silence for a few minutes, drinking our tea while I looked around. The sunlight spilling through the windows shone softly on the plants while jars of medications shimmered like gems. The soft purring of a few mossmews almost lulled me to sleep. This shop felt so different from my barren castle and even more different than the noisy library.

It was peaceful.

Calm.

Quiet.

Everything I enjoyed.

"I can see why Willow loves it here," I said. "It's soothing and warm, just like this tea. I don't think you need to worry about her being a writer or an apothecary. Couldn't she just do both?"

"Of course she can, if she ever lets herself dream big enough to do it. She needs to realize that taking a risk is worth it sometimes, especially when you have someone there to catch you if you fall." The older woman finished her tea and leaned forward with a sparkle in her eye. "If anyone can convince her of that, I bet it's you."

I sputtered, almost choking on my drink. "Me? Why would she listen to anything I had to say?"

Mable got up slowly and patted my shoulder. "You'll figure that out soon enough. Now let me go get Willow's things for you. Keep measuring out that powder and tie the pouches up when you're done."

"You're leaving me alone?" I turned toward the counter and the front door behind it. "What if a customer comes in?"

She was already moving up the stairs to what I assumed was their living quarters, waving a hand at me like it was no big deal at all. I took a deep breath and straightened my shoulders. I was a Demon Lord. I could handle a customer or two, surely.

I went back to work on the hand warmers, being a lot more careful with how much of each ingredient I measured out, before adding the heat stone and tying them up with the red ribbons at the edge of the table. One after another, the completed hand warmers lined the table, glowing faintly as warmth emanated from them.

It felt good to be productive like this. If I'd had something to keep me occupied, maybe the castle wouldn't have been so boring the past few years. The only time I'd had any fun there was with Willow. Her presence had brightened the entire castle, like a fog had cleared and the fires were blazing bright. Actually, that's how the new castle library felt too. Maybe that room had more to do with Willow being there than anything else.

I should ask Misty about that...

The faint footfalls of the apothecary traveled through the floor as she presumably walked around getting a bag together for Willow. The writing board in my pocket started vibrating, so I hurried to view it, eager to see what the message might be.

I could really use those books. When do you think you'll be back?

I grabbed the pencil to write that I'd be back soon, once I was done at the apothecary shop, and then stood up with a sigh. No matter how cozy it was here, I really should be getting back. Especially since time moved faster inside the book than out here. I moved to the bottom of the stairs to call out to the apothecary.

"Sorry, but Willow needs me to go back into the–" I clamped my mouth shut before I spilled any secrets.

"She needs you to do what?" Mable poked her head out of an upstairs room, watching me from the top of the stairs. "Everything okay?"

"Yeah, everything's fine. I just need to head back..."

The apothecary kept standing there, staring at me like she knew I was keeping the real story to myself. She sighed and grabbed a bag, dragging it to the edge of the stairs. "Well, are you going to help me with this or just stand there?"

"Of course, I'll help!" I leapt up the stairs, taking the plump bag from her. She'd packed up half of Willow's things by the looks of it. "Thank you for this. She'll appreciate it."

"Because she won't be coming home for a while?" Mable tilted her head when I nodded, pinning me with a stare. "Or is it because she *can't* come home? Willow has never stayed the night anywhere until now. Not once. So you'd better tell me what's really going on, or you won't be leaving anytime soon. You'd be surprised how many herbs can incapacitate a grown man like yourself."

"That's a joke, right?" A cool chill settled over me. Logically, there was no reason for me to fear a frail old woman, but that threat sounded like something she'd absolutely make good on and maybe already had in the past. I swallowed hard. It was time to tell her the truth, not because of her threat, but because I respected her, and she loved Willow. "Right, well, the thing is, Willow accidentally got stuck in a book. My book series to be precise. The Misty Mountain Library was trying to inspire her to write the last book, but it was the first time the library had used this kind of magic and none of us are really sure how to get her out yet." I held up my hand to stop her inevitable outrage. "We're working on it. The librarians are studying everything they can get their hands on and I'm taking care of Willow inside the book. She's even got a bodyguard and a bunny. She's okay, I promise."

A bodyguard and a bunny. What was I even saying? The need for a bodyguard would probably worry the apothecary even more. I gripped the soft handles of Willow's bag tight, not sure what else to say without digging myself a deeper hole. Only one thing came to mind.

"I'm sorry."

This entire situation was my fault. If I'd never asked her to enter the competition, or never joked about her going inside of my book, she'd be right here with her Gran making hand warmers instead of me. I squeezed my eyes shut, not wanting to see the anger that had to be welling up inside the apothecary. But instead of slapping me or screaming at me, her thin arms wrapped around me in a hug.

She patted my back softly. "Thank you for taking care of her."

My eyes snapped open as I stood there like a limp noodle in her arms. "You're not mad? I'm the reason she's stuck in a book."

"No, I bet Willow's having the time of her life." The apothecary chuckled as she pulled away, shaking her head. "She's loved stories since before she could read and knowing she got to step inside one is just amazing. She's lucky and she'll have no excuse not to write that book now. She literally can't run away." Her laughs grew louder as she started walking down the stairs. "Honestly, it's perfect. You bring these things to her and come back if she needs anything else, you hear?"

I gaped at her. "Really? You don't care that she's missing?"

"Missing is a strong word when we know exactly where she is." Mable held onto the railing as she reached the end of the stairs, turning back towards me. "Does Willow blame you?"

"Well, no, she said it wasn't my fault."

Mable nodded. "Then that's all I need. Stop worrying about things you can't change and work on the things you can. Like giving her a change of clothes."

"Right." I joined her downstairs. This family was so strange. "I guess I'll get going then. I'm supposed to tell you to hire some help though."

The apothecary clicked her tongue against her teeth. "You tell my granddaughter that I've been running this shop for over forty years, so I'll be fine on my own for a few days."

She was just as stubborn as Willow. "Okay, then I'll come back and help you again later. There's not much I can do while Willow's writing anyway."

"I don't need–"

I shook my head. "Doesn't matter. Willow's already got a lot on her plate and I'm not adding this to it. So, I'm going to help you."

Mable scratched her head, frowning at me. "Well, I'm not sure how much help you'll be, but if you insist."

"I do."

She sighed. "Oh, fine. Hurry up and get out of here then. I'll see you tomorrow."

I nodded, feeling accomplished after all these errands. Not only had I gotten everything Willow needed, but I'd secured a spot as the apothecary's apprentice too. She'd probably have to teach me from scratch, but I'd work hard to repay Willow for trying to find me an ending I deserved. And for helping me figure out who I really was. No amount of time I spent with her Gran could repay all of that, but it was a start.

Plus, I was looking forward to coming back. Today had been surprisingly nice.

Chapter 18
Willow

Cinder nibbled at a pile of fresh green hay I'd picked up from town, shuffling the strands around and creating a mess in the Demon Lord's new library. Dain narrowed his eyes from where he silently stood guard across the room, but it was just hay, and I could clean it up if she didn't finish it all. I scratched behind the demon bunny's ears as she tilted her head into my palm.

Since I had so much work to get done, I'd decided to outline the last book in the castle instead of the cafe, but Cinder deserved to play with other bunnies soon. Once I knew what I was going to write, I'd bring her there for sure.

If only outlining was going better. Somehow, the more I learned about this world, the less I understood. That whole humans siphoning magic from demons thing was really throwing me for a loop and I couldn't get myself to write a single word. Sure, I had piles and piles of random ideas, but nothing that made sense or that the fans would go crazy over and talk about for years to come.

At this rate, I wouldn't even have a solid idea by the deadline, let alone an actual book. Gran would never feel comfortable retiring then. I could just see her patting my hand, telling me I needed to give my "real dream" more effort. I had to finish this book, make it amazing, then continue working as an apothecary. That was the only way she'd see where my heart really was.

My grandparents and my parents had all been apothecaries. It was in my blood, and I had to make her believe that somehow. Being an apothecary wasn't an obligation: it was a legacy. One I was proud to continue.

I flipped another book from the Demon Lord's series open, skimming through it for clues. No matter how hard I looked, I couldn't find anything that would explain the kind demon villagers I'd met or the Demon Lord himself. They were always described as monsters who would rather burn your town to the ground than talk to you. Every time a demon appeared in the books, they were doing something evil like attacking villagers or kidnapping people.

It really felt like the hero was doing a good thing. That his actions were right and just, fulfilling his divine mission wonderfully. He was the light that cast out the darkness. He was the chosen one.

I just couldn't wrap my mind around how that worked with everything else I'd seen since entering the book, and I was getting more and more frustrated staring at a blank page trying to figure it out. I'd even finished the newest book at record speed, but that had just made me even more confused.

"Ugh." I flopped back onto the couch, hand over my eyes. "If the hero is so amazing, then why is he fighting the Demon Lord? And why does the Demon Lord seem just as nice as the hero when he's supposed to be the evilest creature in the whole series?"

Dain snorted. I tilted my head to peek over at him, but he was pretending like he didn't notice me at all, just sitting in front of the open doorway with his spear in hand like he was ready to fight.

But that snort meant he had opinions. Opinions I could very much use right about now, even if it was just to bounce ideas off somebody.

"Something you want to add?" I sat up, turning on the couch to face him. "Maybe an opinion on the hero? Or the Demon Lord?" My bodyguard just sat there, statue still. I tossed a pillow at him that he expertly dodged. "Come on, help me out here. The Demon Lord is the one who wants me to write this book, so you should at least brainstorm with me. Didn't he tell you to give me whatever I needed?"

"He did, that's true." Dain set his spear to the side and pulled his chair closer to my couch. "Well, if you really want to know, then I think you're looking at this all wrong. I've heard you mumbling for hours about this great hero of yours, but he's obviously the villain. Why else would he slaughter innocent demons? He hunts us down to steal our magic, forcing us to hide in this one protected city. That doesn't sound very hero-y to me, and yet, you humans wrote thousands of pages about him!"

He shook his head, obviously disgusted with my entire race. I picked another pillow up, twirling it in my hands as I considered that. If the demons weren't the enemy like the books led me to believe, then why was the hero fighting them? What was the point of the war? And what role did the Demon Lord really play?

"Okay, so in your version, who's the Demon Lord then?"

Dain rolled his eyes as he leaned back in his chair. "You've visited our town, talked to our people. You know who the Demon Lord is to us. He's the hero of this terrible story of yours."

I dropped the pillow, eyes wide. The Demon Lord was the hero? Not just a bad guy for a good reason, but an actual hero? That word meant something in this world. It held power and righteous purpose.

"No way." I shook my head, holding my hand up. "I mean, I know he's nice and he's been good to you, but he's not the hero. He can't be."

"Who says?" Dain tilted his head. "Your human priests? Your government? Your Kings? Who cares about any of that, they're probably just as evil as the hero."

My mouth dropped open. If the Demon Lord was the hero, that flipped this entire story on its head. Again. I mean, he was obviously the hero to the demons, but that didn't mean he was the hero to everyone. There were two sides to this story, but somehow, neither side was making much sense. Which kept leading me back to a plot twist...and what bigger plot twist would there be than the Demon Lord being the good guy all along?

The soft crunching of Cinder chewing a giant mouthful of hay mixed with the crackling of the fireplace as my brain kind of broke. Nothing else had gotten me anywhere, so I might as well let the idea play out and see where it led. Maybe it would spark something.

"Okay, so let's pretend you're right." I pulled a pile of blank paper over, nudging Inkheart to wake up. The poor pen had given up on me after hours of debating without actually letting it write anything. "Let's make a list of suspects."

The pen hopped up, scritch scratching across the paper.

Suspects? Now we're talking. Where do you want to start?

I glanced over at Dain who was reading the synopsis on the back of each book before dropping them on the table in disgust. "Let's start with Dain's ideas about the priest and the royal family. If the Demon Lord isn't the villain, then somebody else must be. I don't think it's the hero since there's no hint of it in the books, but maybe somebody's manipulating him."

Ohhh, I called it! Poor himbo hero.

"Really?" Dain's eyes widened as he pulled his chair even closer. "Okay, I'll help however I can."

Seeing him eager to join in felt so nice compared to how stand-offish he'd been ever since the Demon Lord had assigned him as my bodyguard. If we were going to be stuck together for a while, then it would be nice if we could find some common ground.

"Inkheart, are you any good at drawing? Let's make posters for each suspect and pin them up." I laid out a few pieces of paper for the magical pen after it nodded. "Okay, first up is the holy priest who first gave the hero his divine mission. That seems like a classic secret villain based on other stories, but it's almost so overdone that I feel like it would be disappointing."

Dain frowned. "We worship the same gods as the humans, so I doubt a priest would be sending a hero after us. I'm not sure what it would get them."

"That's a good point." I reached over to add the word motive to the papers as Inkheart drew a fairly accurate depiction of what I thought a priest would look like with billowy robes and a holy staff. "Okay, so if the priest doesn't have a motive, then who else?"

"The King." Dain curled his lips. "That family wants our resources for themselves, using our magic to fuel their technology."

That lined up with what we'd heard around town. I nodded, adding the name and motive to the next paper for Inkheart to draw on. Something about it didn't feel quite right though.

"From what I've read, the King is kind of a father-figure to the hero and has actually tried to stop him from finishing the mission a few times." I flipped through a few of the books, trying to find the parts I was looking for. "Ah, yes, right here. The hero has some kind of illness that the King's healers worked day and night to make a remedy for, but even that didn't fully heal him. That's why the King doesn't want him putting himself at risk."

Inkheart's feather swayed as it drifted over the pages of the book, apparently reading the passage I pointed out. I hadn't realized pens could read, but hey, they *were* magical.

Hmmm.....either this King is ultra sus and using some intense reverse psychology or he actually does love the little himbo. I'm rooting for them.

"Well I'm not." Dain scoffed. "Even if he's a nice guy, he's still the one stealing our land."

"True, but if we're adding the King, then we should definitely add the Princess too." I wrote Princess on a new sheet of paper for Inkheart. "She's the hero's love interest, but nobody wants them to marry since he's just a commoner. If he defeated the Demon Lord, that would really raise his station."

Ah yes, the lover. Excellent, excellent.

Inkheart was moving faster than ever as it drew all our suspects out, barely having time for silly commentary. Dain scratched his chin.

"Something wrong?" I asked.

He shook his head, leaning forward to examine the books. "Wasn't there another so-called hero before this one? What happened to him?"

Now that was a very good question. He'd trained the hero in the first book, shaping his entire view of how to be a hero. He'd injured himself before defeating the Demon Lord, so his only claim to fame now was helping the current hero. That had to be frustrating, and I could see him bending the narrative a bit to get the hero to make him seem more impressive than he was.

I jotted that down too, but paused as Inkheart scurried over a few book pages, waiting to see what the pen was so excited about. Eventually, it hopped back onto a sheet of paper and drew the most extravagant sword I'd ever seen. I stared at it, trying not to laugh.

"Ummm, are you implying that the sword is the villain?" I asked with only a hint of a smile in my voice.

The pen fluffed up its feathers.

It's a talking sword! It's obviously possessing the hero, slowly taking control until the sword is the one in charge. Yup, that's what I'd do if I were that sword.

Dain raised an eyebrow. "So you're saying that talking objects tend to take control of their humans and make them do evil things, huh?"

Before the pen could explain that crazy statement away, Dain lifted it into the air, pinched between his thumb and index finger. He stared at it, moving it this way and that, with such intensity that the pen shivered. Then it started jumping and scribbling in the air like it was shouting. It was all so ridiculous that I couldn't help but laugh.

"I think we're safe, so hand the pen over." I held my hand out until Dain reluctantly returned Inkheart. I patted its feather softly before setting it back on its book. "Maybe don't say villainous things with this over-eager bodyguard looming about."

The pen huffed, sputtering ink all over the page.

Well never in my life has somebody manhandled me like that. At least buy me some tasty ink first.

Dain shrugged. "Don't make such evil-sounding statements then."

His tough demeanor cracked a bit as the side of his mouth quirked up. Okay, so he did have a sense of humor. I was starting to wonder about that. I shook my head, chuckling as I gathered up all the pages we had so far and stuck them onto the edges of the bookshelves. I turned back to Inkheart, but the pen was already drawing a picture of the loveable himbo hero for the middle, apparently knowing exactly what I was trying to do here. I grinned and added the hero to the middle of this little mystery board of ours, feeling like a real detective now.

The silence stretched as the three of us stared at our masterpiece. It was missing something. I grabbed a sheet of paper and drew a big question mark on it, sticking it right above the hero's portrait.

"There." I nodded proudly at the sprawled-out suspects. "Now we just need to link their motives up and see who gains the most from sending the hero after the Demon Lord and causing a war." I bent down to grab a few long pieces of hay from Cinder to use in place of string. "Now, the Princess and the King have strong motives that are linked together, but the priest angle still feels pretty good too, especially since he would have had a hand in the last hero's goals as well."

I strung the hay between all the characters, making a web of motives, none of which really stood out that much stronger than the others. The more time we spent brainstorming, the more suspects we unearthed, all with good reasons to manipulate the hero.

At this point, I was starting to feel like the hero was even more clueless than I'd originally thought. Even if there wasn't some secret bad guy, the hero himself was still way too easily influenced. He cared so much about helping people that he'd been led astray more than once throughout the series.

His integrity wasn't in question though, no matter how much Dain tried to convince me otherwise. The hero was brave and honorable through and through, usually to his own detriment. The more we looked into it, the more I felt like somebody really was using him. All the groundwork was laid out in the previous books, from farmers conning him into harvesting their entire crop alone to other members of his party using him for their own personal gains. He was obviously too gullible for his own good.

I flopped back onto the couch again, rubbing my tired eyes. "Every time I think we're onto something, another plot thread pops up. I just can't tell what's important and what's not."

"Your hero is hopeless." Dain fell back into his chair with a sigh. "Honestly, how you think these stories are entertaining is beyond me. I hope you write this last book better."

"Hey, that's not fair. The books are amazing." I tried to sit up and debate more, but I was too exhausted, especially since Cinder hopped up on my stomach and I didn't have the heart to move her. "Nevermind. I wish I could just talk to hero. I'm sure he'd want to get to the bottom of this just as much as we do and talking to him would make this so much easier. He knows a side of this that we'll never understand."

Yes! Chase after the mighty hero! Steal him away from the self-obsessed Princess!

Dain shook his head. "No way. He's got an entire army behind him at this point, haven't you heard? They're camped right outside the Wandering Woods, ready to invade."

"That's fair." I sighed, snuggling deeper into the plush couch while I pet Cinder. The bunny closed her eyes, as if she was also tired after her meal and this long discussion. "Okay, fine, I won't go look for the hero. But I really do need to talk to him. This book won't ever get written otherwise."

"Is he really that important?" Dain asked softly. "Can't the Demon Lord help you?"

I shook my head. "No. The hero is the main character. He's who the story's about, so he's the one I need."

Plus, it would be kind of cool to meet the main character of the series I'd been reading since I was a kid. Even if he was a little too gullible, he still had the heart of a hero. Everything he did was from a place of kindness. Being too kind did seem to get him taken advantage of a lot more than I'd remembered though. Where should you draw the line between being kind and being overly kind?

Dain stood up, gripping his spear tight. "Stay here. I'll get you your hero."

I jerked up, almost throwing Cinder off my lap. "Wait, hold on, what about the army and all that?"

"You said you need him, so I must." Dain took a deep breath, squaring his shoulders. "It's the duty the Demon Lord bestowed upon me: give you anything you need. He even tried to get me to kidnap the hero himself once, but *you* stopped him, remember?"

"I remember trying to save your life, yes." My voice was drowned out by Inkheart's scribbling as the book flew in front of us with far too much excitement.

Oh this is going to be fantastic. You get 'im big guy!

"Not helping, Inkheart." I reached out to stop Dain, but he was already walking out the door. "Seriously, you're going to get yourself killed. Or start the invasion!"

Dain turned back, a small smile on his lips. "Trust me. I'm more capable than you think."

Was he though? I hadn't seen anything to support that so far, but he was committed to his duty that was for sure. I squeezed my eyes shut. "Fine, but come back the moment it gets dangerous."

"Yes, my Lady." Dain bowed low before taking his leave.

Inkheart's feather danced as it wrote.

What an over-eager puppy. I bet he really does start an invasion. All to give you everything you desire. Love triangle time?

I rolled my eyes. "No. If anything, he loves the Demon Lord."

You're so right. How did I not call that from day one?

Speaking of the Demon Lord, I pulled over the writing board he'd given me to communicate. He'd want to know what just happened, but how did I even go about explaining it? Sorry your demon buddy just did a crazy thing and might start a war because of a silly comment I made? No, that would cause a panic and possibly rush him away from Gran too fast.

We need to talk. I'll be in the castle's library waiting for you, no rush.

Chapter 17
Demon Lord

The castle's library looked like a tornado had hit it with papers strewn across every surface, some balled up while others were full of Willow's handwritten notes. Inkheart was collapsed on the table, it's feather drooping like it was exhausted. I moved through the library carefully so I didn't step on any pages and noticed Willow sleeping on the floor by the fireplace.

Her hair was tied back in a ponytail and ink smudged her fingers, with a bit under her eyes too, like she'd been rubbing them a lot. Even more papers surrounded her in carefully stacked piles like she'd been organizing them before she fell asleep. She might have said no to writing my book at first, but she sure seemed committed now. Her Gran had nothing to worry about there.

I wish she'd fallen asleep on the couch instead of the floor though, especially after all those comments about my own uncomfortable sleeping habits. I reached for a blanket, pulling it up over her shoulders. She murmured something that I couldn't make out and curled up under the blanket, almost brushing against my hand.

My heartbeat quickened, and for some reason, I sat next to her. The easy rise and fall of her chest calmed me as the warmth from the fireplace settled against my skin. The castle had never felt this comfortable before and I owed it all to her.

I picked up a few of the pages she'd been working so hard on. The ones farthest from her had even and steady handwriting, perfectly formed like she'd been taking her time, but on the pages closest to her the handwriting curled and looped like she was racing to keep up with her thoughts. I ran a finger over the words, feeling her excitement shining through with each pen stroke.

All her notes were about me and my story. She'd written far more than I'd expected, filling up so many pages with ideas. My eyes widened as I read the words *anti-hero* and *protector* written over and over with mentions of me saving the demons by defeating some hidden bad guy.

She must have been more tired than I thought, because none of that made any sense. I flipped through more of her notes, searching for the real ideas in all her wild sleep-deprived ramblings, but there was nothing. No hint of my glorious demise anywhere.

I dropped the papers, my gaze landing on a group of pictures pinned on the shelves. They were suspects with motives listed for why they'd be manipulating the hero. I stood up, drawn to them like a moth to a flame, surprised a picture of me wasn't hanging anywhere. Instead there were headshots of the priest, the King, the Princess, the old hero, and so many other potential bad guys.

"Does she really think it's not me?" I muttered, staring at those pictures even harder, unable to comprehend what they might mean. "I'm the villain…"

The sounds of Willow shifting pulled my attention as her eyes fluttered open. "Hey, you."

Her voice was thick with sleep still and her hair was messy, just like when she'd woken up on the couch yesterday. Seeing her like that made it feel like we were sharing a moment and my chest ached for something I knew I couldn't have, something I didn't even want to name.

She rubbed the sleep from her eyes and then jerked into a sitting position. "Wait, you weren't supposed to see those yet."

"Oh, sorry." I moved away from the pictures hung on the bookshelves and awkwardly sat on the couch. "I don't understand what you're thinking though. I'm the bad guy, so wasting time on whatever that is just seems silly."

"Maybe." She toyed with the frayed edges of the blanket, curling it around her fingers. After a while, she took a deep breath and lifted her head to meet my gaze. "Or maybe it's not silly at all and the only ridiculous thing is you thinking that you're evil. I mean, let's face it, you're a terrible villain." She held her hands up before I could protest. "No, let me get this out first. You care way more than you let on and you always try to help people, even if you do it with a grumpy attitude. Like when I was worried about my last book and you offered to read it. Or when you didn't execute Dain and ordered him to be my bodyguard instead. Or when you promised that seamstress that you'd protect everyone no matter what."

"That was just–"

She shook her head. "No, it started even before that when the town thought the library was haunted. You could have hurt people to keep them away, but you chose to scare them instead with some shadow monsters. You always choose the less evil route, and I think we need to accept that."

"Accept...that I'm a terrible villain?" A lump formed in my stomach. I'd always felt like a fake, but now that she was agreeing with me, it was so much worse. Because it wasn't just in my head anymore, it was in hers too, and she was the last person I wanted to be thinking that. "No, you were supposed to help me live up to my potential, remember? To make me into the best villain anyone had ever seen."

"But what if you're meant for something different?" Her voice was soft as she stood up and joined me on the couch. She reached out for me, but then pulled back. "I'm sorry, I shouldn't be forcing my ideas on you. I just feel like you're better than you give yourself credit for. Every time I tried to brainstorm you as the villain, something felt off. I spent hours wracking my brain and couldn't figure out a single idea I liked. Not until Dain suggested that you were the hero of the story. Once that clicked into place, it's like my mind was overflowing with good ideas."

"Ah, so this was Dain's fault then?" I shook my head, gripping the couch tight. "Remind me to punish him later."

Willow sighed. "Fine, fine. I'll keep brainstorming ideas for you being the big bad instead."

Her expression was pained as she ran a hand over her face, all excitement for the story obviously gone. Her notes had felt so full of life, and I hated telling her that they weren't good enough, but they just weren't me. At least, that's what I wanted to keep saying, but a small part of me had felt happy when she'd said that I was meant for more.

Knowing that she thought I was a good man deep down made me want to try, even just a little bit, if it meant seeing that excitement in her eyes again. I secretly enjoyed the way her notes had portrayed me, so full of confidence and strength, able to protect anyone who mattered to me. But the only person I really wanted to protect right now was Willow.

"I'm willing to give your ideas a shot."

Her eyes widened. "Really? You're not just saying that to make me happy, right? This is your story, so you're the one who needs to feel good about it."

Every moment we spent together felt good, like I could be anyone I wanted to be instead of the joke of a villain from before. She never expected me to play a role. She just wanted me to be me and she would craft the story around that. It was the nicest thing anyone had ever done for me, and it made me want to return the favor.

"Let's go somewhere," I said suddenly. "Anywhere you want, and you can tell me more about this morally gray hero idea of yours."

"That sounds great!" She lunged forward, wrapping her arms around me in a tight hug. When she pulled back, she was grinning from ear to ear. "You're going to make an awesome anti-hero, I promise."

"Yeah, yeah." I stood and offered my hand to her. "Where would you like to go? Back into town, to the apothecary gardens, or maybe somewhere entirely new?"

"Hmmm...I think best when my hands are busy, so I'd love to plant a garden or something outside."

My lips pulled into a grin. "I thought you might want that. There's a giant garden that the apothecaries of this world use that's overflowing with magic. Apparently, the plants glow with demonic energy and it's a beautiful sight. I bet we can even find a small section where you can garden to your heart's content while you're here."

Her eyes lit up as she slid her hand into mine so I could pull her up off the couch. "Let's get going then!"

She tugged me through the halls of the castle even though she had no idea where we were going. I was glad I'd taken the time to ask about nearby gardens before I'd returned to the castle. Seeing her so full of joy at such a simple thing made my heart soar.

I'd never have thought I could be anything but the villain before, but being around Willow made me want to explore my options and really let myself live for once. Maybe I'd be surprised.

Chapter 18
Willow

Visiting a garden was exactly what I needed after a long day of outlining, like a reward for finally coming up with a good idea for the Demon Lord's book. Too bad he was walking at a snail's pace, so we still hadn't left the castle. I turned back to chastise him, but he looked deep in thought as he stared at a wall.

"The cracks are gone," he said softly, running his hands along the walls that used to be full of cracks and fuzzy spots. They were solid and smooth now, with bright sconces and tapestries lining them.

"It feels warmer in here too. Think it's because of Misty?"

"I don't know." He leaned closer to the wall, as if he was completely entranced. "The castle didn't start changing until you came here."

"Wait, you think I'm changing it somehow?" I bit my lip, not really sure how to answer that. "Well, I mean, I do like the library you have now. But the only kind of magic I have is storytelling, so I think it's probably something else."

"Maybe..." After a few more silent moments, he snapped out of it, turning toward me with a smile. "Sorry. Let's get going before it's dark out. There's no point staring at a wall."

Except it was a wall that had changed completely since the first time I saw it. Whether it was Misty's magic or something else, hopefully his home would keep getting nicer so it wouldn't be so sad picturing him here all alone once I went back to the real world. He deserved a cozy place to call his own, just like everyone else.

The air was cool as we stepped outside, and the sun was already on its way back to the horizon. We'd only have a few hours before it was dark, so I quickened my pace. If these gardens were as cool as he'd described, I definitely wanted to see them. Gran would want to know every single detail.

The Demon Lord led me away from the city to the edge of the forest behind his castle where a sprawling garden laid before us. Magic hung in the air like moisture on a humid day, clinging to my skin and tingling down my throat as I breathed it in. It was a rush, my head spinning from the amount of magic pulsing in the air.

"Whoa." I reached my hand out to steady myself against a tree. "That's some intense magic." I waved my hand at him before he could fret too much. "I'm fine. Just needed a moment to adjust. Let's head inside."

His gaze roved over me, as if trying to decide if I was telling the truth or not. I gnawed my lip and pushed past him as the magic settled against my skin, invigorating me. If just being in the garden felt this powerful, I could only imagine what making medicine with these plants would do. He hadn't been kidding, they were literally steeped in magic, glowing with a faint purple light that I'd come to identify with demon magic. It was beautiful. So many plants filled to the brim with magic, and I didn't even recognize half of them.

Excitement rushed through me. This was like when I'd first started helping Gran and everything was a new and wonderful discovery. From giant flowers that towered over me to delicate herbs swaying in the wind, it was all so bright and full of life. I wanted to learn every plant in this garden and figure out how they could help people and how to tend to them properly. That was my job as an apothecary, keeping the plants and people around me healthy.

The sweet scent of the flowers mixed with the brightness of the herbs and the earthy scent of fresh soil being tilled. I closed my eyes, breathing it in. Even though we were inside a book, literally standing in a demon's garden, I felt so very much at home. I wouldn't be surprised if Gran called out asking if I wanted some tea or if the bell above our shop door chimed, welcoming in a new customer. This was where I belonged, with my feet in the dirt and my hands full of plants.

"I missed that look." The Demon Lord's voice was low and closer than I'd expected.

I opened my eyes to find him smiling at me as if he was watching a flower bloom or a mossmew play in the lavender pots. Heat rose to my cheeks, and I turned away from him. It felt like he'd changed in some crucial way while he was gone. He was more open and comfortable now, like he wasn't trying to pretend anymore.

Which made keeping him at arm's length even more difficult. There was something about a powerful man being so open and sweet that sent butterflies racing in my stomach. He probably had to ask around about this garden, which meant he'd gone out of his way to plan this for me. Nobody had ever put that kind of thought and effort into our dates before.

Not that this was a date.

I cleared my throat and stared up at a bird flying overhead with a long tail of fire, its wings bright in the darkening sky. I'd never seen a phoenix before, but it was a sight to behold! I'd heard their tears could heal most wounds and a single feather could warm a family's house all winter.

"It's beautiful," I whispered, as if a loud voice might scare the creature away.

"So are you." A small smile tugged at the edge of his lips as he watched me. "This was definitely the right place to visit."

I put my hand over my chest, my heart racing as the magic of this garden, and his words, overtook me. It wasn't just the physical magic in the air, but the magic of all the creatures and plants thriving here when the rest of the world in this book was trying to keep them down. It was almost too much to take in and made me even more sure that this final book had to end in a surprising way. There were just too many beautiful and miraculous things in this village to have it end in bloodshed.

As we walked, the Demon Lord filled me in on his trip to the normal world. "Nyssa and Oren are literally buried in books researching library magic while the dragons and knights run around them causing chaos. They were playing tag of all things." He scoffed, but his lips betrayed him with a hint of a smile. "The purple dragon won, of course. He always does."

"That's the one who follows you around, right?" And perched on his horns, which he pretended to hate. I was starting to see through that grumpy exterior though, because he looked pretty proud as he nodded. "I'm glad you got to visit them for a bit. How's Gran?"

"Well, I know where you got your stubborn side from now. She had me working before I even knew what was going on. Planted me in a chair and told me to assemble hand warmers." His laugh was warm as I paused to examine a plant. "Sounds like she chased off a possible apprentice, but she's doing okay. She just seemed worried about you."

I winced. "You told her I was stuck in a book?"

"Well, yeah, but she was fine with that part. Happy actually." He leaned against a tree, watching me closely. "She said it would be good for you to be stuck in one place for a while, so you'd have no choice but to follow your dreams."

"Sounds like her." I shook my head, standing up and brushing the dirt off my hands. "Only she'd be happy her granddaughter was stuck in a book."

Working on this book had been kind of fun so far though. There was something fascinating about learning the story by being inside it. That wouldn't be true for anything else I wrote, but maybe just this once, Gran had been right to push me to do this.

The Demon Lord might have a little to do with all the fun I'd been having lately too. Being able to talk to somebody about my stories again felt really good, like an itch I hadn't been able to scratch in years. It mattered to him in a way my stories had never mattered to anyone, not even my Grandpa. This was personal to him.

So personal that he needed to start making some decisions himself if we were going to finish this story.

I moved closer to the tree he was leaning against. "Remember when I was joking about different names for you?"

"Don't even start with the Lord Shadowbuns again." He covered his face with a hand, sighing. "It just doesn't suit me, okay?"

"Well, I know that," I said with a laugh, "but have you thought about what would suit you? It's about time you gave yourself a real name. We'll need it for the book."

His eyes widened. "Don't you want to decide that? You're the writer."

"And you're the person who's going to have to use it for the rest of his life." I shook my head, leaning against the tree beside him. "No way am I picking that name. I'll help you if you want though."

He gazed up as the setting sun painted the sky in brilliant shades of pink and orange. The phoenix from earlier had landed on a tree on the other side of the garden, flames licking the branches without setting them ablaze somehow. I should ask if the professor had a phoenix I could meet or see if this one was tame.

The Demon Lord took a deep breath. "I'd appreciate help. I have thought about it, but none of the names feel quite right." He glanced sideways at me. "Promise you won't laugh?"

"Promise."

"There's a character in a book I really like named Elias, but it felt too soft." His brow furrowed. "So then I tried to think of evil sounding names like Lord Darkmire or Ashbane the Terrible or Dreadthorne the Undying."

I bit my lip, trying so hard not to laugh, but I couldn't help it. "Ashbane the Terrible?? Is that because you have ashen skin or what?" If looks could kill, I'd be in serious trouble right now. I forced myself to stop laughing and took a breath to calm down. "Sorry. I actually think Elias suits you pretty well, but might not be as imposing as you're looking for. What about the Thorne part of Dreadthorne? Thorns draw the blood of anyone trying to hurt the plants they're protecting, which feels like it suits you pretty well too."

His glare softened. "Thorne, huh? I do like the idea of stabbing anyone who tries to touch you. Like that soldier..." He glanced behind us, turning to sweep his gaze across the whole garden. "Where's your bodyguard?"

Shoot, I'd forgotten to tell him about the whole Dain going off to kidnap the hero thing. "Well, funny story, but remember when you tried to punish him by sending him on a suicide mission to get the hero?" I waited for him to nod before continuing. "Well, I sort of casually mentioned how nice it would be to talk to the hero, and he took that as a command to go finish that mission you gave him. He swears he's got a plan though, and I made him promise to come back if things got dangerous..."

My voice trailed off as he stared at me with a look I couldn't place. It felt intense, but in a soft way, like he was impressed by me for some reason. I took a few steps back, kneeling to look at a black rose that was growing nearby. It had extra sharp thorns just like we'd been talking about and really did remind me of him.

Beautiful, but prickly.

"I'm sorry," I said. "I know he's one of your demons and I didn't have any right to send him away."

The Demon Lord pushed himself off the tree, kneeling to join me by the flowers. It reminded me of that day on the mountain when he'd helped me pick herbs. Now all we needed was playful dragons zipping around and we'd be right back there.

"I'm sure Dain's fine. He seems quite capable." He reached in front of me to pick one of the roses, careful to avoid the thorns. "You have this fascinating way of inspiring people to do great things. First the soldier with an impossible mission and now me with a name fit for a protector." He gazed at the flower, running a finger along the stem carefully. "Thorne. I like it. I like the idea of protecting people by any means necessary, too." His dark purple eyes met mine and the glow of the flowers illuminated his skin. "I'm glad you chose to be my writer. Nobody else has ever looked at me the way you do, never seen me as anything other than a villain. I trust your vision for my series."

My heartbeat thundered in my ears, either from the nearness of him or the way he said he trusted me. Nobody had ever believed in me enough to put their fate in my hands, which is basically what he was doing by letting me write his final book.

He believed in my writing.

He believed in *me*.

"Thorne." I leaned forward before I could stop myself, entranced by the glow of the flowers and the kindness in his eyes. His lips were only a breath away from mine as I whispered, "thank you."

Without another thought, he closed the distance between us, pressing his lips against mine. I should have pulled away, should have kept my distance like I'd been trying so hard to do, but my body had other ideas. Warmth spread through me as I leaned into his kiss, craving him like I'd never craved anyone before.

Everyone always told me that I needed to open up and feel life more deeply. Well I felt *this* throughout my entire body. Every part of me tingled as his strong hand cupped my cheek. I wasn't sure where we'd go from here, but I knew one thing: I didn't want to run away anymore.

CHAPTER 19
WILLOW

The moon was out in full as we walked back to the castle, illuminating our path in the kind of soft light that made every moment feel more magical. Not that we needed much help there. My body was hyperaware of Thorne now, every brush of his finger against my skin or bump of his shoulder against mine sent sparks through me.

I glanced sideways at him, appreciating the beauty of his shadows dancing across the ground like they were trying to merge with the night itself. He was supposed to be a terrifying villain, but all I saw was a man who'd spent the past hour digging around in the dirt with me while I gardened until it was too dark to see clearly anymore.

He'd seemed content watching me work and was so much more at ease than when I'd seen him in the library. Like the further he got away from other people, the happier he was.

A warm, fuzzy feeling filled my chest. We were more similar than I thought.

"You're staring." His voice had the same low, grumbly tone it always did, but hearing it now made my stomach flutter.

"Sorry."

I took a deep breath and clamped down on my emotions. Not wanting to run away from these feelings and letting myself get lost in his shadowy vibes were two entirely different things. I had to keep a clear head until this book was finished. Then we'd see where we stood. Maybe we'd end up together, happy with the wonderful story we'd written. Or maybe we'd realize there was nothing connecting us anymore.

Thorne laced his fingers through mine, tugging me closer. "I didn't say that you staring was a problem. I just wanted to know what was on your mind."

"Well, right now I'm thinking about how much I like your hands covered in dirt." I grinned, brushing my thumb across the back of his dirt-stained hand. "I bet you'd make a good apothecary. Or at least, you'd probably be good at the gardening part. You wouldn't need to interact with anyone and you could be as grumpy as you wanted in total silence, just us and the plants."

Our steps had taken us all the way back to the castle already and he paused just outside the door. "Is that a job offer?"

I laughed. "Yeah, sure. We can always use the help."

He glanced back at me with a look full of longing, far more serious than I'd intended my joke to be. He closed the distance between us, pulling me against his chest and kissing me with enough passion to make my head spin. I clung to him, breathless and hot. His hair tickled my cheek, blocking out the moonlight like a veil.

It was just him and me.

Somebody cleared their throat, and I jumped back to find Dain standing in the doorway, staring at us. Okay, so it was me, Thorne, and apparently Dain too. Heat burned across my cheeks as I stepped into the castle.

Thorne groaned. "You have terrible timing. What do you want?"

Dain slammed his fist against his chest, standing tall and proud. "Welcome home, My Lord."

"Welcome home?" I laughed, letting the awkwardness of getting caught making out on the Demon Lord's front stoop wash away. "You're always so serious, but since you're back, I'm guessing things didn't go well with the hero?" I patted him on the shoulder. "Don't worry about it. I'm just glad you're back in one piece and nothing bad happened."

"It was a difficult task," Thorne said as he moved past us. "Failure was expected."

"But I didn't fail." Dain shook his head, frowning at both of us. "I would never leave a job unfinished. I told you I'd get the hero, so I got the hero."

My mouth dropped open. "Wait, you really brought the hero here??"

"You could start a war!" Thorne's shout echoed off the stone walls as he turned his glare on me. "I just can't leave you alone, can I? How could you send him to kidnap the hero after everything we've learned about the humans?"

"Hey, you told Dain to go after the hero first." I crossed my arms, staring Thorne down. "And besides, kidnap is a strong word." I turned to Dain, smiling at him. "You didn't kidnap him, right? You just asked politely and he came here with you of his own free will?"

"Oh, no. I definitely kidnapped him." Dain grinned proudly. "I threw him over my shoulder like a sack of potatoes and just walked right out of their camp with them none the wiser. Honestly, those humans are far too overconfident. None of them would expect a demon to just walk in and grab their hero. It was easy."

I shrank in on myself, wishing I could hide in the shadows like Thorne. "You're joking, right?"

"I never joke about kidnapping." Dain puffed out his chest. "I just threw a cloak on, pulled the hood up, and said I had an important mission for the hero. They led me right to him."

Thorne's shoulders stiffened. "Where is he?"

"The dungeons, My Lord." Dain's frown deepened. "Well, at least that's what I told him. You don't actually have a dungeon though. I was pretty surprised, so I just stuffed him in the coldest room."

I let out a breath. "See? It's fine—"

"Show me." Thorne's voice was low and commanding, leaving no room for arguments. This was the side of him the author had envisioned, I bet.

Dain marched towards the end of the hallway where the sconces were barely shining and something suspiciously sword-shaped was leaning against the wall. It was wrapped in a thick blanket secured with a belt, but I still recognized the amber gem in the pommel.

"Is that the holy sword?" The fantasy lover in me wanted to rush forward and unwrap it. "I'd give anything to hold it, just for a minute."

Dain shook his head. "I wouldn't advise that. The sword was pretty upset the whole way here because it couldn't seem to repel me with its magic."

"Well obviously not," I said, "that's only for monsters and dark magic. It's got a few other spells we probably don't want to see though."

The sword rattled against the wall like it had some snappy retort. It was one of my favorite characters in the book, so a big part of me wanted to unwrap it and damn the consequences. It was the holy sword of all things! Excitement rushed through me, but Thorne shook his head and nudged me towards the door.

"We're here for the hero, remember?"

My shoulders drooped. "Fine, fine. But I get to talk to the sword later."

"Deal." Amusement colored his voice as he opened the door to reveal a man with blonde hair pacing the room like he was a beast locked in a cage. His bright white armor and amber eyes signaled he was none other than the hero himself.

"You really did it." My mouth fell open, staring at Dain. I had assumed he was a bit silly and maybe not very good at his job, but now I was seeing him in a whole new light. "You're actually pretty skilled, aren't you?"

"Of course, I am." His back straightened. "The Demon Lord wouldn't have appointed me as your bodyguard if I wasn't."

I didn't have the heart to tell him that that was probably a spur of the moment decision without much thought behind it. Thorne wasn't the type of guy who got to know people easily. Now wasn't the time to bring that up though, not when Thorne was glowering at the hero like he was a bug he wanted to squash.

"Vile monsters!" The hero reached for a sword that was no longer at his hip, flexing his hand awkwardly before lunging to the other side of the room like he wanted some distance between us. "I'll defeat you and save this world, once and for all. You never should have brought me here, not unless you're ready to die!"

Thorne sighed and turned back to Dain. "Take him back."

"But My Lord, we haven't even questioned him yet." Dain motioned for me to get closer. "You said you needed to talk to him, so talk before the Demon Lord, in his infinite mercy, sends him away."

The hero clenched his hands at his side. "I'll never talk. Not even if you torture me."

"Whoa, nobody's torturing anyone." I held my hands up. "I just want to ask you a few things. You know, have a friendly conversation."

"No, he's going back." Thorne's shadows filled the room. "Now."

"See reason, My Lord," Dain pleaded.

I nodded. "We already kidnapped him, so we might as well get something out of it. Just let him stay the night."

Our conversation devolved into us arguing about the pros and cons of kidnapping a hero. On the pro side, I'd be able to get all the information I wanted for the book. But there was a pretty big con: his people would probably consider this an act of war and would try to get him back by any means necessary. That hadn't seemed to bother Thorne before, but now that he'd seen how badly the demons were treated here, he probably didn't want the humans anywhere near them again. Which was fair, but it wouldn't help me finish the book.

Cinder poked her head inside the room, completely ignoring all the excitement as she hopped over to the hero, who had sat on the stone bed at some point and was staring at us with a blank look on his face.

"Uhhh, do I get a vote?" The hero raised his hand like a school kid.

"No!" We all said it at the same time, and I couldn't help but laugh at the absurd situation.

I took a deep breath to calm down and smiled at him. "Sorry. What were you going to say?"

He gave me an exasperated look. "That I actually agree with the Demon Lord. Send me back. I promise I won't mention this little visit and I'll save the invasion for later. Tomorrow maybe."

Thorne shook his head. "Well now we definitely can't send him back. He's going to invade my lands either way."

I bit my lip, hoping that didn't mean he planned to deal with the hero permanently or something. I should probably talk to him in private before anyone decided something we couldn't come back from.

"Come with me." I tugged on his sleeve, pulling him into the hallway and lowering my voice. "If you want me to finish this book series, then I need to talk to the hero."

"Really?" He raised an eyebrow at me.

"Yes, really. He's the main character! Don't you think we should ask him about the books? See what his plans are and all that?"

"His plans are to kill me." He stared at the holy sword, leaning down to pull the belt tighter like that would prevent it from overhearing us or something. "I thought you were trying to find a better ending for me." His voice lowered. "For us."

"That's not fair and you know it. Of course I'm trying to find a better ending for you, but to do that, I need *him*. So we're going to talk to him and that's that."

"But he's my enemy." He gave me a look that screamed I was being really dense, but I wasn't about to give in.

"So what if he is?"

"So, this is dangerous, Willow. I can't protect you if an army storms this village."

Ah, so that's what he was so worried about. Now that he'd taken on the role of a protector, this whole situation probably felt a lot different to him. He couldn't just cast the area in darkness and do whatever he wanted anymore. He had to keep his people, and me, safe. I understood his point, but the hero was literally in the next room! I couldn't let this opportunity pass me by.

I tapped my finger against my thigh, watching the holy sword struggle against its bindings. "What if he agrees to tell his party that he's on a mission and will be back soon?"

"And how will you get him to agree to that?"

"That's a problem for tomorrow." I forced a smile that hopefully looked far more confident than I felt. "Let's sleep on it and see where we're at in the morning. After he gets some rest and eats a hot meal, I'm sure he'll be more open to our plan."

Thorne snorted, but didn't say anything else as we walked back into the room. The hero was having a staring contest with Cinder while Dain nudged the bunny closer.

"Uhh, what's going on?" I asked.

"The demon bunny has found its newest prey." Dain smiled grimly. "And she's not going to let him go."

Cinder puffed up her fur and produced three little balls of red flames in the air. The hero leaned back, but then Cinder sneezed, and sparks flew up like sparklers and ruined the whole scary bunny vibe. I laughed and pet her soft fur. She deserved a carrot or two for lightening the mood like that.

"Let's all get some sleep." I shooed Dain and Thorne out of the room, hoping that everyone would be more reasonable in the morning. "You're safe here, hero. So please, rest."

He glanced at the stone bed and barren room. "Right. It feels very safe and cozy in this dungeon."

"It's not a dungeon." Exasperation colored my voice. It had been a long day and this was not how I'd wanted to end it. "I promise, you're safe here. I give you my word."

"And how can I trust that? The Demon Lord is in charge here." The hero leaned down, staring at Cinder as she flipped her ears. "And is this bunny really dangerous?"

"No, she can even stay here and keep you company if that helps." I put on my best smile again and said the only thing that might actually help this situation. "You can trust me because I'm the Demon Lord's consort. My promise means something. So if I say you're safe here, then you're as safe as a well-sealed tonic."

His mouth dropped open. "Wait, Demon Lord! When did you get married?"

The hero's voice was loud enough to reach Thorne down the hall who called back, "I didn't!"

"My spies are terrible," the hero muttered, gazing at me with newfound wonder. "I can't believe he married a human and we didn't even know about it. Hmmm...I'll have to work on our spy network when I get back. Oh, and congratulations!"

The last part was also shouted loud enough to make Thorne grumble and moan, muttering something about annoying heroes. I pressed my lips together to stop from laughing. I'd loved the hero's personality as a reader, and he seemed to be exactly the same in the flesh. Wary when needed, but also happy and genuine, making the best out of any situation. Even congratulating his enemy on getting married.

I could work with that. Maybe I could even get the information we needed without starting a war.

"Sleep well," I said as I walked out the door. "Cinder will keep you safe."

The bunny hopped up on the bed with the hero and snuggled closer to him even as he tried to jerk away. After a moment, he pet the bunny's head with a smile. Yup, this was all going to work out brilliantly. I'd have to congratulate Dain on a job well done. Never in a million years did I think I'd get the chance to talk to the hero.

Now I just had to patiently wait until the morning.

CHAPTER 20
THORNE

Out of all the things that could have happened while I was gone, Dain kidnapping the hero hadn't crossed my mind as a possibility. What was the point of a bodyguard if I couldn't trust him to stay by Willow's side? Sure, I told him to give her anything she wanted, but the hero probably wouldn't be any more help than I was with planning the final book.

Neither of us knew how things were supposed to end. That's how stories worked.

My nose twitched as a delicious scent drifted into my room. I sat up slowly. Was that bacon? I made my way to the kitchen to find Willow by the stove with her hair tied back and Inkheart floating nearby pointing at something on a notebook.

"It's just eggs," Willow said. "I can handle bacon and eggs."

The pen's feather drooped.

"Oh fine, show me the recipes." She leaned over to peek at the notes Inkheart had written for her and smiled. "That actually sounds delicious. Maybe we can pick up ingredients in town today and try it?"

The pen leapt up in excitement, splattering ink everywhere. Watching Willow cook while chatting with that magical pen was oddly soothing. I wished every day would start like this from now on. Willow looked so happy, just cooking and laughing with Inkheart. Every time she smiled, it was like a balm for my soul. I wanted to do something for her, something that showed how much her being here meant to me.

"Morning, Thorne." Willow glanced over her shoulder with a smile. "I hope you're hungry, because we're making a feast."

Hearing her call me by my new name felt so right, like I was finally becoming who I was always meant to be. A protector. *Her* protector.

"Need any help?" I moved closer to the stove, watching the eggs slowly turn from clear to white in the pan as the bacon sizzled. "You didn't have to cook breakfast."

"Oh, were you going to?" She gave me a wicked smile. "I'd pay to see that. We could even get you an apron and everything."

Inkheart fluttered, excitedly writing something on the page. *Ohhh, please make it say "kiss the chef"! I love those aprons.*

"Kiss the chef?" Willow laughed softly. "I doubt he'd wear something like that."

She peeked at me for just a moment before turning back to the pen, but it was long enough to catch the faint rosy hue coloring her cheeks. Like she was picturing what I'd look like in an apron like that. Warmth spread through me as memories of kissing her filled my mind. I'd barely been able to sleep last night, thinking about her in my arms.

I'd never imagined something like that would happen, but it had felt so right. Willow was more than just the woman writing my book, she saw me differently than anyone else. She was the woman I could feel myself falling for. As I moved closer, she reached up into a cabinet that used to be empty and pulled four plates down, lining them up on the counter to pile them high with eggs and crispy bacon.

"Four plates?" I tilted my head, not liking where this was going. "Are you making breakfast for that hero?"

"Well yeah, did you think I'd let him starve?" Willow rolled her eyes, shoving two plates into my hands. "Come on, let's all eat together."

She set the plates on the table next to glasses of water and silverware. Dain marched in shortly after with the hero in tow and suddenly my warm and cozy morning disappeared like a dream I could barely remember.

"Hero." I inclined my head at him as I sat at the head of the table.

He lifted his chin. "Demon Lord."

Willow gave us both a funny look. "Are you two going to do that every time you see each other?" When neither of us responded, she sighed and took Cinder from the hero's arms. "Well sit down before the food gets cold. A good meal makes everything better."

"Unless it's poisoned." The hero sat down at the very edge of his chair and sniffed the food. His eyes widened, but he quickly covered it up with a look of indifference. "It smells good, I guess. But I certainly won't be eating it."

A hungry grumble echoed in the kitchen, and he slapped a hand over his stomach. Willow hid a smile behind her hair as she bent down to feed Cinder a few carrots and a handful of hay. Her gaze flicked up to mine and she jerked her head at the hero like I should do something.

I blinked at her before slowly turning to him. "Well, that's your choice, but it's not like we're fattening you up for the slaughter or anything."

Everyone got really quiet before Dain sat down with a chuckle. "That was actually the hero's first guess before poison."

Willow laughed. "Man, the two of them are so much alike, aren't they?"

"Hey!" I shouted in unison with the hero. He immediately snapped his mouth closed while I scowled at my breakfast. "I mean, no, we are not. We're eternal enemies."

"Right, right, of course." Willow nodded as she finished up with Cinder and joined us at the table. She leaned over to take a bite of the hero's eggs and snag a piece of bacon. "Mmmmm.....tastes wonderful. Not a trace of poison, and I'd know, I am an apothecary after all."

The hero waited a few more moments until she finished every bite of that bacon and then dug in, wolfing his food down like he'd been imprisoned for days instead of spending one night in an unlocked and unguarded room. I bet he hadn't even tried to leave. How was he the man who'd led armies against us and destroyed all our towns?

"This is delicious!" he mumbled through a mouthful of food. "Seriously, it's so good. Thank you for the meal."

Dain nodded. "Agreed. Thank you, my lady."

"You're both very welcome." She smiled and took a big bite of eggs, then stared at me. "Aren't you going to eat too?"

The intense look she was giving me made me think this was about something more than food. I sighed and picked up my fork, taking a small bite of well-seasoned eggs. Her grin widened as she set to eating her food with gusto, bouncing happily as if we were a sweet little family eating breakfast together. It just felt so wrong seeing the hero across from me every time I looked up. Even worse seeing Willow refill his plate with seconds.

This was the man who wanted me dead, and she was practically fangirling over him like all those people had done with me at the library!

If I was being fair, the hero didn't seem as bloodthirsty as I assumed he'd be. He hadn't attacked Dain even after getting kidnapped and he'd done nothing but thank us since he started eating. Maybe Willow was right about the plot twist. Maybe the hero *was* being misled. I couldn't wrap my mind around the story otherwise.

"What are you planning, hero?" I snapped off a piece of bacon, chewing it slowly. "Are you really going to invade our peaceful village? Or are you waiting for me to do something?"

He gulped down half his glass of water before slamming it back down on the table. "Ah, that really hit the spot. What a good way to start the day!" Then he glanced at me with a shrug. "I've got no idea honestly. I'm waiting to hear from the holy priest and the King."

My eyebrows shot up. "So you don't even make your own battle plans?"

"Wait, that's not what I meant." He scratched his head, wincing. "Forget I said that. I am completely prepared to invade this city of monsters, yes."

Wow. He really was oblivious, just like the books made him seem. There was no way he was the mastermind behind all of this.

Willow leaned forward, patting his hand. "It's okay, I didn't hear a thing. But I am curious what got you into this hero business. Did you always want to be one or did a priest just show up at your door one day and hand you the holy sword?"

"A bit of both, actually." The hero ran a hand through his flowing golden locks that only heroes ever seemed to have and smiled. "It all started when I was a child playing hero with my friends. We'd race around the town helping anyone who needed it and doing heroic deeds. But then my mother thought it was a good idea for me to start training with the sword so I could become a knight at the royal castle and suddenly I was too busy training to play hero. I was going to be a hero for real!"

His story went on like that for what felt like hours, and during that time, I noticed a curious thing. Willow was nodding and smiling like she was fascinated, but her gaze kept flicking over to Inkheart who was writing so fast I thought the pages might catch fire as the pen whipped across them.

Was this her casual way of getting information out of him without arousing suspicion? Now that was clever. I leaned back in my chair, admiring her ingenuity. I never would have thought that breakfast and a few choice questions would have him spilling his entire life story when he'd been adamant about not being interrogated last night.

The demons could learn a thing or two from this woman. The way her mind worked was absolutely brilliant.

Willow gasped over something. "Oh no! What happened then?"

"Then I—" The hero froze, staring at me. "Wait a minute, did you put truth serum in my food? Or maybe something to loosen my lips?"

I shook my head, a grim smile on my face. "Oh no, hero, you did that all on your own. Seems like you like to talk."

"Which is a good thing!" Willow kicked my shin under the table. "I love hearing about your adventures."

My leg tingled from where she'd kicked me, but it didn't really hurt. It amused me more than anything, like we were a married couple telling each other to shut up when one of us said too much. I'd seen lots of people like that at the library and had always found their bickering endearing.

The hero's chair scraped against the floor as he backed away. "No, you're his wife! You're just trying to trick me."

"I'll tell you a secret since you've been so open with me." Willow leaned closer to him, lowering her voice. "I'm not really his wife. It's a long story, but I'm not trying to trick you. I really do enjoy hearing about your life. I can prove it. Just give me a minute."

She ran out of the room, leaving me alone with Dain, the hero, a demon bunny, and a magical pen who couldn't help but say the most uncomfortable things. The silence was only broken by the pen's scratching and the pages flipping. What would all its notes say at the end of this?

Thankfully Willow came back before it got any more awkward, her arms full of the books I'd brought from the library. My books. She dropped them on the table in front of the hero, shoving his plate out of the way.

"See?" She grinned, motioning at the covers with handsome illustrations of the hero on them. "I've been reading about your heroic journey for years. They're some of my favorite books."

Favorite books, huh? She was laying it on a little thick, but his eyes were full of stars as he stared at the covers. Seriously, how was he the one winning all these battles when he was so easily thrown off course?

He picked up a book, turning it this way and that. "Hmmm, the artists did an amazing job with these. They really captured my heroic vibes and strong jawline."

I snorted. "Aren't you even curious why she has books about you in the first place?"

"That's a good point!" The hero flipped through the pages, eyes moving back and forth as he read snippets. "Are you a stalker? How else would you know all these details?"

Willow glared at me then plastered a big fake smile on her face. "I'm more of a fan than a stalker. These are..." She looked up at the ceiling as if lost in thought before holding her hand up. "These are part of a biography I'm writing about you! Yeah, somebody has to document your tale, and I thought why not me?"

His mouth formed an O as he nodded. "That makes sense. My deeds are valiant and should be recorded. But this detail is astounding. How did you know what I had for breakfast each day and what I wore?"

"Oh that's easy. I just asked a few people what things you liked and guessed from there." She shot me a dirty look that made me oddly happy. Seeing her maneuver this situation with ease was beautiful to watch. "Sorry if it's weird. I meant it as an homage to your triumphs."

"It's not weird at all. It's glorious!" The hero clapped her on the back. "When can we continue the story? I want to make sure you've got every detail you need."

"Right now, if you want." Willow let out a breath, her shoulders relaxing as I gathered the plates up from the table. "Let's head to the castle library and start from the beginning."

The hero rubbed his hands together, practically jumping with excitement. "This is going to be so much fun. I'll just let my comrades know I'm going to be late."

"Late?" I laughed under my breath. "Don't you think they'll need more than that?"

"You're right." The hero tapped his hand against his hip, biting his lip. "Oh! I've got it. I'll tell them I'm on a secret mission and they shouldn't come looking for me for at least three days. That should give us more than enough time. Well, maybe five days. Yes, five days should do the trick."

I felt myself smiling even though his nonsense should be irritating me. There was just something about him that was difficult to hate, especially after reading all of his books multiple times. Any other hero would be using this time to take me down and end our story once and for all, but he was perfectly content to wait it out and help Willow first. It was weird, but it's what made him the type of hero he was.

"Good luck," I whispered to Willow. "If anyone can find a way to untangle all this, I'm sure it's you."

She smiled softly. "I'll do my best not to disappoint you."

Disappointment was one thing I'd never felt when I was around her. I was far too awestruck by her passion and creativity for anything else to register. Bringing the hero here might actually work out for us.

Chapter 21
Willow

The hero seemed even more excited about writing this book than I was. We'd spent the past few days holed up in the library chatting and having a wonderful time as he explained his life and all his plans to me. Armed with that knowledge, I even managed to get a few chapters written which felt like a huge success. I still didn't know what the big plot twist was, but at least I finally had something on the page that was readable. Everything felt better with words on the page.

Thorne and Dain relaxed in the corner, a silent but steady presence day after day. They still didn't seem to fully trust the hero, but at least they were finally chill enough to take naps, read, or stare into the fire instead of at us non-stop. That had been a very awkward first day. The hero was a very animated reader though, so it was hard to stay serious with him around. He cheered when he got to the good parts of his book, cried when something sad happened, and sometimes even jumped up like he was going to join the battle when there was a fight.

It was all so ridiculous, exactly like the hero I'd grown up reading about. Having him right here in front of me made nailing his personality even easier and the words were flowing with ease at this point.

Or they would be, if Inkheart didn't keep leaping off the page to taunt the hero's holy sword every twenty minutes. The pen swirled across its notebook, writing in even fancier script than usual as it mocked Dawnbreaker, the Eternal.

The pen is mightier than the sword, I'm sorry, but it's a fact!

"And yet, you basically just write fanfiction shipping everyone you see together." Golden light shimmered down the blade as the metal vibrated, casting magic that turned the vibrations into words that we could all hear. "Don't think I didn't notice you writing about my hero with that distasteful Demon Lord. As if that would ever happen." The sword quivered, then stood straighter. "Oh, you misspelled *mightier* too. At least insult me accurately."

Inkheart's feather bristled. *Some of the most well-written stories are fanfiction! You think you're so cool, all glowy and forged by the gods. But everyone knows the hero does all the work, right Sunny?*

"My name is Dawnbreaker, you insufferable excuse for a pen." The sword glowed brighter, as if trying to cleanse Inkheart of evil.

"Calm down, both of you." I put my hands between them to stave off the inevitable bickering match. "Don't you think this argument has gone on long enough? You're both mighty in your own way." I nudged Inkheart onto the page we'd been working on. "Back to writing the actual story, okay?" The sword shimmered beautifully, as if it had won something here, so I shifted it to the other side of the hero's chair. "And you, go back to...guarding the hero or whatever it is you do."

Inkheart huffed but continued writing where we'd left off on chapter 4. I took a deep breath, ready to move on to chapter 5, when I realized the hero hadn't reacted at all to that whole exchange. Usually he was the first to chastise his sword for being confrontational, but this time he'd just sat there, book forgotten by his side as he squeezed his eyes shut in pain.

"Another headache?" I asked softly. "You've been getting those more and more lately."

Dawnbreaker lurched around to stare at the hero. "Have you fallen ill?"

"I'm fine. My medication just doesn't seem to be helping as much as usual." He rubbed a hand over his face, holding it there like he was blocking out the light. "Maybe I need a stronger dose. I should head back to the capital and check in with the healers."

"Or maybe get some sleep and see if it gets better?" I asked hopefully. I wasn't ready for him to leave yet, but I also didn't want him to be in pain. "I could always make you something for it too if you want. I'm an apothecary, so it's my job."

He peeked at me between his fingers. "Really? You'd do that?"

"Of course. You've already done so much for me." I studied him for clues as to what was really ailing him, knowing that the book alluded to a mysterious illness he'd had since he was a child. Nothing stood out besides his headaches though. "What's your medication for? Migraines?"

"They're just a symptom." He sighed, slipping deeper into the plush chair. "I've actually got miasma sickness."

Dawnbreaker vibrated. "Apparently he inhaled too much miasma as a baby and can't tolerate it anymore. Maybe that's why it's worse. This land is full of it."

"Miasma sickness?" I hadn't seen that mentioned anywhere in the books, not a trace of it. "What's—"

"It doesn't exist." Thorne's voice startled me. He'd been so quiet, I'd almost forgotten he was there. "Miasma is just a cruel word humans use for our magic. Demonic magic is beautiful and pure, the very essence of our world, it would never sicken a child."

The hero shrugged. "Well, I have it, so it must be real. That's all I can tell you."

Shadows whipped around Thorne and Dain like a storm cloud.

"Whoa now." I held my hands up, feeling like all I did lately was break up fights. "I'm sure he's not trying to insult you. He's just answering my question. If they told him it's miasma sickness, and you say that doesn't exist, then that's another clue." I stared at Thorne, willing him to understand. "This is a *good thing*. Every clue helps me unravel this story."

His jaw clenched, but he nodded. "Fine."

Things got a bit tense after that as I asked the hero for all his symptoms. The sword provided a few the hero missed, but they seemed to be all over the place and vague. No wonder it had taken the healers a while to cure him because in my world, these didn't add up to anything specific. It was like his body was fighting itself, but not in any way I'd seen before. Thorne was getting more and more irritated every time the hero blamed miasma.

"Okay." I clapped my hands together to get everyone's attention. "I think this would go a lot better if we could all start acting like more of a team. I can't think straight with all this tension."

They all averted their gazes like children being yelled at by a teacher. Even the holy sword tilted to the side so I couldn't see it properly.

I sighed, turning to Thorne. "Please? For me?"

His gaze softened and he was about to say something, but then his eyes glazed over like he was lost in his thoughts. He looked up at the ceiling, his jaw clenched even tighter than before. It was like he heard something that we didn't, something that bothered him far more than the hero and his ailment.

"Is everything okay?" I rested my hand on his arm.

His gaze jerked back to me. "Sorry, but I need to leave for a bit. I'm going to go check on your Gran and see if she needs help at the shop."

"Wait... now?" I shook my head, holding onto his sleeve tighter. "That doesn't make any sense. What just happened?"

He leaned closer, whispering in my ear. "The library is calling to me. Misty needs help with something."

Ohhh, so that's what that look was. He must have been communicating with the Misty Mountain Library somehow. I'd have to ask him more about it later, but for now, I pulled away and made a shooing motion with my hands.

"Well hurry up then, Gran needs her assistant! And bring me back some of her scones too."

A small smile tugged at his lips. "Always giving me orders. I kind of enjoy it."

"Wait..." The hero's eyes widened. "You're telling me the Demon Lord is an elderly woman's assistant? The surprises never end in this town."

"It's almost like you know nothing about demons." Thorne shot him another dark look. "Before you attack us again, maybe you should figure out who we really are. Helping the elderly, creating beautiful works of art, and growing plants that can heal the masses are just a few things that demons do. It wouldn't be a surprise if you had ever tried talking to us instead of fighting us."

I winced. He had a point, but with the hero in pain and Misty calling to Thorne, it didn't feel like the right time to make it. "Please, go help Gran. I'll take care of things here."

He caught my gaze and held it for long enough that heat rose to my cheeks, but he eventually nodded. On his way out of the room, he turned to Dain. "Watch out for that hero. Don't let him hurt anyone. And continue taking care of Willow too."

"Yes, sir." Dain saluted him, standing tall and proud. "You can count on me."

He glanced back at me one more time before sweeping out of the room and taking his shadows with him. The air seemed to lighten, and the hero released a deep breath. I hated how much conflict there was between them when it felt like they could be best friends if they'd grown up in different circumstances. The story had forced them to be enemies, and I still wasn't sure why. What was the point of all this?

Wondering about that had done nothing but make my head spin, so it was time I focused on something I could fix: the hero's headache.

"Okay, let's head over to the apothecary gardens and gather ingredients." I held my hand out to help him up with a smile. "I'll banish that headache in no time and then we can get back to work in the morning after you've had some rest."

"Sounds—"

"Like a terrible idea," Dain said. "The hero can't roam our village unattended."

"So, attend him?" I shrugged. "It'll be fine. We'll just make him wear a hood and nobody will notice he's a human, let alone the hero."

Dain raised an eyebrow. "Is that like how nobody noticed *you* were a human? Because that only took a few moments."

"Yeah, and you stabbed me, remember? So I think you owe me one." I tapped my cheek, which had fully healed by now, but Dain looked horrified. I waved him off with a smile and walked into the hallway. "We're going with or without you, so if you want to keep your word to the Demon Lord, then you'll have to come with us."

The hero followed me without hesitation. Dain's sigh was so loud it would have impressed Thorne if he were here. Hopefully everything was okay with the library. Maybe it had finally found a way to take me out of the book or something. My shoulders tightened, oddly hoping that wasn't the case. I was finally getting real answers, so this would be the worst time to leave.

At some point, living inside this book had started to feel normal. The only things I really missed were Gran and the shop...

I took a deep breath, handing the hero a cloak to hide his face. Dain pulled the hood down so far that I doubted the hero would even be able to see where he was going. I shook my head as we stepped outside, our ragtag group ready to take on this stealth mission together.

CHAPTER 22
THORNE

I stepped out of my book and immediately stumbled as the floor of the library moved, groaning and sliding like something was ripping the library in half. The shelves quivered and the books huddled together like an earthquake was trying to shake them apart. I made my way downstairs, pausing every time the floor shifted, until I found the others.

Every story spirit was circled around the great book tree, hands on its bark as they murmured words of encouragement. Lisa waved me over as Mochi ran high into the branches to console the tree. The golem wrapped its arms around the tree too, the side of its face pressed against the bark like it was holding on for dear life.

"Everything's okay," the golem said loudly. "It's all okay, Misty. We are here. For you."

I stormed over, feeling Misty's panic in my chest like it was my own. Our connection flickered but calmed a little when I added my own hand to the tree's bark. I closed my eyes, trying to bring our connection into focus. Bright green wild magic surged through the tree, twisting around the golden library magic like roots that wouldn't let go.

"It's all the patrons," Lisa whispered. "There's been so many people reading here every day that Misty's magic has exploded. None of us know what's going to happen next."

An ache swept through my chest, for Misty and for Willow. She was stuck inside a book with no way of getting out. I'd assumed that Misty and the librarians would figure it out, but if the library's magic was this chaotic, then who knew what would happen to her. I couldn't let her get stuck there, never to see her Gran again.

"Misty." My voice was hoarse, full of emotion for this library that had believed in me enough to call me here in its hour of need once again. "It's time to embrace your magic, all of your magic. Just let go and see where it takes you. We're all here. We'll help however you need us to."

Lisa nodded. "Don't fight the wild magic, it'll just get more chaotic otherwise."

The tree shuddered, clinging to us with its branches. Another rumble, far greater than the rest, rocked the library as the sound of creaking wood and fallen shelves made me wince. The floors were expanding, growing larger and larger by the minute. The library was growing!

Nyssa ran towards us, breathing heavily. "The patrons are all outside and Roan's leading them down the mountain. We're fine, so do whatever you need to do."

"About time you showed up," I grumbled. She was the librarian, but she seemed to care more about the patrons than the library itself. "What happened to set this in motion?"

She rolled her eyes. "Hello to you too, Demon Lord. Are you here to mock or to actually help?"

My connection to Misty warmed, like the library was seeking me out for something. It reminded me of the first night I'd woken up in the library when the wild magic storm was raging out of control, ripping holes in the roof with lightning crackling all around us. Misty had felt desperately alone then and terrified of the storm that was hurting it.

The library had summoned us not just to protect it, but to keep it company. Maybe now Misty needed us for more. Needed us to be its strength.

"Join hands," I commanded, turning back to find the dragons clinging to the shelves. "And you guys, come over here."

One by one they flew over to us, landing on our shoulders, heads, horns, anywhere that they felt safe. The knights came next, lining up along the base of the tree and climbing up the golem's arm until they were securely in place. I reached out my hands, putting them on either side of the great book tree on top of Lisa's hand and the golem's. Mochi rushed down, booping his nose against our hands as well.

Together we encircled the tree with love and trust. We wouldn't exist without the library and we wouldn't ever forget it. Misty was part of us, the best part of us. We'd all been so focused on other things, from the overflow of new patrons to the story contest, that we hadn't had as much time for the library as usual.

I leaned forward, bowing my head against the great book tree's bark. "Misty, we're here for you. You have nothing to fear. I'll slay anything that tries to harm you, scare off any foe. I'll be your shield and your protector, just like I've always been."

"I'll be your librarian and your friend," Lisa whispered, resting her forehead against the tree as well.

The knights lifted their swords as one from on top of the golem's shoulders. "We continue to be at your command. We will fight for you and stay by your side. We are your friends."

"Library is my friend," the golem rumbled, gripping the tree even tighter. "Best friend."

Mochi chittered the same, producing Misty's favorite tea to pour onto the tree's roots. The dragons soared, dipping in and out of the branches. We'd all come from different books, but there was one thing uniting us: our love for this library.

"You're safe with us." I tried to send as much warmth and reassurance through our bond as I could. "Just relax and let the magic flow through you. Share it with us if you need to. We can handle it."

Golden light fell from the branches above us like little orbs of sunshine, floating through the air and bathing us in a brilliant light. My connection to the library grew stronger, even more vivid than before, as we each took a bit more of its magic, stabilizing it. Misty would never have to bear this burden alone. We were just as much a part of this library as the shelves and the books.

We were story spirits.

The floor slowly stopped shaking and Misty's branches relaxed, resting lightly on our shoulders. I pulled back with a smile as Lisa and the others grinned.

"That was amazing," Nyssa whispered, her eyes wide as she spun around to take in the new library. "It's so much bigger! Look at all those new rooms!"

She was right, there had to be at least six new areas and a double wide set of stairs that looked like it led to a lower level that hadn't existed before. The Misty Mountain Library had grown, that's for sure. A sense of calm washed over everyone as they wandered around to explore the new growth, but I stayed by Misty, not ready to walk away just yet.

This all could have gone much worse, but we weren't totally out of the woods yet.

Willow was still stuck in my book against her will.

A book flew past my head with a tiny knight riding on it like it was a horse, whooping and hollering like the library hadn't just gone through an emotional and magical crisis that changed the entire shape of the building. I shook my head, watching as the purple dragon who so loved perching on my horns chased after the knight. He flipped tail over head when he saw me though, flying back as quickly as he could. The dragon cried out, spreading his arms wide to latch onto my shoulder with tiny little claws.

"You again." I patted the flying lizard's head reluctantly, knowing they never left unless I showed a little affection first. "Now go back to chasing that knight of yours."

The dragon nuzzled against me for a moment before taking off, flying after the knight to continue their game. The dragons and knights were always up to something from tag to wrestling to some kind of fireball game. Maybe this was a race and my distraction would make the purple one lose. Hmm...I didn't love that idea. I followed his flight long enough to see him pounce on the book carrying the knight. They all went down, landing on a soft couch that I didn't remember being there before.

"You're something else, Misty." I closed my eyes and let my mind wander, getting lost in our connection. It felt like the library was still a little unstable though, like it hadn't given us as much magic as it could have. I ran my fingers across the bark. "Were you worried you'd overwhelm us earlier? That's nonsense, I'm the Demon Lord. Give me as much magic as you want."

Our connection warmed as the library did exactly that, trusting me to protect it like I always had. My entire body felt like it was lighting up, humming with magic like never before. I kept my eyes closed and relaxed into the tree, letting myself drift off as Misty and I shared a dream filled with beautiful library magic.

After a while, I woke up, blinking in the soft light of the library. How many hours had passed? I stood up, my body stiff like it had been at least a few hours. I stretched my arms, loosening the tension that had built up in my muscles. The library was so quiet, like it used to be before all the patrons had returned, and I found myself feeling quite at home again.

"Nyssa was looking for you." Lisa sipped a cup of tea at a table nearby, giving me a strange look. "I've never seen you fall asleep like that. You seemed so peaceful and content. We didn't have the heart to wake you."

I sighed. "Well you should have. I needed to talk to her about Willow."

Lisa shrugged. "Well, go find her then. She's holed up with Oren researching just that." When I was almost out of earshot, she called out one last thing. "And thank you for coming back. We all appreciate it, Demon Lord."

My eyes widened, but she was already back to reading her book when I turned to look at her. I hadn't done anything special, but it felt like we were closer somehow. Like family. I didn't hate that idea and felt myself walking back.

"My name's Thorne now," I said softly. "Not Demon Lord."

She lifted her gaze, smiling brighter than I'd ever seen her smile. "That's wonderful to hear. Thorne is a good name."

I nodded and cleared my throat, not sure why I'd even told her that or what else I should say. So I said nothing. I just walked away so I could look for Nyssa. Lisa hummed behind me, and it made me smile for some reason. It felt like I'd been gone for months instead of weeks, and seeing the story spirits again wasn't so bad.

Walking through all the open areas felt surreal though, like this was an entirely different library than before. There was so much room for extra shelves and hundreds more books. Maybe even thousands. All I needed right now was answers though, and there was only one person who could give them to me: Nyssa.

I found her and Oren surrounded by books, all flipped open in a circle around them as they sat cross-legged on the ground. Ink stained Nyssa's hands and smeared her face as she wrote notes on various pieces of parchment scattered around. Her hair was tied up with a string, but wisps of it were falling out like she'd been tugging at it. Roan sat outside the circle, leaning against a pillow wall with his eyes closed as he calmly pet the three-headed beast everyone loved so much.

Cerberus' tail started wagging when I stepped closer. I gave him my best stern look to remind him to stay put, but he hopped up and came by me anyway, licking my hands and jumping up so his paws were on my legs. His mouths were open in big goofy puppy grins. He'd start drooling on me soon if I wasn't careful. I scratched behind his ears before pushing him down.

I'd forgotten what a handful these story spirits were! But it was nice that they'd missed me...

Roan opened his eyes, inclining his head when he noticed me. "Demon Lord."

"Adventurer," I answered back. We hadn't bonded like him and the other story spirits had, but I respected his desire to protect them and the library. Plus, he had been useful at times. "I'm looking for an update on the Willow situation."

He motioned at Nyssa and Oren with a shrug before closing his eyes and apparently going back to sleep. Okay, maybe he wouldn't be so useful this time. I turned to the others who were bent over books, so lost in whatever they were reading that neither moved to answer me. I absently pet the three-headed beast while I waited for one of them to snap out of it, but after a few minutes, I'd had enough. Each minute we wasted was another Willow had to spend away from her family.

"Can you rescue Willow or not?" My shadows crossed the little book circle of theirs, sweeping over the text they were trying to read. "That is what you're working on, right?"

Nyssa finally glanced up at me, her forehead scrunched up. She rubbed her eyes and tilted her head like she was coming out of some kind of trance. "Yeah, we've been working on it a bit each day."

"So can you get her out or not?" I asked.

Oren took his glasses off to clean them as they shared some kind of silent conversation, staring at each other and shaking their heads.

"Well, about that..." Nyssa stood up, brushing the wrinkles out of her clothes. "We've tried a few things, different artifacts and spells, but nothing's worked. And with the library's magic going a bit haywire lately, we haven't had as much time to figure it out as we'd like."

Logically, that made sense, but I didn't like hearing that she wasn't their priority. She deserved better than that. "She's literally stuck in a book. If word got out about that–"

"Don't even think about it." Nyssa shook her head firmly. "I am still trying to get Willow out, yes, but the library's growth needs to be looked into as well. I'm guessing it's all connected. Misty has never had this many patrons before and the tree is literally overflowing with magic."

I knew that, but it didn't make me feel any better. Misty obviously didn't know how to control its wild magic, not yet, so I couldn't force the library to bring Willow back. All I could do was rely on these librarians to figure something out. I needed somebody who could see the big picture, but they were too overwhelmed to do anything but put out fires right now.

"Just get her out." I took a deep breath and forced myself to walk away. Threatening them wouldn't get me anywhere. "I'm going to visit the apothecary."

"Aww, that's so sweet of you." Nyssa grinned, waving goodbye. "Tell Mable we say hi and we're doing our best for her granddaughter."

If only their best was a little better. At least Willow was happy, getting all the information she could ever want from the hero. They'd been thick as thieves the past few days, laughing and brainstorming better than I ever could. They'd find a good ending to my story, I could feel it. Even if the hero had done nothing but irritate me since he arrived.

Willow was too good of a writer to fail.

Chapter 23
Willow

The trip to the gardens had gone off without a hitch so far, which was probably because we'd left Inkheart and Dawnbreaker at the castle. Their bickering was a surefire way to get us caught and I really didn't want anyone questioning why the Demon Lord's human consort was entertaining the hero as a guest.

The longer we walked, the more I started worrying if I could actually help the hero too. It had taken the royal healers years to figure out a medicine that worked for him, but here I was claiming I could pull it off in one day? Maybe if I studied the tonic he'd brought with him, I could work backwards and identify the herbs inside.

"Do you still have some of your medication left?" I asked the hero as we finally made it to the garden. The plants were even more beautiful during the day, pulsing with dark purple magic like they were alive. "It could be useful when we're looking for new remedies."

He handed me a bottle with a few drops of dark liquid in it. "That's all I've got. Not that it's been helping anyway."

I held it up to the light, staring at the beautiful swirls of purple running through it that looked far too familiar. I'd bet my title as an apothecary that this medication was made with herbs from this very garden. Or at least, herbs that had been infused with demonic magic. We wandered deeper into the gardens, smiling and waving at the other apothecaries without a word, hoping they wouldn't come over by us.

This tonic definitely looked demon-made though. "Dain, have you ever—"

The hero clutched his hand to his chest, doubling over. I sank to the ground in front of him to support him. Sweat beaded his forehead and his breathing was labored.

"What's happening?" he asked through clenched teeth. "It feels like my chest is going to explode."

I held a finger against his wrist. His pulse was racing. I might know about illnesses because of my job, but I wasn't a doctor. It had been foolish to take him here.

"We need to get him to the capital." I shot Dain a frantic look. "Now. Before he dies right in front of us."

He moved to lift the hero over his shoulder, not even second-guessing my request to visit the human lands, but the hero screamed, and Dain dropped him back down. The hero curled into a ball, holding his head like it was splitting.

"This isn't normal." Panic had my own heart beating fast. How had he gone from having a headache to this? "We need to get him out of here. His symptoms started getting worse the moment we stepped into the garden."

How could I have been so careless? I should have left him at the castle where he'd be safe, locked away from most of the demonic magic in town. But instead, I dragged him to a place that was literally overflowing with it. The magic was so strong here you could practically taste it in the air, like a faint metallic note on your tongue.

The hero screamed again, his body convulsing as Dain tried to carry him out of the garden. Small white horns sprouted from the hero's head along with fluffy ears. He kind of looked like... My mouth dropped open as Dain stumbled back, glancing at me with wide eyes.

Was the hero actually a demon? No. That couldn't be right. Except, a fluffy tail sprouted from his lower back too as if his body was saying he absolutely was a demon.

The hero took a few deep breaths like he was no longer in pain. He just stared up at the sky, breathing in and out like that was all he could manage right now. At least he wasn't screaming anymore. Dain ripped the bottle of medication from my hands, sniffing the tonic inside. He cursed and threw it away.

"It's Veilshade." He spat the word out like it was disgusting. "It seals a demon's aura so completely that their demonic aspects slowly die off. They appear human, but at the price of a much shorter life. It's a banned substance, so nobody here would have made it for him."

"Then who?" I was still having a hard time wrapping my mind around it, but the horns and tail were hard to dispute. "Who would go that far to hide that the hero's a demon?"

The hero blinked up at me then started laughing. "What did you just call me?"

"Um, a demon?" I bit my lip as his laughter grew louder. "Don't you...feel any different? Maybe your head? Or your backside?"

"Well of course, they don't hurt anymore." He sat up, grinning as if the pain was but a memory now. "But I needed a good laugh, so thank you."

Dain scratched behind his horns. "Uh, I hate to shatter your worldview or whatever, but you're definitely a demon. Half-demon if I had to guess."

"This isn't funny anymore." The hero stood up, brushing the dirt off his clothes. His cloak had fallen off entirely, revealing those beautiful shimmery-white horns poking out of his blonde hair. His hand brushed against his tail and he froze. "What's that? Get it off." His voice rose a few octaves as he tried to pull it off him, but he winced in pain. "What's going on?"

He spun around, trying to spot his tail behind him. It was fluffy and white-blonde, just like his adorable ears, and the whole thing reminded me of a dog chasing their tail. I covered my mouth with my hand, determined not to laugh at him when he was in such a shocking predicament. But he just kept spinning and flipping his head over his shoulder like he couldn't comprehend what was behind him.

"It's a tail." I said in as serious of a tone as I could. "You have ears now too and, um, horns. But just tiny ones. People will barely even notice, I'm sure."

His eyes bulged as his hands clamped down on his head. "No, no, no. This can't be happening. What did you do to me??"

"Nothing!" I picked up the bottle Dain had thrown away. "It was all this medication you were taking. It was hiding who you really were this whole time."

Dain nodded. "It's poison. Nobody should have ever given that to you."

"It was helping me!" The hero's shouting was starting to draw unwanted attention from the other people in the gardens, but I wasn't sure how to calm him down as he kept patting his new ears and horns. "You turned me into a...a monster!"

Dain's eyes narrowed. "I know this is hard, but you're going too far now. We are not monsters and if you keep talking like that, we're going to have a problem."

"We've already got a problem," the hero moaned. "I'm supposed to be the hero of this land! How can I do that while looking like this?" He rushed over to me, clutching my hands in his. "Take pity on me. Make him turn me back to normal."

"You *are* back to normal," I whispered. "This is who you've always been. You just didn't know it." His hands gripped mine even harder as he started to tremble. I felt terrible for him but wasn't sure what to do. Maybe Thorne could help. "Why don't we go back to the castle and sort this out?"

He leapt away from me, shaking his head so hard his ears flopped around. "No way. I'm never stepping foot in that place again. You tricked me with heroic stories and tasty food, but this was your real goal all along, wasn't it? To turn the hero into a terrifying monster!"

"Come on, your tail and ears are far from terrifying. Honestly, they're kind of cute."

His mouth fell open. "Cute? You think these are cute??"

Now we were definitely drawing too much attention as apothecaries came toward us from all directions. Dain sighed and hit the hero on the back of the neck, knocking him out. He slung the man over his shoulder like a sack of potatoes, threw the cloak over him, and walked straight out of the garden like it was totally normal.

"Dain! You can't just knock him out like that!" I hurried after him, making sure the hero was still breathing and okay. "We're trying to gain his trust, not lose even more of it."

"Do that once you're back at the castle," he grumbled. "I swore I'd protect you and there's no way I can do that if this fool keeps screaming about being the hero and hating monsters and all that."

He had a point, but it still didn't feel right. I pulled out my writing board to let Thorne know what was going on.

Get back here as soon as you can. The hero is actually a demon. We need help.

Hopefully he'd see it before the hero woke up because I had no idea what to say and there was no way I was going to lock him up. Dain would, but not me. I couldn't just let him run back to his people either though, not until he calmed down and we had a chance to talk about this. The beginnings of an idea started forming in the back of my mind, tugging at me to write it down.

If the hero was secretly a demon, then that changed everything. I'd been looking for a plot twist, sure, but this felt like a plot wrecking ball, and I had no idea where to even begin.

Chapter 24
Thorne

I'd dropped everything when Willow sent me that ominous *we need help* message, leaving her Gran elbows deep in a mess of herbs and poultices she swore weren't supposed to be that potent. I'd probably messed something up again, but she told me to go help Willow and not worry about it.

Images of Willow being attacked or the hero running rampant through the castle raced through my mind, but when I stormed into the castle's library, they were all just sitting quietly.

Well, the hero did seem to be mumbling something over and over in a state of shock while Willow hovered over him with a stressed-out look that screamed she was in over her head. She seemed to be a master of getting into trouble every time I left. I took a deep breath and tried to make my way to her, but Dain stepped in front of me.

"Welcome back, my lord." He saluted me, his face as serious as ever. "I made the mistake of letting the hero travel with your consort to the apothecary gardens while you were gone. The magic there overwhelmed the Veilshade potion that had been suppressing his demon side and chaos broke out. Giving him more Veilshade will kill him, slowly but surely, so I couldn't allow him to leave." He knelt on the ground, bowing his head low. "I have failed you, sire. Please punish me how you see fit, even if that punishment is banishment."

"He was a demon all along then, huh?" I shook my head as I stared at the hero's tiny horns and ears. "Who gave him the Veilshade?"

"I don't know." Willow's eyes pleaded with me to do something, anything, to fix this situation. "I know he's your enemy, but he's also one of your people now too. Can you help him?"

That look tugged at something in me, making my chest hurt. I hated seeing her so helpless, but she was right, he was my sworn enemy. He'd done nothing but hunt my people relentlessly. How was I supposed to show mercy on him now and solve all his problems? I should just send him back to the capital and let them sort it out.

"Turn me back." The hero lifted his head to glare at me, but the tears in his eyes lessened the effect and made me pity him more than I wanted to. "I promise I'll tell people how kind you are. We can even work on a truce, if that's what you want. I'll have to run it by the King, of course, but I'm sure I can convince him."

"Desperate people really are willing to say anything." I let out a breath as I stepped around Dain. "I can't change you back into something you never were. You're part demon. There's no getting around that." When sobs shook his shoulders, I sighed. "But I can get revenge on whoever gave you that cursed tonic and lied to you for your entire life. Give me a name and it's done."

Willow raised an eyebrow. "Really? You think killing them is the answer?"

"What else do you want me to do here?" I stared at their exhausted faces while she shrugged. How long had they been in this library wallowing over this? "Maybe I can show him the good parts of being a demon?"

"Yes!" Willow grinned. "Do that. Show him around town and bring him to that cafe or somewhere else he'd like. Once he sees how kind everyone is, maybe he'll be less freaked out. I really do think the two of you would get along great if you just tried talking to each other."

The hero frowned. "You do realize I'm still here, right? And that I'm not a child? You can't just pretend that demons are good and make me okay with this. The King would never have given me medication that would hurt me."

"Ah, so it was the King then." I walked over to Willow's board of suspects, jabbing my finger at him. "Guess we know who the real villain is now. Always good to put a face to a name." I turned to Willow. "Does this help with your story?"

"Well yeah, I think you're secretly supposed to team up and work together to defeat the true villain, but..." She nodded her head at the hero and lowered her voice. "I can't really write when he's upset like this. It seems kind of heartless, you know?"

That was fair. He did seem pretty overwhelmed. He reminded me a bit of myself actually, with his entire world crashing down around him and no idea who he really was. Why would the King have hidden his true identity this whole time and let him believe demons were evil, when he was actually one of us? It was beyond cruel, worse than any torture I could dream up. Humans really were the true monsters in this story.

But if Willow thought we were supposed to work together, then I had to at least try to reason with him.

I moved closer to the hero, resting my hand on his shoulder. "Come on. Let me show you the truth about demons and I promise you'll see this all differently. Then we can talk more about this truce thing."

"Really?" He looked so lost as he gazed up at me, not even shrugging my hand off like I expected him to. "You swear this isn't all a trick?"

"I swear."

He nodded and followed me outside while Willow sank onto a chair mouthing the words, "thank you."

She'd been working so hard to finish my book, so showing the hero around town was the least I could do to help her. It felt kind of nice being useful actually, like I was helping write the story, even if it was in a small way. I grabbed a cloak and tossed it over the hero.

"Hey! Do I really need this still?" He pointed at the white horns protruding from his head. "Aren't these enough to blend in now?"

"Sure, if you don't mind people recognizing you." I opened the doors to the castle, motioning for him to step outside into the daylight. "I mean, you might be the hero in the human realm, but you're definitely not anyone's hero here."

His eyes widened. "Oh, I guess you're right. So does that mean... that *you're* their hero?" He laughed as he walked outside. "The Demon Lord as a hero, what a funny thing to think about."

"Hey, it could happen!" I let the doors slam shut behind us and stormed off into the city. If he couldn't keep up, that was his own problem.

The hero jogged after me, keeping pace extremely well. "Sorry. That was rude, wasn't it?"

"It's fine."

As we walked, various street sellers waved at us, offering everything from roasted nuts to blown sugar art. It felt so different than I'd imagined walking through town would be back when I was too nervous to leave my castle. I sadly had to push past them as quickly as we could without being rude though, otherwise we'd risk the hero being recognized.

Thankfully our destination was right up ahead. The scent of freshly baked bread and sweets drifted out of a cozy little bakery with a sign hanging by the door that had a giant cleaver stuck in a loaf of bread.

The hero raised an eyebrow. "The Destroyer's Bakery?"

"Just go inside. You'll see why we're here soon enough."

A loud thunk made the hero jump as a giant, hulking demon slammed a massive cleaver on the counter, cleanly slicing a loaf of bread. The demon picked the weapon up and slammed it down again and again until the entire loaf was sliced evenly and perfectly.

The hero's mouth dropped open. "That's Varnok the Destroyer!"

A woman laughed. "Noki's mostly the destroyer of diets now, so there's no need to worry." The voice was coming from behind the counter, but we had to look down to notice the petite demon baker, Miri, who had married the Destroyer a few years ago. She smiled warmly at us. "What can we get for you today?"

The hero gaped, turning from Varnok to me. "But he's one of the six great demon generals! And he's just...baking bread?"

"And pies," Miri said. "He makes a delicious apple pie. The secret is a good caramel sauce and multiple kinds of apples for variety. But don't tell anyone else that."

Varnok the Destroyer grunted and nodded at me. "Back again, huh? I didn't realize our lord had such a sweet tooth."

"Well, Willow does." I shrugged, not wanting to admit to such a weakness myself, but I did quite enjoy the pie here. "We'll take a loaf of bread and a cherry pie to go." I glanced over at the hero. "What about you? What kind of pie is your favorite?"

He blinked at me. "My favorite pie? Um, well, probably apple?"

"Excellent choice." Miri clapped her hands together, bumping her hip against Varnok's. "See? I told you today was a day for apple pie."

The big demon smiled softly as he patted her head. He was so tall that she only came up to his waist, but the way they looked at each other was full of love.

This was what I'd wanted to show the hero, that even the demons he thought were monsters had people they cared about. The hero couldn't seem to stop staring at Varnok's broken horn though, so I nudged him.

"Stay calm, you're fine," I whispered.

"But I'm the one who shattered that horn." His voice was full of panic and so quiet I almost didn't hear it. "It's literally hanging on my wall as a trophy!"

"Oof, don't tell him that." I turned back to Miri and handed her a few coins, shaking my head when she tried to protest. "If you don't let me pay, I can't keep coming here and then I'll have to bake for Willow instead and we both know how that would go."

A soggy pie. I'd tried it once while Willow was busy writing, and it was more than a little disappointing.

"Let me do the baking." Varnok laughed a big belly laugh as he slammed his cleaver to cut up some apples. "Grab a seat while I finish this."

Miri led us to a table by the window and set out two plates of cherry pie. "To snack on while you wait. Oh, and have your consort try this with the bread!" She handed me a jar of strawberry jam with red frilly fabric on the top. "It's extra sweet for her."

"Thank you." I took a bite of the cherry pie and couldn't help but make a happy noise. "It's wonderful yet again, Miri. You two are amazing."

"Oh stop." The petite demon slapped my shoulder as she laughed. "You're always welcome here."

I dug into the pie as she went back to help Varnok with the other pie, but the hero just sat there with a dumbfounded look on his face.

"Eat already." I nudged the plate closer to him. "You don't want them to think you don't like it, do you?"

He snatched his fork up so fast I thought he might knock something over. He took a wary bite, reminding me of the first breakfast he'd eaten at the castle, but then his eyes widened.

"This is amazing!" He wolfed the rest of the slice down as Miri smiled at Noki. The hero turned to them. "Ma'am, could I please try another kind of pie as well? This was delicious."

He didn't even ask me, the one paying for that pie, but at least it meant he was comfortable here. That was the goal today, to show him that even the worst enemies he'd ever fought had another side to them. A softer side when they weren't being forced to fight because of the humans' fool of a King.

"Do you see now?" I asked. "Not all demons enjoy fighting. Some do, sure, but most of us just want to live in peace and focus on the things we love. Demons as a whole work hard on their art whether that's baking, gardening, glass blowing, or anything in between. We're a people who love beautiful things and enjoy sharing the warmth of good food and good art with others. You can't just label us monsters because of how we look and call it a day."

"Of course not." The hero wiped crumbs off his mouth with a frown. "But I've seen your generals hurt people." He leaned over the table to whisper. "Varnok didn't get the nickname the Destroyer for no reason, you know."

I'd read the books, so I knew that, but I also knew that he'd never do that on a whim. He was so at home here in this bakery with Miri, so for him to have gone to war, there had to be a good reason. After spending enough time with the villagers, I think I knew what that reason was too: to protect our people.

"What if I told you that was self-defense?" I asked, taking another bite of pie. "Or more accurately, a rescue mission gone bad?"

"A rescue mission?" The hero leaned back in his chair. "Well, maybe I could see that. But why would he need to rescue anyone?"

I sighed. "Because the King makes a habit of kidnapping demons. Honestly, do you even know him at all? I thought you were supposed to be close."

His shoulders slumped. "So did I, but I guess I'm as gullible and clueless as everyone says after all." He rested his head in his hands, looking utterly defeated. "I thought I was doing a good thing. Thought I was *saving* people. But the more I see of you and this village, the more I think I've been tricked and used for some nefarious plot."

That had seemed obvious from the moment we realized he was part demon, but now was not the time to rub it in. Miri came over with more pie, chocolate cream this time, patting the hero on the shoulder even though she had no idea what was going on. He took a bite, and his eyes lit up.

"Thank you," he mumbled around the pie. "You're all very kind and I will never forget this."

Varnok slammed his cleaver into the counter again with a grunt and a glare our way. Had he figured out who the hero was yet? I gripped the table, ready to step in if I needed to, but the big oaf of a baker just shook his head.

"Nobody forgets our pies," he said solemnly. "Or else we'll just have to feed you more to jog your memory."

Miri grinned. "Pies and threats, it's our own little charm. Don't take him seriously."

"Right." The hero nodded, taking another bite. "I'll eat as many as he requires. I'll come here every day if I must."

"Hear that, Noki?" Miri called out. "We've got a customer for life now!"

As they laughed, the hero settled back in his chair with that helpless look he'd had at the library. "What do I do now?"

"Figure out who you are and what's really going on in the world before you try saving anyone again." I sighed as he fell back against his chair. "Don't look so discouraged. I'll help you."

"Like a mentor?" The hero's eyes lit up again. "Or a teacher?"

"Whatever gets you to pay attention. You can still save people, you just need to learn which ones really need saving first. Because from how I'm looking at it, the demons are the ones who need you most right now."

The hero stared at Noki and Miri putting our apple pie in the oven to bake. The Destroyer wrapped an arm around her, picking her up to kiss her cheek. She giggled and kissed him on the mouth with so much passion that we had to look away before things got awkward. Their love shined brighter than the fire in the oven, blazing hot every time I saw them together. They were such a lovely couple and if this war continued, they'd probably be ripped apart. I didn't want to see that, and I hoped the hero didn't either.

He took a deep breath. "You know what, I think you're right. It's about time I fought for all people, not just humans. If you help me, I bet we can make this world a much better place."

I almost choked on my pie. "Help you? But you're the hero, this is *your* job."

"Pretty sure you're a hero too, in your own way." The hero grinned as I coughed, drinking a whole glass of water. He chuckled warmly. "Let's show that King who's boss around here. If the most powerful hero and the most powerful demon work together, I bet there's nothing that can stop us. That's what your consort wanted, right?"

True, that did seem to be where Willow wanted to go with this story, and I hated to admit it, but after getting to know the hero, I had absolutely no urge to fight him anymore. All those visions of our great battle were just gone, like a dream I couldn't quite remember. He was still infuriating, but in the annoying younger brother kind of way instead of the arch nemesis way.

"Okay, we can try working together," I said. "But only if you let me decide who's telling the truth or not. You are far too gullible for your own good. We should work on that."

The hero blushed as red as the cherry pie from earlier. "Fine. That sounds reasonable."

"If we're going to work together, then you should start calling me by my real name," I mumbled, pushing a few pie crumbs around on my plate. "It's Thorne."

"You are pretty prickly, so that makes sense." The hero's eyes widened when I glared at him, then he smiled and laughed. "Kidding. It's nice to meet you Thorne. My name's Leo. Glad we can move past this whole hero and Demon Lord thing."

I nodded. "Leo suits you. Like the golden lion hero." I squinted at his fluffy ears and tail, thinking about his eager personality and energetic vibes. "Or maybe a golden retriever is more your style?"

Leo slumped over in his chair with a dramatic sigh. "You wound me, Thorne. I thought we were allies! But you apparently see me as a dog."

"Dogs are nice though. I like dogs." I felt myself smiling just a bit at the absurdity of this conversation. I never would have thought the hero and I could joke around like this. It felt nice, like what friends sounded like. I held out my hand to him. "Let's save this forsaken world of ours together."

That perked him right up as he reached out to shake my hand. "Yes! But first, let's try a few more pies. Who knew this place would have such good food?"

Miri beamed behind the counter. "Make sure to tell all your friends. The Destroyer's Bakery is the best in the business."

Varnok loomed over her, cleaver in hand as he nodded. They made such an odd pairing, with him literally overshadowing her in every physical way, but her bright personality and cheer was exactly what he needed to open up. Miri reminded me of Willow, actually. I really wanted to take her here soon and share this special place with her.

Maybe once she was done writing the book we could come back here and have a good conversation. Maybe it could even be our first official date.

Chapter 25
Willow

Inkheart and I had been holed up in the castle's library for the past week, writing non-stop and only sleeping when we had to. I'd had idea after idea since realizing the hero was a demon, and I refused to miss a single moment of inspiration. It was too rare of a feeling to waste, like a gift from the gods telling me that I was on the right track finally.

I was really glad Thorne and Leo had come to an agreement too, which meant I could finally use both of their real names without Thorne glaring at me like I'd said something offensive. Between their new partnership and my ideas, I was already on my way to the midpoint, which I was basing off what had happened with Leo in the garden.

After entering the demons' land, the magic would overwhelm Leo and reveal who he truly was: half demon, half human. He was going to spend a while coming to grips with that and his party would probably shun him, but he'd realize that his unique perspective was exactly why he'd been chosen as the hero in the first place.

Only a man who was both human and demon could end the war and unite the people as one. Which was why the King had hidden it from him, to ensure the war continued.

"Inkheart! You're missing all the good stuff!" I nudged the pen awake as a thrill of excitement shot through me. "This story is going to be epic!"

The pen teetered left and right like it was drunk, its feather frazzled.

What's in those drinks that demon's been bringing you, straight caffeine? How are you still this fired up?

"Funny. It's just some of Gran's tea that Thorne brought back for me." I glanced at the empty mug and plate on the table, realizing I hadn't seen him in a while. "I wonder if he'll be bringing more soon."

He'd been stopping by a few times a day to bring me food and drinks, often before I even realized I was hungry. He never stayed long, but it felt like he was checking in on me to make sure I took care of myself. It was extremely sweet, and I found myself looking forward to our little food breaks more and more.

Inkheart scribbled something but hesitated to show me it. I frowned, leaning over to get a better look.

So, when are you going to let him read what you've written? I can tell he's curious.

I flopped backwards onto the floor, listening to the crackling fireplace instead of answering. I could tell he wanted to read it too, but I just wasn't ready. Not yet. The story was still in its infancy and if he told me he hated it now, I'd lose all my excitement for the story. I'd probably never write another word if it felt anything like how horrible reading that note from the story gods had felt. That kind of rejection was hard to get over and it stung even now.

I curled onto my side as Cinder hopped over, her little bunny nose wiggling.

"Hey there," I whispered, reaching out to pet her soft fur. "Sorry I've been ignoring you lately." She tilted her head and nosed my fingers like she was looking for food. "Okay, okay, I'll go get you something tasty in a minute."

Oh sure, you feed the bunny but not yourself. Inkheart fluffed up before writing another note. *Just remember that no first draft is ever perfect, okay? No matter what you write, you can always edit it later, so you shouldn't be afraid to show it to him.*

That's what people always said, but it didn't make the disappointment sting any less when your first draft ended up being terrible. Until somebody read it, I could stay blissfully ignorant and believe that this story was the best thing I'd ever written. It really did feel that way too, which was probably because I knew the characters and their stories so well.

Now I just had to nail their ending and this whole adventure into Thorne's book would be worth it.

But first, carrots.

I stood up to go grab some food for Cinder, but paused as noises drifted over from down the hall. It sounded like Thorne and Leo were struggling with something, cursing and breathing heavy. It almost sounded like they were...

"Stop fighting!" I shouted as I ran down the hall, freezing in place when I saw the mattress they were carrying. My face burned. "Oh, you're bringing a mattress in. Ignore me, I'm sleep deprived."

"It's good to see you out and about." Thorne smiled and rested the mattress against the corner wall they were trying to maneuver around. "How's the book going?"

"Hey!" Leo's shout was muffled behind the mattress where he was presumably pinned. "You can't just pretend like I'm not here! That's not how teams work!"

Thorne raised an eyebrow, leaning close to whisper to me. "He keeps telling me that teamwork makes the dream work and I just had to do something."

I barely covered up my laugh as I moved to free the hapless hero from his cushioned prison. His face was rosy and his hair was mussed up, but he was grinning like he was having a pretty good time.

"Thank you, my lady." He squeezed out from behind the mattress and bowed to me before turning to Thorne. "You need to work on your manners. Being a demon doesn't mean you can go around squashing people with extremely cozy mattresses." He pushed his hand deep into the cushion, his eyes wide. "Honestly though, where did you get this? It's the most comfortable thing I've ever been pinned behind. I'd sleep like a baby on this."

I grinned. "Demons love being cozy, so there are multiple mattress stores in town. We'll have to show you sometime. Maybe you can even purchase some for yourself and share the news about how wonderful everyone here is."

Thorne rubbed his chin. "Now there's an idea, spreading peace through comfortable bedding. I wonder if anyone's ever tried that."

Leo and I glanced at each other, not sure how to take that deadpan statement, before we broke out laughing. This was exactly what I wanted for the end of the book, to have these two being ridiculous together and saving the world one mattress at a time. If the humor was good enough, the readers would hopefully overlook any issues they might have with them teaming up and by the time they were done reading it, they'd be too in love with their vibes to care that my plot twist sounded insane.

Or at least, that's what I was banking on.

I frowned as they picked up the overly large mattress and started carrying it awkwardly through the halls again. "So, why didn't you just get delivery? I'm sure somebody would have helped the Demon Lord set this up."

"Oh, they tried." Leo chuckled. "But it seems like *somebody* is a little self-conscious about his castle. Something about not wanting his people to see how run-down it was, but it looks pretty nice to me."

The castle really did look nicer than when I'd first come here. I had a feeling that had something to do with Thorne, like his journey was connected to the castle itself somehow. Or maybe his emotions were? That would make sense since Misty was linked to him and not the rest of us. The longer I stayed here, the more questions I had, but now was not the time to think on them.

I rushed forward to tilt the mattress before it took down one of the new sconces on the walls. "Be careful! You almost lit this thing on fire."

"And that would be such a shame," Thorne said in a dry voice. "It's a good thing I purchased two of them."

"Two? Why would you do that?" I asked.

He paused, shifting around the mattress so he could look me in the eyes. "One's for you, of course. Did you really think I'd let you keep sleeping on the couch when I had a nice new bed? I want you to feel at home here."

My breath caught as he suddenly dropped the mattress, reaching out to brush a strand of hair behind my ear. He was so close, close enough to feel the warmth radiating off him, as his fingers grazed against my cheek.

"Flirt on your own time," Leo shouted. "I can't carry this alone!"

The mattress wobbled and started tipping over. I rushed forward to catch it, my face hot again. Thorne had spoken so casually about something that felt huge. He'd bought a *bed* just for *me*, and my heart wouldn't stop racing. He hadn't assumed I'd be sharing his bed like some other men might think, but he also hadn't wanted me to be uncomfortable on the couch. He'd given me a place in his home, somewhere I could call mine.

What kind of guy did that?? Just gave the woman he liked a room in his house like it was nothing.

"Thank you." I hefted the mattress up to hide my embarrassment.

"Thank the gods," Leo said. "I bet she'll be a lot more reliable than you." He peeked around the mattress at Thorne. "Since I'm helping, do I get a bed too? I'd love a big fluffy one that you can get lost in."

"Of course you would." Thorne sighed as he took the mattress from me, our hands brushing against each other. "Fine, if you help me carry hers in too, I'll get you a bed."

"Awesome!" Leo picked up the pace, hurrying to Thorne's bedroom humming a little tune about cozy beds.

I shook my head, laughing as I followed them. Every day here was so ridiculous and wonderful and I owed it all to the Misty Mountain Library.

Chapter 26
Willow

My hands were practically shaking as I rushed to write the big climax of the story. Leo and Thorne had revealed the King's dark secrets to the world by freeing every demon prisoner in the dungeons, letting them rush into the town so everyone could see their fear. These weren't monsters to be killed, but people just like them.

When the King saw his subjects turning on him, he used all the magic he'd collected to cast Thorne down, blaming it all on him and his demonic ways. But Thorne wasn't alone, the hero was by his side wielding Dawnbreaker, fighting magic with magic. The two of them took down the King, showing everyone the power of both sides joined together. In a last ditch move, the King almost killed Leo, so Thorne cut him down with no remorse.

Thorne, blood-soaked and terrifying, declared peace from this moment on and every person in the city cheered, demon and human alike. The Demon Lord had saved the hero by taking out the true villain: the evil King.

A shiver ran through me as I flopped onto my bed, sinking into its cozy mattress with a grin. Everyone loved a good hidden villain revenge story, so I knew the readers would enjoy this ending.

I'd finally gotten past the hardest part of the book!

I hugged the pages to my chest as relief washed over me. This ending was all Thorne had ever wanted since I'd met him. He'd wanted an impressive ending, one where he wasn't just a foil to the hero, but a real character. I'd managed to give him that and made him a savior to boot! Nobody would ever overlook him again or act like he was just some cookie-cutter bad guy.

He had depth, so much more than I could even show in the book. I turned to my side, glancing at the vase of sunflowers and daisies he'd picked from Gran's garden for me. The more sucked into my writing I got, the more he'd visited her, and he'd always bring me back something so I wasn't homesick.

It was the nicest thing anyone had ever done for me and this ending was my way of saying thank you. Maybe I should let him read the book now.

I sat up, rubbing my eyes which felt far heavier than they should. The book wasn't completely done, but he'd been so patient with me the past few weeks, and we hadn't really gotten to talk much lately. I missed that.

If I brought him the book *now*, it would give us a reason to have a conversation. Maybe dinner too...

I hopped out of bed before I could change my mind and burst into the hallway. The sconces were even brighter than usual, lighting my way to Thorne's bedroom right next to mine. He'd said it was so he could protect me better, but I noticed he put Leo and Dain in rooms on the opposite side of the castle. Having my bodyguard that far away felt like the opposite of protection, but I couldn't help but smile remembering his blush when he'd shown me which room was mine.

He wanted me next door for more than just protection. And I had to admit, I kind of liked it.

Knowing he was right next door had sent my mind buzzing more than once when I was trying to fall asleep, so it was about time I made use of these side-by-side rooms. I raised my hand to knock on his door but stopped before my knuckles touched the wood.

Was this really a good idea?

Once he read it, I'd know how he really felt about the story. No more wild dreams of everyone loving it, no more fantasy about him thinking it's the best story ever. After how much time he'd spent dissecting my last book, I knew he'd take notes on every aspect of this one too. He wouldn't leave anything out, no matter how tough it would be to hear.

I paced from his room, to mine, and back to his over and over as my mind raced. I really thought he'd like the ending I chose, but what if I was wrong? What if he hated the entire book? There wasn't enough time to start over, not if I was going to submit it for the competition. He needed this book to be perfect. Every character I'd met since coming in here did.

This wasn't just a story to them, it was their lives, and somehow I'd let Thorne convince me to make sweeping decisions that would affect all of them.

"This is way too much pressure." I clutched the manuscript, pacing even faster and muttering to myself. "Way, way too much. Why did I think I could do this?"

I froze at the sound of Thorne's door creaking open. I slowly turned around, plastering a smile on my face. "Oh, hello. How are you doing tonight?"

"Better than you, it seems." A bemused smile graced his lips as he leaned against the doorframe. "You talk to yourself a lot, you know. Usually when you're stuck on a scene or you're worried about something."

He was far too observant, which meant there was no chickening out now.

I sighed and pushed the thick stack of pages at him. "I was hoping you'd read my book."

"You want me to read it?" He almost dropped the pages and had to use his shadows to catch a few of them. "Does that mean you're done?"

I crossed my arms over my chest, feeling weird now that the pages were gone. "I'm almost done. I think you're going to love it, so I wanted to share it with you, that's all."

"Oh, well come in then."

He turned, allowing me to step inside, but I caught the smile on his face before he did. He looked happier than a mossmew in lavender pot and it made all my worries wash away. Thorne believed in my writing more than I did. It's why he picked me to be his writer, so I should have nothing to worry about.

I hadn't been in his room since we'd brought the mattress in, which felt like a week or so ago, but I couldn't be sure. I'd completely lost track of time once I really dug into the second half of the book. His room looked different though, cozier.

The bed had thick pillows and the end table looked like it was part of a set with mine. There was even a plush rug on the floor and a fireplace!

"Stop gawking," he said with a laugh. "I just got a few things that seemed interesting. The woman at the store helped me when we went back for Leo's mattress. And then again with Dain's."

I grinned. "You are such a softie. Honestly, you're going to have half the town living with you soon."

"It was practical." He set my manuscript on the table and motioned for me to sit on the bed. "Are you hungry? I can make us something to eat."

His bed was just as comfortable as mine, pillowing my body like it was made for me. A yawn escaped before I could stop it.

"Sorry." I stretched my arms out as exhaustion hit me like a brick. "Dinner sounds nice, but I'm afraid I'd fall asleep before I ate it. Maybe we could make breakfast together in the morning?"

"Deal." He joined me on the bed, his weight shifting the mattress just enough for my shoulder to brush against his. "I bet your muscles are stiff from being hunched over your manuscript all day, right?"

"You have no idea," I groaned. "We should have gotten a desk and a comfortable chair while we were shopping."

"You're absolutely right." He moved further back on the mattress, resting his strong hands on my shoulders. "Let me make it up to you."

His whispered promise sent tingles through me as he carefully swept my hair to the side so he could massage my shoulders. Each press of his hands hit one of my tense spots perfectly, releasing every pent-up bit of stress I'd accumulated over the past few weeks. I let out a soft moan as his hands expertly dug into my back and his shadows gently drifted over my skin like velvet.

"How are you so good at this?" I asked softly as his hands swept down my back. "Nevermind, just don't stop."

His quiet laugh danced across my skin, his breath warm as he encircled me in shadowy comfort. Everything about him was so kind. I leaned back against him as my eyes grew heavier and heavier.

"You're falling asleep, aren't you?" he asked.

"Mmmm..."

His arms wrapped around me, making me even more comfortable as he kissed my temple softly. We sat there for a little while enjoying the moment until he shifted, swinging his legs off the side of the bed. "Let's get you back to your room."

But his bed was so comfortable and the walk all the way back to my room felt like it would take forever.

"Or I could just stay here?" I covered another yawn and laid down, but when he didn't respond, I cracked an eye open. He was hovering between getting up and sitting back down, like he couldn't decide what to do.

"I don't bite," I said with a laugh. "You can read the book while I get some rest."

"Okay, if you think you can sleep like that." The bed shifted again as he reached over me to grab the manuscript, but there was a devious smile on his lips as he looked down at me. "I know I'd have other things on my mind if I was the one trying to sleep with you here."

Heat washed over me. I suddenly felt far more awake than I had a few moments ago. My heartbeat raced as I propped myself up on my elbows, my lips so close to his that I could practically taste him.

He leaned down, trailing kisses across my cheek until he whispered in my ear. "Sorry, but I've got a really good book to read."

"You're horrible." I fell back onto the bed with a sigh. "Maybe you really are a villain."

"Only for you." He laughed, settling down next to me and pulling me close to him. "Sleep now. We can pick that back up in the morning if you want."

Mmmm...I definitely wanted, but he was right. Every bone in my body felt tired now that I'd let myself close my eyes for that long. If I was going to be intimate with Thorne, I wanted to be fully awake for it. I snuggled up against his side and closed my eyes, listening to his deep, even breathing and the soft turning of pages.

When I was just about to drift off, his arm tightened around me. I frowned as the page flips grew louder, like he was snapping the pages. I rubbed my eyes, blinking against the light of his fireplace.

"Is something wrong?" I struggled to sit up, my body yelling at me for ignoring sleep yet again, but something about Thorne seemed off. His eyebrows knit together, staring at my manuscript like it was written in a foreign language. "What's going on?"

"You had me kill the King? You really think I'd do that?"

A sinking feeling swept over me as I realized he'd skipped right to the end instead of reading the entire book I'd worked so hard on. "If you read the rest, you'll see why I did that."

"But I'm not the villain, remember?" His voice was rough as he sat up straighter.

The bed didn't feel nearly as comfortable with all this new tension in the air between us. I stared at the mattress, not wanting to see that strange look in his eye anymore. Like he blamed me for writing it wrong.

"I thought we decided you were a morally gray anti-hero type character." I gestured at the pages in his hands. "This is exactly what that kind of character would do."

"Well then I'm not that." He shoved the manuscript back at me. "I just don't think I'd kill somebody, not if I didn't have to."

"But this is what you asked for." The weight of the pages in my hands felt like a rock as I stared at them. Did he really not see how amazing this ending was? "You said you wanted to go out with a bang and to be remembered by everyone for doing something amazing. Killing the King did that! I didn't even need to kill you off either. I thought you'd appreciate that."

My heartbeat echoed in my ears, and my face grew hot. I thought I'd done such a good job, given him everything he asked for, but it still wasn't enough. Just like at the Tales and Tomes Festival. What was the point in writing a book if nobody liked it? Maybe if I'd finished it like I'd planned, if I'd waited until it was perfect before letting him see it, then he'd have understood.

But no, I'd been so excited to see him that I let my emotions get the better of me and had let him read it before it was ready.

Now his silence could only mean one thing: he hated it.

"I never should have let you read it before it was done," I whispered. "I just really wanted to share it with you tonight, but an incomplete story won't impress anyone." I swallowed the lump in my throat as I moved off the bed. "Just forget about it."

"Wait!" Thorne reached out to me, but I pulled away. His expression turned pained as he dropped his hand. "I'm sorry. I don't think that's me, but that's not your fault. I didn't realize it myself until I read that chapter and felt weird. You couldn't have known that."

That's right, I couldn't have known *that*, but I had known all along that I was too inexperienced to write this book. No matter how amazing my ideas might be, my writing wasn't good enough to hold up. I was just an apothecary stuck in a fantasy world with dreams of being a famous writer.

I clutched my hand to my chest. This series was so much bigger than me, and I had no right to try and finish it. Even Grandpa would have told me it was too much for me to handle right now. He might have been a dreamer, but he always knew where the line was between optimism and foolishness. I, apparently, did not. But there was still time to fix that. I just had to stop fooling myself.

"It's fine, Thorne." I took a deep breath and moved off the bed. "Since you don't like it, I won't submit it. I won't write another word in fact. I never wanted to be a writer anyway."

"Wait, no, that's not what I meant." He jumped up. "I still think you're an amazing writer, so I'm sure if we just tweak some things, it'll work. We can lock the King up or something like that."

"Really?" I shook my head. He'd read so many books, but somehow still didn't understand the fans of his series at all. "The readers wouldn't be happy with a blah ending like that. They're looking for something big and memorable. You were too when we first started this."

"Don't let it end like this." His voice was so quiet I almost missed it.

Did he mean the story...or us? And was there even an us without the book?

The sad expression on Thorne's face was too hard to look at. Giving up on writing this book would hurt him, but if I submitted it and the fans hated it, it would hurt us both. How had I let this all get so messed up? I never should have gotten so close to him. If we weren't together, then I could have just told him the ending I chose was right and I didn't care what he thought.

Except I did care. I cared so much it hurt.

This wasn't what I signed up for.

"I'm done." I crossed my arms over my chest, gripping my sides tight. "I'm just not cut out to be a writer, so there's no point in finishing the book. I quit."

I tossed my manuscript on his bed as golden light filled the room, enveloping me in magic that felt very familiar. Then it was gone and so was Thorne. I blinked, turning to take in all the bookshelves and tables and the many patrons filling the Misty Mountain Library.

Relief flooded my body. I was back. I could finally go home!

I turned, half expecting to see Thorne standing there, but he hadn't followed me out of the book. I knew deep down he wouldn't. I'd seen that pained look on his face before. In the mirror.

My eyes burned from exhaustion and from the hot tears welling up. I started making my way outside but stumbled across Nyssa and Oren in a circle of books on the floor surrounding the great book tree.

"Willow!" Nyssa leapt up, pulling me into a hug as a grin spread across her face. "I'm so glad you're back safely!"

"But how is she back?" Oren took his glasses off to clean them as he squinted at me. "Did you figure out how the magic worked or use a relic or something?"

Nyssa winced. "Relics definitely didn't work for us. We kind of exploded a few trying to get you out."

They seemed so happy, but I could barely process their words. The look of agony on Thorne's face was the only thing on my mind.

"I have to get home, sorry." I pushed past them as fast as I could. "I'll come back later and we can talk!"

The moment I was back in the forest I loved so much, I let the tears fall. I cried so hard I could barely see as I stumbled down the mountain. This was why I never got close to anyone. It always ended in disappointment and someone hurting the other.

It was easier to be alone.

Chapter 27
Thorne

The fires in the castle were burning low and a chill hung in the air. The darkened hallways reminded me of the first time I'd woken up here, the cracks in the walls leading me along. I ran my fingers across them, feeling every crumbly piece. I thought they all disappeared, but maybe the cracks were just hiding behind a pretty exterior for a while, fooling me into thinking this place was cozy. Like how I'd fooled myself into thinking I could be something other than a villain.

Why couldn't I have just gone along with Willow's plan to kill the King? I'd never wanted my story to end with me as some kind of golden hero unwilling to do what was needed. I was supposed to do whatever it took to protect the people I loved, even if that meant killing somebody who obviously needed killing. The King would just keep harming my people if he was alive. She'd written a perfectly fine ending, going above and beyond what I'd asked of her.

So why had my blood run cold when I read it?

Everything in me had screamed that something was wrong, that that wasn't me, but it was exactly the version of me that Willow and I had discussed so many times. What else had I expected?

And why hadn't I followed her when she got out of the book? I should be happy for her, elated that Misty finally figured out how to bring her back to her own world, but the ache in my chest wouldn't go away no matter how I tried to rationalize it.

She'd quit. Not just on the book, but on me. On us.

"My lord!" Dain shouted as he ran over to me, sliding to his knees across the rough stone floor. "I am so sorry. I brought the hero back to his people like you said, but I lost track of him after that." He bowed his head low. "I am a terrible bodyguard and should be punished."

"Calm down." I grabbed his arm, trying to get him to stand up. "He's the hero, so I'm sure he's just fine. Asking you to watch over him was unnecessary and with Willow gone..."

I couldn't bring myself to finish the sentence. Saying it would mean she wasn't coming back.

"My lord?" Dain moved a little closer, as if he was going to offer some kind of support, but thought better of it. He stood at attention instead. "Tell me what you need, and I'll get it done. I'll find a way to bring her back if that's what you desire."

"Just go home." I shook my head, moving past him toward the kitchen. "Willow's gone, so I don't need your services anymore. Tell everyone that the castle is closed. Nobody comes in and I won't be going out anymore either."

If I set everything back to the way it was before I'd started feeling all these emotions and interacting with people, then maybe the pain would go away. I'd spent plenty of alone time here without feeling lonely, so why was this eating at me so much now? She'd only been gone for a few days, but it felt like weeks.

Willow wasn't coming back and without her writing, my fate was sealed. I'd be the villain forever.

Behind me, Dain shuffled like he couldn't decide if he should stay or go, so I turned back to give him my final command. "Leave this castle and don't come back. I appreciate all you've done for me, but your services are no longer required. Spend time with your family and friends, enjoy your life. Just stay away from the castle from now on."

His face fell, but he pressed his hand to his chest anyway in a salute, bowing to me for the last time before he left. A lump formed in my stomach as he walked away. Apparently, I'd grown attached to him as well. Willow's presence had opened me up to far too many attachments.

"Did you have to be so mean?" Leo's voice startled me as he hopped off the kitchen counter, finishing off a slice of apple pie like he lived here. "Really, that soldier deserved better. And what's all that about Willow leaving?" I must have given him a funny look, because he shrugged and scooped up another slice of pie. "What? Voices carry in this castle. Now tell me everything."

The eager look on his face cut through my pain and filled me with irritation instead. He was the reason I'd been written as the villain in the first place, to make him shine brighter and give him somebody terrifying to defeat. My entire purpose in life was to make him look good. I should hate him for that, but after spending so much time together, I'd started feeling a sort of kinship with him. And that really set my teeth on edge.

"I want to be alone." I nodded at the door, hoping he'd take the hint. "Shouldn't you be with your people anyway? They must be worried about you."

"Ehhh, they're fine." He brushed crumbs off his face with a goofy grin. "My party's handling things and they don't need a half-demon like me screwing that up for them." He grinned as he took another bite of pie. "Mmmm, this really is amazing. I should coax them into opening a shop in our lands."

I snorted. "Right, because the Destroyer would definitely be welcome."

"If he kept making pies like this, you never know." He laughed, eating the last crumbs on his plate. "Okay, I'm all done and ready to listen. What happened with your wife?"

"She's not my wife." I groaned and left the kitchen, trying to put as much distance between his nonsense and me. "Just go back to the humans already. I don't need you here."

"Too bad, because I'm not leaving." He followed me down this hallway and that like that annoying three-headed puppy back at the library.

Maybe if I threw the hero a ball, he'd run off to fetch it and I could lock the door behind him. I could see his tail wagging now and that big goofy grin of his as he chased after it. I chuckled, wishing I actually had a ball to test it out. At least he'd be gone then, and I could go back to how things were before. Just me and this castle.

This game of follow-the-leader got very old quickly though. I spun around and stopped so fast that he ran into me. I pushed him back with my best glare. "You need to leave."

"But you're my friend and you're in pain." Leo rubbed his nose like he'd injured it crashing into me. "Well, now I'm in pain too, but that's not the point. I saw how much you cared about Willow and if she really did leave, then you must be devastated. Let me help you. I can make dinner or go get more pie at least since I polished the last one off." He gave me a sheepish look. "What? It was tasty and you shouldn't be alone right now."

"I shouldn't be alone, huh? I'm the villain, of course I should be alone."

I pushed past him again as we walked by the room that had been the warmest and most full of life. The library. My stomach sank and I couldn't get myself to walk inside to see if her notes were still there or if the board of suspects had crumbled into ash. The rest of the castle had gone back to the way it was before she came, so I assumed that room would too. Memories flooded my mind: Willow lying beside the fire resting, her brow furrowed with frustration as she glared at a blank page, and the sheer joy in her eyes when she came up with a good idea.

I'd miss that joy the most. For somebody who'd experienced so much pain, she still found happiness in little things like a beautiful plant, soft dirt, or a good idea.

"You know, I've seen a lot of bad guys," Leo said softly, "but none of them acted like you. You could have tortured the answers out of me or kept me locked away in a room somewhere, but instead, you fed me, helped me through my issues with being part demon and my world crumbling around me, and now you've got a broken heart. It's all so very..."

"Don't say it."

"Human," he finished, smiling as I groaned. "You're a nice guy, what can I say? Seeing you act like this is depressing."

My shadows flickered, snapping at him with barely any oomph. I couldn't even muster up a glare, not while I was so close to this library of hers. All I felt was overwhelming sadness and I really didn't want Leo to be right about that.

"Just go," I repeated. "Leave me alone. We are not friends, you fool, we're enemies!"

He stood in my path so I couldn't storm off again. "If you really mean that, then I'll go, because I've had enough friends shunning me as it is. So if you're just doing your whole grumpy demon thing, then stop, because once you truly push somebody away, there's no going back."

His words cut deeper than any blade and the anguish on his face was real. Dain said he'd lost Leo shortly after bringing him back to his people and Leo had mentioned something about them not needing a half-demon like him screwing things up. Had they shunned him because of who he was? No, he was the hero, that didn't happen to people like him.

At least, it wouldn't have before I started messing with the story. Maybe it was time to finally tell him what was really going on.

"You and I are characters in a story." I took a deep breath, hoping he didn't run off and scream this to the world. "Those books Willow said she wrote as a biography are actually what created us. Another author wrote them, and a magical library brought them to life. We're not real and I can't just be a good guy, not when the author wrote me as the villain. Sure, I thought Willow might be able to write me as something else, but that was foolish. I am what I am, and you are what you are. Accept it and be the amazing hero you were always meant to be."

Leo stared at me and then started laughing. "Right, sure, we're just fictional characters in a made-up world. Wow, you really went off the deep-end, huh?"

I stomped into the library and picked up one of the books in our series, showing it to him. "Do you really believe Willow guessed all these things about you? That she knew what you ate for breakfast every single day and exactly what every person said to you and how you fought each enemy blow for blow? You read it, was there anything she got wrong?"

"Well, no, it was pretty perfect actually." He took the book from me, his face scrunched up in confusion. "But that doesn't mean we're not real. It just means she has good spies."

"No spies are that good!" I let out a breath, flipping to different pages and showing him specifics there was no way people could know. "Look, you were alone here, all by yourself in a locked room. How would somebody know what you were thinking in that moment? Even a spy can't read your mind."

He took the book from me, reading it carefully. He was silent for so long that I worried I might have broken him. He sank onto the couch while I stood there awkwardly. I'd been trying to get him to believe in himself again and leave, but I had a feeling I might be stuck with him even longer now.

The sound of a bunny keening pulled my attention to Cinder, Willow's little pet who was sitting right where she always fed it, looking at us with big sad eyes. I grabbed some hay from a shelf and set it in a pile on the floor, remembering how Willow said she couldn't just let the hero starve. I felt the same about this bunny now and something eased in me when she started munching on the hay, her cheeks full to the brim.

Willow had a knack for bringing in strays, first this bunny, then Dain, and then Leo too. Who was going to deal with them all now that she'd abandoned them? It certainly wasn't going to be me. Right after that bunny was done eating, I'd take her to the bunny cafe. Coco and her mother would care for her just fine and yet another reminder of Willow would be gone.

"Okay, hero, time to go." I pulled the book from his hands, nodding at the door. "You know what you are now, so there's nothing else for me to say besides get out."

"Just hold on a minute." He pushed himself further into the plush couch, defying me with every move. "Say we are characters in a book, that doesn't mean we're not real. If that magical library you mentioned really did bring our books to life, then we're just as alive as everyone else." He leaned to the side and pushed a vase off a table. It shattered on the floor. "Did an author make me do that? No, of course not. I have free will, and so do you."

I stared at the broken pieces of the vase mixed with the sunflowers I'd picked for Willow right before she left. They were dried out now, crumbling like they were weeks old. Seeing them lying there all withered and lifeless was like a punch to the gut. Why did her leaving have such an effect on my castle? If Misty was playing games, I did not appreciate it. It felt like it was something more though, like my sadness was being thrown back in my face. Slowly, the sunflowers crumbled to a fine dust that disappeared into the floor as if it was never there.

I'd wanted every trace of Willow and the others gone and it seemed like the castle was responding.

To me.

Maybe the castle wasn't linked to Misty at all. I knelt next to the shattered vase, slowly picking up the pieces. Could the castle be linked...to my emotions somehow? That would explain why it had gotten warmer the longer Willow was here, but that was ridiculous. It was a castle, not a mood ring.

Leo helped me pick up the pieces. "Sorry. I didn't mean to break it, I was just trying to prove a point and got carried away."

"It's fine. Villains don't need flowers."

He groaned. "Not more of this villain talk. You say you're a villain because the author wrote you that way, then you wanted Willow to make you into a good guy instead, but you never seem to take your life into your own hands and work for what you want." He held up a shattered piece of glass. "This vase proves we have a choice. It proves that you can decide who you want to be. Don't let some author tell you that and certainly don't rely on your wife to turn your life around. You need to do that yourself, otherwise you aren't worthy of being my arch nemesis." He stood up, putting the vase shards on the table. "You wouldn't be worthy of being my friend either. So tell me, what do you want most right now?"

What did I want most right now?

I sank to the floor, leaning against the bookshelves as I twirled a piece of glass in my hands. I wanted Willow to write my book, but not just for me. I wanted her to write it because she loved writing and never should have given up on it. I wanted to spend more time in her apothecary shop, enjoying the warm and comforting vibes there without all this pressure. I wanted people to stop thinking I was a villain, but I also didn't want to have to hurt people to protect others. I glanced up at Leo, remembering him joking about me being the demons' hero.

Is that what I wanted? To be a hero in my own right? To be somebody who could protect the people he cared about without harming anyone and who other people looked up to? No, that didn't feel quite right either. Being a hero was a whole big thing and I just...wanted to live my life.

Memories of the townsfolk greeting me warmly as I walked by or Willow's Gran putting me to work because she knew I could help her came to mind. That was what I wanted more of, and I didn't want to worry about the whole hero or villain nonsense. I just wanted to get to know people better and have genuine interactions with them.

I wanted friends who cared about me. I was tired of being alone.

Leo held out his hand. "Did you figure it out yet?"

"Maybe." I grasped his outstretched hand, letting him help me to my feet. "I think I want to be more like you, actually. The kind of guy who fights for what he wants and never lets the heroine give up on her dreams."

Leo's eyes widened. "You want to be like me?"

"Nevermind, forget I said that."

"Aww, it's okay, you can admit you think I'm cool." A grin stretched across his face. "Nobody would blame you for wanting to be more like the great hero of the story."

"Oh shut up." I pushed past him. I needed to find Dain to see if he wanted to join us. If I was going to do this, then everyone I cared about should be part of it. Especially the overzealous bodyguard I'd grown to appreciate. I turned back to Leo. "Bring the bunny too."

"You are such a softie." He laughed and picked up Cinder, cradling her in his arms as the bunny nuzzled against him. "I like your new determined vibe, but where are we going?"

"To talk to Willow. We might not be able to change her mind about writing the book, but I've got to try. Not just because I'm looking for a good ending, but because she loves writing and if she gives up on it now, I'm worried she'll never try again." I made my way through the castle as sconces flickered back to life, illuminating the castle with a new light. "Instead of expecting her to do this on her own, I'm going to offer our help. This is our story, so we should write our own ending."

"Ah, so you were listening to me." Leo rushed to catch up with me, nodding. "I like the plan, but I thought you said Willow was gone?"

"Then we'll just have to go out of the book and find her."

I threw the big castle doors open, grinning as I found Dain standing at attention right outside. For all my faults, I'd somehow found a solid group of people I could call friends. This castle didn't need to be my hiding place anymore. It was time I stepped outside for real and took advantage of this life Misty had given me.

Willow deserved that version of me just as much as I did. I never should have given up on us so easily, without even chasing after her to talk about it. If the ending to my book was the only thing standing between us, then screw my book. I wanted her more than any fancy ending she could ever write for me.

She was my happily ever after.

CHAPTER 28
WILLOW

Now that my little writing side quest was over, I could focus on what truly mattered to me. The apothecary shop was busier than ever, giving me the perfect excuse to dive into work and not think about anything else. Herbs needed grinding, plants needed watering, and orders needed packing. It all felt so wonderfully familiar.

Or it would have if there weren't so many strange things in the shop that hadn't been there when I left. Notebooks full of unfamiliar handwriting, a garbage bin labeled "failures", and shelves of elixirs marked for training next to the old flash cards I'd used when I was studying as a teen. I leaned closer, staring at the handwriting in the notebook.

"Is this all Thorne's?" I asked Gran after she finished up with a customer. "Were you training him?"

"Of course. Did you think I'd keep a terrible apprentice like him around otherwise?" Gran harrumphed but smiled fondly at the section of the shop that seemed to be Thorne's now. "He messed up every single task I gave him for the first few days, making nothing fit for consumption and setting fire to more than one project. But he was determined to help, and I didn't have the heart to say no." She moved closer, resting her hand on my shoulder. "I assume he did it for you..."

I trailed my fingertips over the label on a bottle of energizing tonic, pausing at the little note that said *For Willow*.

Tears pricked my eyes. He'd spent so much time helping Gran when I was too busy pretending to be a writer. I should have been the one here, not him. I gripped the bottle tight, forcing myself to empty it in the failure bin.

Gran gasped. "What did you do that for? That one was practically usable!"

"He won't be coming by anymore." And yet, I couldn't seem to bring myself to dump out the rest of the bottles. My eyes were so blurry that I could barely make out his little corner of the shop. "Sorry we wasted your time, Gran."

A pained look was her only response and that bothered me even more. I shouldn't be worrying her like this. I wiped my eyes and grabbed my mortar and pestle to grind up some fresh ginger root. I pounded the plant over and over, crushing it to loosen it up. The harsh sound of the pestle slamming against the mortar was oddly satisfying. Gran had promised that if I hated writing she wouldn't bother me about it anymore. So at least I wouldn't have to feel like this ever again.

"I'm done writing, Gran." Ginger juice splashed against my hand, but I kept slamming the pestle down over and over. "And I'm done with Thorne too."

"Oh Willow." Gran grabbed my hands, forcing me to stop and look at her. "He was a good man. I'm sorry."

She pulled me into a hug that made it all so much worse. I thought I could just leave the book and forget about Thorne, but remnants of him were everywhere, even in how she talked about him. Tears ran down my cheeks, soaking into her cardigan. Gran patted my back as my shoulders shook and I finally let it all out.

"I don't even know what happened," I said, half sobbing still. "One minute we were great together and the next we were arguing about the book. Then I was back in the library, and it all fell apart." I took a deep breath and pulled away from her, wiping my eyes. "He hated my version of the story, and he didn't even bother following me when the library finally pulled me out. That's all I really need to know I guess."

"Is it really? I feel like there's probably more to the story." Gran stared at me with that intense look of hers that always made me squirm, like I was a kid and she was trying to get me to admit I'd broken a jar. "Let's close early today."

"But we never close early."

"Well today we do." She made her way to the front door and flipped the open sign to closed, turning back to me with her hands on her hips. "The Demon Lord was here almost every day, remember? That man went from lost and kind of sad to confident and glowing with happiness. I know that was because of you, so if you felt even a little bit of what he did, I can't imagine you'd just give up on the book you two were working on that easily."

My mouth dropped open. "You think I'm the reason he was glowing with happiness?"

"Of course, he's in love with you." Gran put a kettle of water over the fire while I stood there, dumbfounded. "You're always so focused on work that you miss what's right in front of your face. I've watched every man who falls for you go from excited to downright gloomy once they realize you'll never pay them the kind of attention you pay your work. But that demon's different." She glanced back at me, her expression soft and kind. "You made him happier the longer you were together. Was it the same for you?"

"Just how much time did you spend together?" I muttered, heat sweeping over the back of my neck. "We weren't in love. We barely even dated. We were just stuck together and we let the excitement of the book get to us."

"Don't do that," Gran chided. "Don't belittle his feelings or yours."

She was right. Even as I said the words, I knew they were a lie. I did have feelings for him, strong ones. Nobody had ever made me feel like that before, which was why it had stung so much when he rejected me. Well, rejected my ideas, but those felt like one in the same at this point.

"It doesn't matter if I liked him or not." I grabbed two mugs and sat down at the table. "I put everything I had into that book and he still didn't like it. He actually just skipped to the climax and didn't even bother reading the rest, which is so rude."

"Well, that is rude, I agree." Once the kettle started whistling, she carried it over to the table and added a few scoops of tea leaves to it. "What didn't he like about it?"

"That I wrote him killing the King." I crossed my arms on the table and rested my chin on them. "I don't get it though. We talked about him being a morally gray character and then he seemed so shocked when I wrote it that way. He said it wasn't him, but honestly, I don't think he really knows who he is."

"You keep calling him a character, but he's a real person Willow. With real feelings."

"I know that." I traced the whirls in the wooden table, wishing we were talking about anything else. Because I had feelings too and they hurt. "Can we just drop this and have some tea?"

She clasped my hands in hers so tight it almost hurt. "No, we can't just drop this. I've let you drop too many things for far too long and it has to stop. You can't keep running away when things get hard. That's not how writing or relationships work. Nothing's ever perfect, especially not on the first try, but if you really care about something, you need to be willing to fight through those hard times. Because you'll never have anything worthwhile if you don't."

I sat up straighter. "What's the point when it all ends bad anyway? Look at mom and dad or you and Grandpa. Nobody's happy."

"But we *were* happy." She let go of me with a sigh and poured us both a cup of tea. "We were happy until the end and that's better than most people can say. I think you were happy too, with Thorne."

"You never even saw us together."

She pushed a teacup at me. "No, but I heard the way he talked about you and the stories he told me. He said you spent time gardening together, helped him find a mattress that finally let him sleep well, and you even took breaks from your writing to eat meals with him." She smirked at me. "I've never seen you take a break like that for anyone, not even me when you're really in the zone. But he said you stopped what you were doing every single time he brought you food. What's that if not happiness?" She leaned closer. "You enjoyed spending time with him and that blush on your face confirms it."

"Gran!" I turned away, hiding my face behind my tea as I took a sip of burning hot liquid. She was right though. I enjoyed those meals far more than I'd ever told him. I'd wanted them to drag on longer and longer each day. "Okay, fine, I was happy. So what?"

"So you should go after him!" Gran jumped up so suddenly she spilled her tea. "Who cares if you finish the book or not? He's the important part. Don't you dare lose him because you're afraid to let yourself care!"

"It's not just that." I leaned back, refusing to get swept up in her excitement. "He cares if I finish the book. It's his life after all. And I just can't do that if he doesn't like my ideas."

"So come up with more ideas." Gran pinned me with a stare. "Find something you both agree on and write that. Unless..." She sat down again slowly. "Unless you really don't want to write anymore. I don't want you to change your mind just because I pressured you or because you feel like you owe Thorne anything. If you keep writing, it should be because you want to."

She was right. If I was going to try again, it had to be for me. No more making excuses and pretending like I only did things because she nagged me about them. I started writing after Grandpa passed away because I wanted to be closer to him. I wanted to feel that connection we used to have and make it into something others could see too.

Talking about my ideas with him had been one of my favorite parts about storytelling, but I hadn't let myself open up like that again, not really. If I had, I'd have let Thorne see the messy middle instead of just hoping he'd love the ending. I would have asked him what he thought about killing the King before ever putting pen to paper.

I was just too afraid to do it.

Afraid he'd hate my ideas, afraid we'd lose the competition, but most of all, afraid that I'd never be good enough to write something worthy of being added to a book series I loved so much.

I stared into my tea as steam curled around the cup, slowly growing colder as Gran waited patiently for me to respond. Grandpa had hated plenty of my ideas over the years and I'd hated a lot of his too. We'd never let that stop us from brainstorming new ones though. It was the opposite actually. We usually came up with even better ideas later on.

Not every idea was right for every story, but that didn't make those ideas bad. It just meant there was something that would work better for that story. So why had I given up so easily? Not just on Thorne's book, but on my own before that. One bad reaction from the story gods and I'd thrown my book away like it was garbage.

Garbage.

My gaze drifted over to the bin Gran had set up for Thorne's failures. It was full to the brim of different herbs, mixtures, and broken glass. He must have spent so much time trying different things to see what would work and what wouldn't. I was the same way when I was learning. Sometimes you had to mess up a few potions to understand how things worked.

Just like Grandpa and I sometimes had to come up with the wrong ideas to discover the right ones.

I reached over to pick up the empty bottle with Thorne's writing on it. He'd written the label so carefully with his little note about how it was for me. He'd tried to support me as much as possible, and then I just shut him out and ran away. I hadn't even really asked why he disliked killing the King so much or what else he might want to do instead.

"I think I should go back and talk to Thorne." I slipped the bottle in my pocket and finished my cup of tea. "Are you okay running the shop for a bit longer on your own?"

Gran grinned. "Absolutely. Go get him, Willow. Dream big and don't let anything hold you back."

I stood up, giving her a hug on my way out. I didn't know if Thorne would forgive me or if we could figure out a better way to end the story, but I knew one thing for sure. I was done running away from the things I cared about.

The bell above the door chimed softly as I opened it, ready to charge up the mountain and beg the library to send me back into Thorne's book, but there he was standing right in front of me. Excitement rushed through me. It was like he knew I'd changed my mind and wanted to work things out, but how?

"What are you doing here?" I asked softly.

A faint blush swept over his cheeks. "I was just coming to find you..."

"He means we," Leo added. "We came to find you."

Dain nodded. "Our Lord thought you might want help with your story."

"Don't give up on your writing." Thorne reached out, taking my hand in his. "I'm sorry I put such a burden on you, expecting you to figure out who I was. *I* should have been the one to do that. If you let me, I want to help with the book. We all do."

Behind him, Leo and Dain were both smiling, but they weren't the only ones. Inkheart was darting around, scribbling about how I should kiss the demon already and Cinder was tucked into the hero's shirt, poking her head out like she was just waking up from a nap. Even Dawnbreaker was here, looking extra shiny on the hero's hip.

They'd all come out of the book for me. I'd always thought writing was supposed to be a solo process, but maybe, just maybe, it was better with friends. Writing a perfect ending didn't feel so scary knowing they'd all be by my side. Especially Thorne.

"I'd love to write with you." I leaned in close, kissing him softly. "Thank you for coming here."

"About time!" Gran shouted from behind me. "But don't think you're all going to fit in here. I've got a business to run, you know."

I laughed, glancing over my shoulder at her. She was beaming with joy, happier than I'd seen her in years. She was the best Grandmother I could ever ask for and it was about time I started listening to her about love.

"Let's go back to your book," I said. "I'm sure we can find somewhere for us all to write together."

Thorne's eyes sparkled. "Oh, I think something can be arranged. Roan mentioned that hot springs are a good place to gather your thoughts, and I know the perfect inn to visit. It'll be like a writing retreat for us."

Hot springs, Thorne, and writing?

Nothing had ever sounded sweeter.

Chapter 29
Willow

After a lot of debate, we decided that going back inside the book was the best plan for finishing this series. It would give us a little extra time to write while being grounded in the source material. Plus, it was their home, and I liked it there, too. There was a magical quality to their world that just couldn't be replicated outside.

Nyssa and Oren had grumbled about it, but the library had thankfully overruled them. Misty believed I'd get out when I really wanted to, just like the last time.

Which was how we'd ended up at this beautiful hot springs inn, walking down the rich wooden halls on the way to our rooms. A faint mineral scent drifted on the air, making me want to explore outside as soon as possible. The back of Thorne's hand brushed against mine, sending a pleasant shiver through me. This was the first time I'd fought with a guy and actually kept seeing him. Usually when we called it quits, that was it.

Thorne was too important to let go of that easily though. I laced my fingers through his, securing him to me. His eyes widened, but before I could say anything our hostess stopped.

"This will be your room for the duration of your stay," she said. "Staff will bring meals three times a day at the appointed times, but feel free to visit the springs whenever you'd like."

She slid two large pocket doors open to reveal a room that looked like it was meant for a large group. Dark wood flooring stretched out in front of us with cushions scattered everywhere and at least six futons stacked in the corner. A table in the middle already had snacks on it with a steaming pot of tea ready to drink.

The hostess bowed like she was about to leave us there, but I turned back. "Wait, we're all staying together?"

She paused, glancing at Leo with a confused expression. "I thought that's what you wanted?"

"Absolutely." Leo grinned. "It'll be a great team-building experience. Nothing like sharing the same space to get in each other's minds and really work together well."

That was so not how life worked, but I didn't have the heart to crush his excitement. Besides, staying in the same room as Thorne wouldn't be too terrible... I glanced over at him, but his shadows were already filling the room as a deep sigh escaped his lips.

"I never should have let Leo handle our reservations." He glared at the hero before turning to me. "Sorry about this. I can get you a room for yourself if you want."

Dain stepped closer, fist over his heart. "Leave it to me, my lord. I'll resolve this matter quickly."

"But where's the fun in that?" Leo asked, leaning Dawnbreaker against the wall. "What do you think?"

The sword hummed, glowing faintly as its words reverberated through us. "I think I'm going to rust if we stay here too long. Where we sleep doesn't matter."

Inkheart swooped in front of us. *Didn't think a holy sword would be scared of a little steam. Just wait until you fall in love, then you'll really be in trouble.*

While Dain and Thorne glowered at the room, everyone else started settling in. Even Cinder hopped from cushion to cushion, arriving at a small plate of hay the staff must have left just for her. It was sweet and I couldn't picture a better place to write this last book in.

"It's perfect." I squeezed Thorne's hand softly. "I usually write alone, but this will make sure I'm surrounded by wonderful people. I love it."

Leo beamed at me from across the room. "See? I knew she'd like it! So get on board, shadow boy."

"Shadow boy??" Thorne's voice rumbled as his shadows coiled around Leo, practically drowning him in darkness until Dawnbreaker lit up to banish them.

The hero held up his hands, laughing. "I'm sorry! Let's just get along and work on the book, okay? Where should we start?"

Thorne pulled my manuscript out from his robes. "You start by reading this. You and Dain need to catch up before we can talk."

I frowned. "Don't you mean all of you do? You only read the last chapter I wrote."

"No, I read all of it." His eyes softened. "Every word, Willow. I'd never miss out on something you wrote. I was just too curious that night, needing to see where my story ended. Now I know that it doesn't matter, because my story ends with you."

Inkheart scrawled a message as butterflies danced in my stomach. Thorne seemed so confident now, so in charge of his life. Gone was the man who'd worried about what he should say or do. He seemed to know exactly what he wanted now and apparently, that was...me.

Maybe you two should find a cozy hot spring to yourselves for a while. Get a little alone time, if you know what I mean.

"That actually sounds great." I grinned at the pen before moving to the other side of the room. Beautiful sliding doors opened up into a garden viewing area outside and the mineral scent grew stronger. "Care to join me, Thorne?"

"More than anything." He pressed my manuscript against Dain's chest and followed me outside without another glance at anyone else.

Dawnbreaker and Inkheart started arguing the moment we left the room, but I let it all drift away, wandering through the gardens hand in hand with Thorne. It reminded me of the last time we'd been in a garden. The sun had been setting back then, too. Soon we'd be in a beautiful moonlit hot spring together and my stomach was already in knots just thinking about it. I'd never let a man in like this before, not really. He'd seen my good sides and my bad and he was still here, walking along beside me like our fight never happened.

Was this what it meant to be in an actual relationship? It felt really nice, like we had so much room to grow from here. I finally saw what Gran had been talking about. I'd cut myself off from having a real life and any real relationships long ago. It was about time I let myself experience more of what this life of mine had to offer.

The air grew more humid the closer we got to the hot springs and different scents filled the air, some floral, some citrusy, and even a hint of chamomile, which meant the inn probably had multiple baths to choose from!

Thorne laughed softly. "Which bath do you want to try first?"

"Herbal, definitely herbal."

He nodded as we finally reached the changing area. I went into the women's side and left my clothes in a basket before I showered and pinned my hair up. Then I wrapped a thin towel around myself and stepped into the wonder of the real hot springs area. The air itself was invigorating, like health and healing vibes were filling me up before I even stepped into the water.

Thorne joined me a few moments later, his upper chest completely bare with just a small towel slung around his hips. Suddenly, the thought of bathing alone with him under the moonlight was making me a little light-headed. A drop of water ran down his arm, slowly falling off his finger to the ground. I swallowed hard. This bath was going to take all my self-restraint.

A faint blush tinged his cheeks. "Uh, are you ready to go?"
"Mmhmm."

A non-verbal answer was about all I could manage. I didn't trust myself not to say something ridiculous like how absolutely beautiful he was. Honestly, whoever made him a villain didn't know what they were talking about. Not unless it was supposed to be a romance novel.

The scent of herbs surrounded us as we moved toward a faintly green bath with herbs floating in it. The scent of lavender and chamomile relaxed my senses as I sat down at the edge of the bath, dangling my legs in the warm water to slowly acclimate to it. Steam rose around us, carrying the wonderfully earthy aroma of plants. It made me feel like we were back home again, in the shop surrounded by herbs.

Thorne joined me, leaning back on his hands as he gazed up at the sky. "I'm glad you came back with us. I didn't like the idea that one thoughtless comment from me might have ruined your dream."

"It's not like that." I scooted a little closer until my shoulder almost brushed against his. "I was actually on my way to find you when you showed up at the shop. I wanted to apologize for leaving like that, without even asking what you meant or what you were feeling." I stared at a chamomile flower floating across the water, lowering my voice. "I never meant to tell you who you should be. I've always wanted you to be whoever you wanted to be, and I'm sorry I let my fears stop me from checking in with you more on that."

He pulled his gaze from the sky to look at me. "Were you really coming back?"

"Of course I was, but you beat me to it." A smile tugged at my lips as I bumped my knee against his. "Thank you for that. I was so surprised to see you there, but it was like we both knew we needed to see each other again at the exact same time."

"The castle wasn't the same without you," he mumbled before sliding into the water. He leaned back, offering me his hand. "I'm not the same without you. You make me better, and I hope I can do the same for you."

I slipped into the water next to him as the heat overtook me for a moment. "Does this mean…that we're together now?"

"I would like nothing more, Willow." He took my hand again, pressing it against his lips. "I'm yours for however long you want me."

Steam curled around us, hiding the fact that we'd both left our towels on the ledge. It wasn't proper to take them in the bath, but now I felt more exposed than ever. Except, I wasn't nervous about it or awkward. I wanted him to see me for who I really was, every fear, every anxious moment of doubt, and every joyful win. I wanted him to know every part of me, more than anyone else ever had.

"Then I want you for forever," I whispered. "Somewhere along the line life stopped being fun without you around. I want our story to keep going, with all its twists and turns. I want to know the real you, the you that you are now and the you that you'll become. I want all of it." I reached out to brush a damp strand of hair behind his ear, running my fingers over his strong jawline. "I'm in love with you, Thorne."

He cupped my hand in his, pressing it against his cheek as his eyes closed for a moment. He kissed the inside of the wrist, his lips soft and tender. When his eyes opened, they were shining with the moon's reflection. I could get lost in those purple eyes of his and I felt myself moving closer.

He leaned down, his hair brushing against my bare shoulder, but he paused. "Are you sure about this? I don't think I can handle it if you disappear again."

"I'm sure. I'm not running away anymore, not from you, or my writing." I wrapped my arms around his neck and kissed him, hoping he could feel my sincerity.

Being with him had changed my life in so many ways. He'd given me the courage to go after what I wanted even if it hurt. That pain was just a small ripple in the water compared to all the wonderful moments in life, and I knew there would be so many of those with him by my side.

"Let's write something amazing together." I smiled against his lips, not afraid of the ending this time. Because with Thorne, the possibilities were endless.

CHAPTER 30
THORNE

Our room at the inn had been crowded and noisy all week, which was exactly what I'd grown to dislike about the library. I leaned against the wall, picking at the bright purple robe the hero had insisted I wear to fit in with the rest of them. I hated to admit it, but the fabric was so soft that I'd almost asked the inn's staff where they got them from more than once.

Willow's robe was leaf green, matching her eyes perfectly. A ray of sunshine fell through the windows, casting her in a warm glow as she leaned over the table to write. She was working on the final chapter, and I couldn't be happier for her. Through the chaos, we'd all managed to come together and get a surprising amount of work done.

Even the ridiculous holy sword and the pen were getting along now. Dawnbreaker was doing dramatic readings of the chapters while Inkheart edited them. Leo was sleeping like a rock through the whole thing, his tail wagging occasionally like he was having good dreams. It was all so...cozy and honestly kind of nice. Nothing like the cold empty castle I'd spent so much time in.

A knock at the door pulled my attention.

"I'll get it." Dain leapt forward with his spear in hand and his robe hanging down around his waist like he couldn't be bothered to use the sleeves. He opened the sliding door, revealing the hostess who'd first shown us our rooms along with two other women carrying trays of food that smelled delicious.

"Once again, we are not invading," the woman said with a laugh. "Please put the spear away."

Willow sighed. "Put some clothes on too. You can't keep answering the door half naked like that."

Dain shrugged as he snagged a fresh bread roll off the serving trays and led the group inside like he was their guard. He'd sure come a long way from the soldier who wouldn't even eat some roasted nuts while on duty. Every day he relaxed a little more, like we were finally getting to know the real him.

And what about me? Was this cozy chaos what I truly enjoyed? It felt so different from the buzz of fans at the library, always wanting answers about my book or demanding to take a picture with me. This was more like a group of friends spending time together.

Maybe a Demon Lord in soft purple robes was exactly who I was supposed to be.

I smiled as I moved closer to Willow. "You should eat something."

"In a minute." She gave me a quick smile, but didn't stop writing. Her pen was practically flying across the page and excitement radiated off her. "I'm almost done."

These intense writing sessions of hers either seemed to be full of anxiety, with more of a gloom and doom kind of vibe, or full of pure joy like today. Writing was a lot harder than I'd realized and seeing her experience so many different emotions throughout the process made me even more impressed that she'd stuck with it. She was making something magical here and putting her heart and soul into it.

She'd even let us read the chapters as she worked on them this time, incorporating our comments as she went. It was so much more fun than when she wrote the first draft, like we were part of the story now instead of on the outside looking in.

"There." She let out a breath, leaning back with a big smile on her face. "It's done."

Leo jerked up from his nap. "Did I miss it? Did we win?" His nose twitched. "Ohhh is that breakfast I smell?"

Willow leaned close, whispering to me. "He looked just like Cinder with his nose twitching like that, didn't he?"

Her shoulders shook with silent laughter as we watched the demon bunny use her flames to add ambiance to the meal, her chubby cheeks chomping down on a plate of fruit just for her. I felt myself laughing along with Willow as the hero stuffed a roll in his mouth, cheeks just as chubby as the bunny's.

"He really does." I sat down next to Willow, handing her a plate of food. "Congratulations on finishing the book! You're even in time for the competition too."

She took the plate from me, her fingers lingering on mine. "You know I wasn't working so hard just to win a competition, right? I was doing it for you." She turned to the rest of the group. "For all of you. I might be the one writing it, but this is your story. I hope I did it justice this time." She picked up the scattered pages on her desk, tapping them to make a neat pile before she handed them to me. "I want you to read it first. Let me know what you think."

Those pages were the most precious thing anyone had ever given me. I wiped my hands off before taking them, leaning back to read while she finally took a break to eat and relax with everyone.

As I read over the last chapter, my eyes started getting misty at the perfect resolution to this whole crazy story. We beat the King without bloodshed, freed all the demons he'd been keeping locked away for their magic, and the hero even renounced his role, saying that it couldn't be on one person to stop a war. Everyone had to join together to keep the peace going, and peace was exactly what this last chapter was full of. Demons and humans mingled in the streets, eating at the Destroyer's Bakery and laughing as they swapped stories of better times.

It was exactly what I wished for our little demon town.

"It's beautiful, Willow." I wiped my eyes, handing the pages back to her. "Absolutely beautiful."

Inkheart swooped over, jumping excitedly. *Me next! Let me edit it to perfection!*

"Wait, wait, wait," Leo mumbled around a mouthful of eggs. "I'm curious too! Let Dawnbreaker read it out loud so we can all hear."

The sword shimmered with brilliant light. "I, Dawnbreaker the Holy Sword, take on this task willingly. Let me bring your words to life, dear author."

Willow blushed, smiling softly. "Well, if you want, that sounds good to me."

"Oh, we definitely want." I put my arm around her shoulder, pulling her close to kiss her temple. "You deserve all the praise we can give you."

She put her hand around mine, leaning against me as we settled in for the reading of her final chapter, narrated by the holy sword that had once wanted to end my life. It was all so surreal, going from being a villain just because the author wanted me to be all the way to trying to be a hero because I thought that's what Willow wanted.

But everything *I* wanted was right here in this room.

I wanted to be with Willow, to be surrounded by friends, and to be comfortable in a way I never thought I could be back when I was alone in my castle. I wanted this moment to last a lifetime and to always appreciate the little things in life.

It felt like I'd grown beyond the character from my book and become a real person finally. The Misty Mountain Library had given me a body, but Willow? Willow had given me my heart.

Chapter 31
Willow

A week after we'd finished the book and submitted it to the competition, tickets to a festival celebrating the series were delivered to the library. No news on who won the competition, just four golden tickets with our names on them. I clutched mine, trying not to let my nerves take over as we stood in line. There hadn't been any buildup for this festival, no news, no excited fans, no nothing. It's like they just came up with the idea a few days ago.

But even with only a few days, the place was crowded.

Thorne's arm brushed against mine. "Everything okay?"

"I honestly don't know." I stared at Leo decked out in his most brilliant armor, at Dain who looked torn between curiosity and annoyance, and at all the other people in line behind us. "It's just so weird. Events like this are usually planned months, even a year in advance. I'd understand if they wanted to do a big reveal to build hype, but why wouldn't they wait for the book to be published? Something's going on..."

"Then we'll be ready for whatever comes." His gaze swept over the crowd as if seeing it for the first time before coming back to me. "We can handle this."

"Even if we don't know what *this* is?"

He smiled. "Even then."

"Okay, enough flirting," Leo said, practically vibrating with excitement. "We're almost there! Get your tickets out!"

His excitement bled over to me just enough for a smile. Being in line with them reminded me of all the times Grandpa and I had waited for new releases together. There was a bond formed in lines like this that only true fans would ever understand, and I should be focusing on that instead of my own insecurities. It didn't matter if our book won or lost, what mattered was that these wonderful people had supported me all the way. I might even be brave enough to write another book of my own after this.

Maybe.

The ideas had been flowing, that's for sure. I'd probably need a new notebook soon. Maybe I could get a custom one here.

We finally made it to the front of the line and handed our tickets to the ticket taker. His eyebrows rose as he glanced from us back to the tickets. "Welcome! Please give me just a moment." He turned back to grab an envelope with my name on it. "Here you go, Willow. Please head inside and find the authors' corner. The others are waiting there too."

"The author's corner?" My heart raced. Did that mean they'd chosen me to write the last book?? No, he'd said there were others… "How many authors are here?"

"The top five contestants were invited for this special event. It's all in the envelope."

I moved off to the side to open it. The first page was a note from the author's family apologizing for not being able to choose a winner. Apparently a few of the books were so good that the choice was too hard to make so they wanted to let the fans decide instead. This event was going to be a reveal of all the best story concepts. Authors were free to meet and greet with fans to talk more about their ideas, but in the end, the fans would decide our fate by voting for the story they liked best.

My stomach sank. "The fans are going to decide who wins now."

"What?" Thorne leaned over my shoulder to read along with me.

Leo wedged himself between us to do the same. "Ohhh, that could work in our favor! Once everyone sees how awesome we are, they're sure to pick your book. Trust me." He grinned, tapping his chest. "I'm the hero, we won't fail."

A passerby laughed. "If he's the hero, I'm the King. Look at those horns! No way is he going to win that look-a-like competition."

"You're no King, sir!" Leo puffed up his chest, but his frown ruined the whole image. "What's a look-a-like competition?"

I bit my lip as I sorted through the paperwork, handing him a pamphlet for the event. "It's like a cosplay contest where everyone tries to be you."

"But *I'm* me."

Thorne clasped him on the shoulder. "Exactly. So go be the best *you* you can be and put that annoying cheerfulness to work, okay?"

"I can do that!" Leo beamed at him before wandering off holding the map up on the back of the pamphlet.

After three wrong turns, Thorne sighed. "Dain, could you go with him?"

"Of course, my lord." He nodded and followed after Leo with more pep in his step than I'd expect.

Maybe he was excited for the contest too. The whole festival seemed to be brimming with anticipation as people whispered their theories about the final book. But nobody, not a single person, was guessing *my* ending for it.

I'd convinced myself that losing this competition would be fine since nobody would know about my story except for the author's family, but now that all these other people were involved too? I wished I was anywhere but here. Thorne and the others had worked so hard on the story with me though. I couldn't abandon them now.

This story was about more than just my feelings. It was about them, and I had to fight for that. Even if it meant people hating my ideas and probably saying that straight to my face.

I cringed. Whoever thought of this festival was horrible. The whole concept was gut-wrenching and should have come with a huge warning label! I took a deep breath, steeling myself for the emotional rollercoaster that was sure to come.

"Let's go," I said with more confidence than I felt. "Time to face the music."

Thorne's lips pulled into a grin, and he took my hand, bringing it to his lips to kiss. "That's my girl. Here I was thinking you might want to leave, but you really are done running, aren't you?"

My breath caught in my chest and words completely failed me. He continually flipped my world upside-down with things like that. Kissing the back of my hand like I was some kind of princess. I felt myself smiling as I tugged him along, so happy he was by my side. I never would have been able to stand my ground without him. He'd believed in me so much that somewhere along the way, I'd started believing in myself too.

I was a good writer and my story was exactly what fans of this series needed to read. They might not know it yet, but this ending was beautiful, and I wanted to share it with them.

The authors' corner was more of a big open area than a corner, with five giant booths set up. Most of them had dashing images of the hero and Demon Lord fighting their final battle. It was all light versus dark everywhere I looked until my gaze landed on the one empty booth with something a little different. The artwork on mine had them holding hands.

I agreed with the symbolism of that, but the artwork was so bright and tranquil compared to the other booths that it barely looked like they were from the same series. Mine felt almost like a slice of life comedy instead of the epic fantasy it was supposed to be. This was definitely going to confuse people...

One of the other authors walked away from their booth, smiling as she made her way over to me. "Hey, I'm Ava Knightly. Now that you're here, I think they're going to start letting fans in soon."

"Thanks."

I managed to squeak out a single word before my throat tightened and my mouth went dry. Ava Knightly was famous! Her books lined my shelves and I wished I had one for her to sign right now. How could I be standing here next to an author like her expecting anyone to choose my book?? I glanced around the room, recognizing the other authors too. It was like a who's who of epic fantasy writers and then me, a no-name romance writer.

My palms started to sweat. Ava was still talking, chatting about something I hadn't really caught. I cleared my throat. "I'm sorry, can you say that again?"

"I was just saying it's brave of you to write a story so original for this competition." She read through the synopsis on a nearby poster. "It isn't like any of ours, and especially nothing like readers will expect."

"I'm doomed, aren't I?" I laughed a little, feeling the weight of my decisions fully on my shoulders. "It's a good story though, I swear. The artwork might not look like it, but the classic epic fantasy tropes are there. Big battles, tough decisions, all of it. It just questions who's the real villain of the series because it's definitely not the Demon Lord. He's way too much of a softie for that, I mean, he loves pie and hates upsetting people he doesn't even know." I glanced over at Thorne who had a small smile on his face that made me want to hide under a table. I was rambling in front of one of my personal heroes! I turned back to her, my face hot. "Sorry. This is the Demon Lord right here, if you wanted to meet him."

Her smile froze like her mind was racing with what polite thing she could respond with and had nothing. That's probably the reaction I should expect from everyone, either that or straight up laughing at me. But I had to get them to see Thorne for who he really was somehow. Before I could, Ava got pulled away by some fans and the crowd started piling in.

My shoulders drooped. "Well, that could have gone better."

"Maybe, but it could have gone worse too." Thorne's shadows curled around me as if they were giving me an out if I wanted to disappear. "Tell me what you need and I'll do it."

His gaze held mine, as if telling me that offer covered more than just convincing fans my story was the best. I had a feeling he'd run away if I asked or douse the entire room in shadows. Whatever would make this experience better for me. My heartbeat slowed and I leaned against his side for a moment, drinking that dark intensity of his in.

"Let's show them who we really are." I gave him a determined smile before turning to the fans milling about, eying our table before passing by. "Hello everyone. I'm Willow and this is Thorne, the Demon Lord you've all heard about. I wrote this book for him and the other story spirits who've come to life with the help of a wonderful magical library named Misty, so I'd appreciate if you took the time to listen."

A few people stopped by our booth, but they mostly seemed to think Thorne was a cosplayer I'd hired and that story about the library was some kind of gimmick. At least they were looking at the story I guess. I talked with more and more people over the next hour and even got a few to drop their voting stones in the jar on my table. They glowed with a soft blue light that eased my spirit. Even though the other jars were filling up far faster than mine, a few people at least thought my idea was good.

We were probably still going to lose, but at least I'd go down swinging this time. Thorne did his best to be the grumpy and adorable demon I knew everyone would fall for eventually if they gave him a chance. He glared at some, thanked a few others, and even laughed once. His gaze kept wandering back to me between people and he'd give me a smile that he seemed to reserve just for me.

That smile sent butterflies racing through my stomach every time, like it was a private little moment just for us even though we were surrounded by people.

Eventually, a sea of people dressed like Leo started overtaking the area, which probably meant the cosplay contest had ended. I welcomed as many as I could to our booth and a few dropped their voting stones in, but most laughed and pointed at the image of Leo with ears and a tail. When Dain led a very depressed looking hero over by us, I could pretty much guess what had happened.

"So you lost, huh?" I patted him on the shoulder. "Sorry. I probably should have warned you about looking different than people thought you would."

"But I'm the hero!" His eyes were misty like this was hitting him harder than I'd expected. "Just because I look different doesn't change that. I'm still me and nobody, not even *that guy*, can be a better hero than me." He gestured vaguely at one of the shiniest heroes of the bunch. "I just don't get it."

I opened my mouth to say something, but Thorne shook his head, leaning close to whisper, "I think this is about more than the competition. His party shot him down too while you were gone. I found him back in my castle pretending like it didn't matter. And eating all the pie."

Yikes, well that sounded doubly awful. I'd actually thought about having his party turn on him, but hadn't had the heart to put it in the book. They just didn't feel very heroic whenever I thought about it, but apparently, they never really were to begin with.

I pulled Leo into a hug. "I'm sorry. People don't always handle change well, but you're still my hero if that means anything. You're still the one who saves the day in my book. Well, you and Thorne together, but you get what I mean."

"Thank you." He held onto me for a bit and then pulled back, glancing at the mostly empty jar of voting stones. "Now what are we going to do about that?"

A few minutes ago, I'd have said nothing. I already had everything I could ever want, so actually winning didn't matter like it did before, but that didn't feel true anymore. Winning would mean people accepted Thorne and Leo's ending, accepted the ending we'd chosen together. No other ending would do, not when it might change who they'd become throughout this journey of ours.

I pulled them all together into a huddle. "Okay, so here's the plan. If they don't believe any of you are real, then we'll just have to make them. Thorne, use your shadow magic. Leo, use Dawnbreaker. Dain—" I paused, tilting my head. "Ummm, be yourself?"

"I can do that." He nodded, his fist over his chest just like the first time we met.

"Great, let's get to it then!" I turned back to the crowd, raising my voice. "Many of you haven't believed our story, and honestly, why should you? We're surrounded by amazing cosplayers and fantasy stories. But the people here aren't just cosplaying." I nudged Leo and Thorne forward. "They're the real deal, brought to life by a magical library. They've lived the story we all love so much, and they've chosen how they want it to end. I might have written it down, but this is the story they've chosen, and I urge you to do the same."

An awkward hush fell over the room until one man in a hero's outfit spoke up. "Isn't that the guy who made a big scene at the cosplay contest?"

Leo sighed. "Yup, that's me, the overeager and always tripping over his own feet hero. But if you ever actually believed in me, then believe in me again now." He drew Dawnblade from its sheath and the bright light of the sun shimmered from its blade. "This is my story, and I promise you'll enjoy it just as much as I did."

"Unless you've forgotten what it means to be a hero." The sword vibrated as its voice filled the room louder than I'd ever heard it. "A true hero is more than flashy looks and a nice smile. A true hero is willing to change their mind when presented with new facts. A true hero is honorable and kind." Dawnbreaker's light grew almost blinding. "I chose Leo and now I expect you all to choose him too."

Stunned silence filled the room broken only by the sound of a stone clinking into our jar. Relief shot through me. We'd convinced one person at least and more would follow, I was sure of it.

Ava, the author I'd been so impressed by, stepped closer. "And what about him? Did the sword choose the big shadow daddy too?"

I smothered a laugh as a blush swept across Thorne's face. "Uh, no, I think that was more because every hero needs a good villain. Or at least, they need somebody to look like the villain."

"Be grateful I'm not," Thorne said ominously. "What do you think a villain would do in my position?"

The silence said it all.

"I've really struggled with who I am since the books didn't let me speak." Thorne frowned but took a step forward. "But I know I don't want to fight Leo. There's no point, we're both just trying to protect our people. The guy you should really hate is the one who made us think we had to kill each other in the first place."

Murmurs swept through the crowd. He'd pulled their curiosity wanting to know who was pulling their strings. Another clink pulled my attention as a stone fell into our jar.

Ava's stone.

"I'm all for surprise endings," she said with a smile. "Just make sure your story doesn't let me down, okay?"

"I will!" Hope surged in my chest. One of my favorite authors had actually chosen *my* story. Even if we didn't get a single vote more, that felt monumental, like I wasn't just a fan anymore. I was a real author, one worthy of her reading my story.

As people started finally talking to Thorne and Leo, the votes started rolling in. It was hard to say they were just cosplayers when their magic was literally on display.

Thorne's shadows drifted across the room like playful smoke, pulling people's attention every time they wandered off. And Dawnbreaker was giving out speeches like they were candy. It was probably good I hadn't brought Inkheart, otherwise they'd have been bickering like children by now.

I smiled, picturing them leaning over the pages of my book together, tag-teaming the editing like they were pros.

I really did love this little group we'd formed together. No matter how this all ended, I was proud of us.

Chapter 32
Thorne
A Few Months Later

Willow walked into the library with a radiant smile, clutching a book to her chest. "So, you know how winning the competition kind of felt like a dream, right?" She held the book out to me. "Well guess what came in the mail today! Another dream!"

I ignored the book for a moment to admire how beautiful she was when she was this happy. Her joy was infectious, and a smile spread across my face before I even knew what she was so happy about. Ever since Willow dropped the walls around her, she seemed to feel life to the fullest, letting every emotion wash over her completely. She was full of life, and I loved seeing her like this.

"Come on, read it!" She nudged the book at me, vibrating with barely contained excitement. "It's the advanced copy of our book!"

My eyes widened. I'd seen the heroic artwork on the cover once before when the publisher asked Willow for approval, but seeing it again now, in my hands, was an entirely new experience. I ran my fingers over the title, tracing the swoops and arcs of the letters fondly. This was the book we'd made together. It was the story of how Willow and I fell in love, even if our love story wasn't on the page itself.

"It's amazing." I cracked the book open, and the smell of new pages washed over me. "You really did it. I know it was hard and I'm so proud of you for sticking with it."

Willow dipped her head, still smiling. "Thanks for being with me through it all. It made a big difference."

As we browsed through the book, appreciating all the little pieces of art the publisher added to make it really shine, Nyssa and Oren walked over to take a peek too. They ooohhed and ahhhed over it like I expected them to, but Oren was obviously distracted by a box he held in his hands. It looked like what they stored the library checkout cards in.

"What's with the box?" I asked.

Oren grinned mischievously. "Oh, just a little something for Willow to test out."

"If she's willing," Nyssa added. "Which I think she will be."

Willow raised an eyebrow. "Willing to do what?"

Oren opened the box with such a look of delight that I half expected to see gold or jewels inside. But no, it was filled with checkout cards like I thought.

Nyssa pulled one out and wrote the name of Willow's new book on it before handing it over to her. "We think we've figured out a way to stabilize your trips into the book."

"Misty seems to keep you there until your goal's finished," Oren said. "So, if you check the book out and write the return date down, that should count as a finished goal. You'd basically be saying how long you want to be inside. Kind of like a book vacation plan."

I frowned, staring at the very basic checkout card. "Can a little slip of paper really do all that?"

"Guess we'll see, won't we?" Nyssa grinned. "If it works, this library might have a whole new adventure for patrons."

Willow picked up a pen and signed her name carefully on the first line, adding a return date two days later. She slipped it into her book and glanced over at the great book tree. "Hey, Misty? Mind sending me inside my new book for two days?"

"Me too. There's no way I'm missing out on this adventure." I laced my fingers through hers with a smile and she squeezed my hand tight.

The branches on the book tree swayed as if there was a wind blowing through the library and golden light fell from its branches. The advanced copy of Willow's book glowed too, enveloping us in the comforting library magic I'd grown so accustomed to. I blinked, readjusting my eyes to the castle's dimmer light. We were back in my bedroom of all places.

"Well, this feels familiar, doesn't it?" Willow sat on the plush mattress, leaning back with a sigh. "But it's so much better than the first time. You're not as grumpy anymore either, so it really must have been the bed the whole time." She winked. "Think anything's different since we came in with a new book?"

"Only one way to find out." I offered her my hand, pulling her up beside me again. I pressed my lips against hers in a quick kiss. "Let's go outside and see."

She laughed. "Look at you wanting to go exploring. I remember a time when you couldn't even open your front door!" She laced her fingers through mine and gave my hand a squeeze. "I'm glad you're more comfortable now."

"Me too."

My days of hiding away in this castle alone were gone for good. I didn't need to impress anyone or put on a show. I was just me and that was enough.

"Demon Lord!" a far too familiar voice shouted. Leo ran out of the kitchen carrying a plate of pie, crumbs clear on his face. "And Willow too! Welcome back."

"When did I say you could move in?" I grumbled. "You're here more than I am."

He brushed crumbs off his face with a shy smile. "Uhhhh, Thorne, oh great and mighty Demon Lord, can I move in?"

Willow covered up a laugh that sounded more like a snort. "Oh, come on, let him stay. He'll take care of the castle while you're out."

"I would definitely do that for you." Leo nodded, leaning closer to whisper. "But don't tell Dain. He might think I'm stealing his job."

"I heard that, scoundrel," Dain called out from the kitchen. "Nobody can take my place. I'm the bodyguard of the Demon Lord's consort, remember? Not this castle."

Consort. That's a word I hadn't heard in a while, but it settled in my chest with such a rightness that I didn't even try to correct him. Willow glanced sideways at me, smiling like she thought the same thing. Maybe we should have a talk sometime when all these people weren't crowding us. Discuss the finer points of the bond...

"So, is that a yes?" Leo asked, his eyes big like Cerbie's when he wanted me to throw his ball.

I sighed. "Oh fine. You can both officially move in."

Leo high-fived Dain and they both grinned while Willow and I headed outside. Just because they were moving in didn't mean we had to spend all of our time together. Except, the two over-eager puppies were following us out the doors and into the city.

Willow laughed softly and pulled me closer. "Let's go on a date soon. Just you and me."

My heart raced. We'd spent time together, but never anything official like a date. That felt like a new thing for us and one I very much wanted to experience. Where should we go? My gaze drifted to Leo who was always gobbling up sweets and I suddenly knew exactly where to go.

"Have you heard of the Destroyer's Bakery?" I slid my arm around her waist. "It's run by the two most loving people I've ever met and has the best food. It's where I got all the sweets I brought you while you were writing."

Her eyes lit up. "That sounds amazing."

I smiled and started going in that direction, but something about the town seemed different. I couldn't put my finger on what though...

"There are humans here," Willow whispered in awe. She turned to me, gripping my arm excitedly. "Humans! In the demon village!"

She was right. Humans milled around, talking to demons as if it was no big deal. Some looked a little awkward, but it didn't seem like any fights were going to break out at least. I nodded at Coco and her mother welcoming a human into Bunny Brews and they waved back with bright smiles. The mattress shop owner was beckoning people to come in and try her magical mattresses unlike anything the humans made, and she was catching more than a few curious people.

It was a subtle change but meant everything.

"Your words did this." I curled my shadows over her shoulder, brushing softly against her cheek. "Thank you for bringing everyone together. It's perfect."

Her smile widened and she leaned against my side. "It is pretty nice, isn't it? I'm glad the ending worked out. Well, mostly." She glanced back at Leo who was oddly quiet behind us. "There's one more thing I wish I could fix..."

Knowing her, she was hoping for a good resolution with his old party members, but I didn't see that happening. They'd shunned him out of fear, and it was hard to come back from that. Making amends would have been easier if she'd written it in the book, but she hadn't let them treat Leo like that in the first place. Only this book world's version of them had done that.

Dain must have noticed us staring, because he stepped closer. "If you're worried, don't be. I already took care of it."

"Took care of what?" I asked.

"You'll see." He gripped his spear tight with a confident smile that looked far too familiar. The last time he'd looked like that was when he'd brought the hero to the castle...

I groaned, running a hand over my face. "Please tell me you didn't kidnap anyone again."

Willow laughed. "Oh, please tell me you did. And it better be that horrible party of Leo's."

Dain's eyes twinkled as he nodded at a group of humans slinking into town. Their armor and weapons were so flashy that it had to be Leo's party, nobody else would be foolish enough to walk into a demon city dressed like that. Another sigh escaped me. Dain better know what he was doing with this little plan of his, otherwise it could ruin the careful peace that looked like it was developing in town.

Willow pulled Leo away from the stall he was looking at and motioned to the newcomers. His entire body tensed up and the cookie in his hand crumbled to dust. Dawnbreaker lit up, ready for a fight. I wouldn't let it come to that though. I wouldn't let them crush his spirit again either.

I stormed over to the group, letting my shadows flow around me like a cloak of darkness. "You are not welcome here."

They flinched and one of them actually dared to point her weapon at me! I snatched it away with my shadows, flinging it safely into the ground. A hush fell over the townsfolk as they gave us a wide berth. This was about to get ugly, and they knew it. I glanced back at Dain, expecting him to step in and deal with this, but he just shrugged. What was he thinking?

"Don't you want to say hi?" Dain asked Leo, nudging him a bit to get him moving. "They came all the way here to see you."

And fight me by the looks of it.

Leo's expression hardened. "You should leave. All of you. There's no place for you here. You made that very clear."

The guy in front winced. "Sorry. We just needed time to process, okay?"

The woman I'd stolen the sword from nodded. "Yeah, you didn't really give us any time. You just showed up all demony and expected us to love it right away."

"So it's my fault?" Leo asked softly.

"No, that's not what we meant," she said, then sighed and turned to Dain. "We're doing this all wrong. Can you help?"

Leo frowned at the sneaky bodyguard. "Why would you help them? How do they even know you?"

Dain shrugged. "I might have visited them."

"Might have?" The woman exclaimed. "He threw us in a sack and dropped us off at the edge of town!"

Another kidnapping then. Great. This didn't look good for peaceful relations. Before I could say something, the guy in front spoke up again.

"We're glad though." He nodded at Dain. "We'd been wanting to apologize for a while, but didn't know how. He seemed to know that and gave us the push we needed." He bowed to Leo. "We're sorry for failing you. We're the hero's party and we should have stood by your side no matter what. We should have fought the King with you, created peace with you, and finished this whole mess together."

The others nodded and Leo's eyes widened. "That's why you're here? To apologize?"

"Why else would they be?" Dain asked. "I wouldn't have bothered if they were going to be rude again."

A smile finally cracked Leo's hard expression, and he nodded. "Thanks, Dain." Then he turned to his party. "Let's go somewhere quiet and talk. Bunny Brews makes the best coffee."

"And has bunnies?" The guy in front's eyes lit up. "Sounds perfect."

Leo turned to me. "Is it okay if they stay for a while?"

They all held their breath like I was still the great villain they'd spent so much time hunting. I dropped my shadows. "It's fine, but they are *not* staying at the castle. I've already got enough of you roaming around, and I don't need any more."

"That's fair." Leo grinned, his shoulders loosening. "Come on guys, let's go."

"You're in charge of them!" I called out after him. "If they get into trouble, you'll be cleaning it up."

He held a hand up in the air, waving like he agreed. A tightness in my chest loosened. Seeing him with his party felt right, like the last piece of the story that needed mending. Dain glanced at Willow with a questioning look, and when she nodded, he trailed after the group quietly. It was like they'd had a whole silent conversation.

"Since when did you two get so familiar?" I asked.

"Jealous?" She grinned, looping her arm through mine. "Let's head to that bakery you mentioned, and I'll get a little *familiar* with you too."

Her wink sent sparks through me. Why was I wasting time on Dain and Leo when Willow and I were finally alone together? We walked in happy silence, just watching the curious new additions to the town, until we found our way to the Destroyer's Bakery. The sound of a massive cleaver thunking into the counter and the sweet smell of apple pie filled the air. Willow inhaled slowly, her eyes closed, and a smile on her face.

She was beautiful, content just being in a cozy little place like this. It reminded me of how she'd looked in the apothecary gardens and gave me an idea.

"Have you ever thought of writing cozy fantasy?" I asked, nodding at Miri and Noki as we sat down. "I think you'd be really good at it. You've got a peaceful vibe to you and even managed to bring that into our book. I bet more people would enjoy stories like that."

Her eyes sparkled. "I was actually thinking the same thing." She pulled a notebook out of her bag, showing me dozens of pages of notes about a cozy fantasy she'd been planning. "Being with you made me realize that if I really care about something, it's worth risking a little pain for the ending I want."

Warmth spread through my chest. "Are you talking about us or the book?"

"Both?" She grinned and scooted her chair over to my side of the table so we could look at her notes together. Her arm pressed against mine and her fingers toyed with my shadows like they were hers.

I'd never dreamed of having a moment like this, but now? I wouldn't give it up for anything.

She'd claimed my story and my heart, so if she wanted my shadows too, they were already hers.

Because I was her Demon Lord, and she was my consort.

Epilogue
Willow
One Year Later

Sunlight reflected softly off the jars in the apothecary shop and the mossmews batted at them playfully. Thorne smiled, bending to pet a moss kitten fondly. He used to only do that in secret, but he was far past pretending he didn't find them adorable. They even joined us in bed half the time, curled up at the end like our own little guardians.

Thorne finished filling the last bottle of sleeping tonic and handed it to me to label.

I grinned. "You should really work on your handwriting skills."

"Baby steps, okay?" He glanced back at the bin that used to be full of his failures. "At least I'm not setting anything on fire anymore."

"True." I laughed and gave him an honest smile. "You really are doing great, you know. You didn't have to work so hard to help me out after Gran retired. I could have hired outside help."

"I know." He glanced around the shop, from the herbs hanging from the ceiling to the jars of remedies and ingredients, and gave me a soft smile. "But I like it here. It's soothing on the mind and so quiet, but the comfortable kind of quiet. I even like helping the customers. It all feels so simple, but incredibly worthwhile."

That's exactly what I thought too. Taking over the shop had been such a monumental moment, a time when Gran could finally get some rest and experience life without working so hard, but the days hadn't gotten hectic like I'd thought. Because of Thorne, the easy partnership Gran and I had had just kind of continued on. Thorne helped me with the gardens, picked herbs on the mountain, made remedies, and everything else out of the sheer joy of it.

I never thought I'd find somebody who enjoyed being an apothecary as much as I did.

The bell above the door chimed as Professors Ashford and Min walked in, arm in arm like usual. I glanced at Thorne, but he was already moving to box up their order like he knew what I needed before I asked. He really was catching on so fast, like he'd been here for years, and hopefully would be for years to come too.

I took the box from him with a smile before turning back to the professors. "Welcome to Bloom and Bramble Apothecary. We've got your order ready to go."

"Oh, thank you," Min said, nudging her husband to take the box from me before making her way to a new bookshelf in the lobby. "I was hoping to get your newest book too. Signed if you don't mind."

Thorne grinned but had the decency not to say *I told you so.* It had been his idea to add the small bookshelf to display not only his series, but my own as well. I'd managed to publish a new trilogy of cozy fantasies, with the last one coming out just a week ago. I pulled a copy off the shelf and carefully opened the cover to sign my name, wishing Inkheart was here. The magical pen loved to sign books with me, always adding a little extra flourish to the page.

Inkheart had been spending a lot of time with Dawn-breaker lately though and I suspected there was something more going on there. They might have started off bickering all the time, but after our little hot springs writing retreat, they'd grown closer. Most of their bickering sounded like flirting now and I was so happy for them.

I handed the book to Professor Min. "Here you go. I hope you enjoy it."

"The others have been wonderful, so I'm sure I will." She showed the book to Professor Ashford with a grin. "Look dear, she even signed it! Ah, my friends will be so jealous. I'll have to send them over soon."

A surge of happiness overtook me and my grin was so wide it hurt. "Thank you. That means more than you'll ever realize."

All those years I'd spent dreaming about this moment, and all the hard work I'd put in making those dreams a reality, had finally paid off. I was an author now and people were not only reading my books but loving them too. It was more than I'd ever thought possible.

While I finished ringing up their order, Thorne put a hand on my shoulder as if he could tell I was getting a little emotional. His steady presence was like a balm to my soul. He'd known this day would come all along. I was the one who'd kept doubting even after my first book and my second had come out. It just didn't feel real.

I was a published author, but I was an apothecary too. Both parts of my life melded into beautiful harmony, and I couldn't be happier.

"Remember to take these once a day." I pinned Professor Ashford with a stare. "Don't let the slimes drink them all, okay? We added some extra valerian root again as a treat for them."

He dipped his head with a bashful look. "Thank you."

I leaned back against Thorne as they walked out the door, chatting about how excited Min was to read my book. I put a hand against my chest, enjoying the warm and fuzzy feeling I got whenever a reader enjoyed my stories. It never got old, no matter how many times it happened. Writing something that made people happy was one of the best feelings in the world.

"You look happy." Thorne rested his chin on my shoulder and wrapped his arms around my waist. "Think we should close a little early? Maybe head back to the castle for the weekend?"

"In a minute."

I closed my eyes, breathing in the wonderful scents of fresh green herbs in the shop. All the dreams I'd worked so hard for had finally come true, but the best one was still being written. I trailed my fingers over Thorne's arm. I hadn't been looking for romance, but sometimes the stories you're not expecting end up being the most satisfying of all.

I opened my eyes, turning to catch his gaze. "Okay, I think I'm ready now."

He leaned closer, pressing his lips to mine with a promise of more to come when we got to our castle. I smiled against his lips and led him to the front door, flipping the sign from open to closed.

With every new chapter comes a new beginning, and our story was only just getting started.

PANDORA PIERCE

writes cozy fantasy where the monsters are charming, the magic is whimsical, and the adventures are delightfully low-stakes. She has a weakness for slimes, red pandas, and other adorable creatures that inevitably sneak into her stories.

When she's not writing, she streams as a VTuber, connecting with readers, writers, and gamers in a space as cozy and lighthearted as her books.

Website and Merch Store: www.**pandorapierce**.com